THE

SUCCESSION

THE

SUCCESSION

Douglas King

E-PRIDE Books • Beaumont, Texas

Printed in the United States of America. For information address E-Pride Books, 451 Yorktown Lane, Beaumont, TX 77707-1873.

ISBN 978-0-9882671-3-8

First Edition

Prelude

The sleek black form of Her Majesty's private train sliced cleanly through the thick pre-dawn fog. Two military helicopters paralleled the tracks about a thousand yards ahead; their sophisticated heat, sound and motion sensing hardware trained on the surrounding hillsides, seeking any evidence of activity. Occasionally one of the aircraft would veer off to the side, penetrating the haze with laser guided flood-lights frightening an occasional rabbit or deer into the nearby brush.

The train itself never slowed as it pursued its high speed course toward London. The machine gun turrets and armored plating about the security cars made it more fortress than train. Her Majesty's private car was no exception. Armor plated as well, it had the appearance of a giant black strongbox on wheels. The occasional glint off the muzzle of an assault rifle signaled the otherwise invisible presence of military sharpshooters balancing on the narrow platforms between the cars.

The impression from inside the Royal Coach, however, was quite different. Being heavily soundproofed, there was little noise and only a hint of vibration in the floor, thanks to a well-engineered hydraulic suspension. The interior mimicked a modest, comfortable, English country drawing room encased with dark walnut paneling. A small Waterford chandelier cast a warm glow about the room, its crystals rustling like a delicate wind chime from the ever so slight vibration of the train.

Her Majesty the Queen sat over to one side at a small writing desk next to a window. Her small hands lay folded in front of a large well-worn Bible that was open on the desk. Occasionally, one of the thin, onion-skin pages would turn with the recirculating air from the overhead vent, as if guided by an unseen hand. The Queen stared out of the window into the darkness. Her eyes glazed with a prophetic vision only she was privy to.

She had been unable to sleep after leaving her Scottish retreat at Balmoral. No one showed any inordinate concern about this, as she was always nervous and on edge before having to give her speech for the opening of Parliament. But her anxiety now was for another reason. It wasn't nervousness—neither was it fear. Ever since she had made the decision, her mind had been overcome with a deep and insurmountable anguish. She would never be sure her decision had been the right one.

She glanced down at the Bible. It was open merely out of habit as she could quote its contents by heart, having read each of its pages at least a hundred times in her eighty-six years. But even this life-long source of strength and comfort to her failed to lift the oppressive burden of anguish that now inhabited her every waking moment.

The sound of laughter from the other end of the car pulled her back from the other world to the present. The Prince of Wales and his much younger wife were engaged in a board game with two secret servicemen and the Prince was in the process of toasting a winning move. He had spent the better part of the ride to London toasting such moves, even those of his opponents, and he was becoming louder and less coherent.

Married for four years, the young couple was still childless. With the increasing tension between the two, rumors abounded that he was probably impotent—or worse. As a result, in the previous year he had begun his preferred Royal retreat into various vintage brandies and cognacs. Also in that year, two younger siblings had been assassinated in renewed terrorist bombings making him the only immediate, therefore possible, heir to the throne.

The Queen shook her head sadly at this possibility and turned back to her scriptures for comfort. Her elected governments had failed her, but God had given her a way out . . . a plan—The Plan. Divine intervention had been what she prayed for. The pseudo-religious war between her government, the resurgent, political terrorism by a new and corrupt Irish Republican Army, and Muslim extremists centered around Al Qaeda cells at home and abroad, had stagnated the economy.

With each passing moment she grew more and more sure of the Plan. The Royal Family was nothing more than a target now for every aspiring terrorist in the country—not to mention the determination of certain anti-monarchy factions in the Commons to do away with the ancient, hereditary institution. The future of the Succession was, to her, a duty—a sacred trust. She was the anointed one and there must always be another.

She turned back to the open book before her and gave the appearance of studying it intently. But her eyes had long since turned inward, searching deep within herself, turning over each doubt and fear. Her Silver Jubilee was a past memory. Her health, now failing, portended the inevitable ascension to the throne of one who, even though he was her own son, would be an abomination as monarch. That is why she was now chief apostle for the preservation of her lineage. No faith was greater than hers that this was God's will as surely as it now was hers. Certainly she felt a worthy sacrifice for, after all, she was the Queen.

She fondled the delicate, pressed four-leaf clover that served to mark her place. Overhead, the air kicked on again, and in response, another translucent page of scripture turned. She glanced down at the page and smiled, recognizing the familiar passage.

Greater love hath no man but that he lay down his life . .

PART I

Virtuous and vicious every man must be,
Few in th' extreme, but all in the degree;
The rogue and fool by fits is fair and wise;
And even the best, by fits, what they despise.
'Tis but by parts we follow good or ill;
For, vice or virtue, self directs it still;
Each individual seeks a several goal;
But Heaven's great view is one, and that the whole.

From *Essay On Man*, by Alexander Pope

1

Aidan Ennis pulled the thick, auburn hair from his face and admired his sculpted profile in the Florentine wall mirror. He turned slowly, posing, making mental notes about what areas he would work a little harder on at the gym. A muffled moan pulled his attention away from the mirror to the oversized, four poster bed that dominated the spacious loft apartment. A figure lay in its center, partially wrapped in sheets, snoring lightly.

For a moment Aidan watched the rhythmic rise and fall of the man's breathing. He sat down on the side of the bed and then slowly stretched out beside his partner to fit his body against the sleeping man's side. Snuggling, he entwined his fingers in the red and ginger colored hairs curling up the man's belly and lightly caressed with his lips the nape of his lover's neck. The sleeper stirred slightly and Aidan nipped hungrily at the man's ear with his teeth—his hand moving lower beneath the sheets.

With annoying familiarity, the phone on the nightstand began to beep softly. Aidan froze for a moment, his body tense and hard. Then, with mechanical precision, he rolled off the bed and walked stiffly into the other room to the extension.

The redheaded man in the bed cursed in protest at the interruption and sat up groggily on his elbows, yawning. He glanced at the night stand by the bed and blinked his eyes, trying to squeeze the sleep from them. For a moment he thought he had been dreaming until he realized he was alone in the bed. As his senses cleared he became aware of the sound of Aidan's voice coming from the kitchen.

"I'm awake, Aidan, if it's for me," the man called out, swinging his legs over the side of the bed and pulling himself up. He sat there for a moment, listening for Aidan's response, but all he heard was the phone hanging up and the soft padding of Aidan's bare feet across the kitchen tile.

Aidan stopped at the bedroom door, his face in the shadow. He leaned against the door dizzy for a moment, his breathing slightly accelerated.

The man in the bed was fully awake now as he looked appreciatively at the masculine outline of Aidan's near-perfect body in the doorway. Self-consciously, the man pulled the sheet over his lap to cover himself. Aidan was quite comfortable with nakedness and when he was home, almost never wore a stitch. On more than one occasion Aidan had playfully chided his partner's highly developed sense of modesty. Now, however, the man was aware of a certain tenseness in Aidan's face, which the younger man quickly erased.

Slowly Aidan walked over to the bed, aware of his partner's gaze on him, not to mention the effect he knew it was having on the man. "Go back to sleep, Dennis," he said.

"Don't you have to go to work?" Dennis asked, reaching out for Aidan.

"Perhaps I might take the day off and spend it here with you." Aidan took Dennis' hand into his own and drew his partner to his chest, stroking his partner's fiery red hair with his hand. "The shop can stay closed one day without the world coming to an end."

Dennis embraced Aidan tightly, pulling the younger man into his bed and reveling in the boy's scent and masculine firmness. He laughed.

"What?" Aidan asked.

"I was wondering if Daphne Bates would be able to appreciate this little vignette."

Aidan tweaked Dennis' nose. "Well, love, you said she was always berating you to settle down."

"Yes, me darlin'," he said in his best imitation of Irish brogue. "But I think she had something entirely different in mind." It was only a few months ago that the Prime Minister's wife had chided him on his lack of consistent female companionship at one of her innumerable parties.

"I just don't look good in white," Aidan said. He played with the hair about Dennis' nipples. "Besides," he added, smiling. "You're much too busy hobnobbing as the PM's number one." His lip pouted. "This press conference, that press conference, this cabinet meeting, that cabinet meeting, Parliament this, Parliament that . . ." He pulled at Dennis' hair.

"Ouch!" Dennis grabbed the boy's hand laughing. Dennis had always thought his lifestyle was too busy, too full to make room for anyone else in it for any length of time—but Aidan was someone different all together. "I always have time for you," Dennis said. "Mr. Hoity-Toity Couturier to the Rich and Powerful."

Aidan lay back on the bed. "You can bloody well thank your lucky stars, too. If it weren't for my dresses, you wouldn't be having all this fun."

Dennis leaned over to kiss him. "And I *am* having fun."

"Want to have some more?" Aidan took Dennis' hand and stroked his own forming erection with it.

Dennis looked long at the younger man, enjoying the sensation his partner's soft skin brought to his hand. "My life's been on top of the world since you came into it," he said hoarsely.

Aidan smiled up at him and Dennis bent down to nibble on his breasts. Usually when Dennis woke from sleep, his mind turned automatically to the day's work schedule. Dennis was very proud of the fact that he had, in essence, redefined the position of Chief of Staff secretary to the Prime Minister. The news media had taken to referring to him as Dennis Perkins, shadow Prime Minister, and Dennis more than felt he had earned that singular insinuation—but there had always been something missing.

It had been a long way up from obscurity and the small, Northern Irish country hamlet he was born in, but he had managed to break the class barrier after some ten years of menial but backbreaking work on every level of the House of Commons, acquiring various connections and an intimate knowledge of the British bureaucrat's mentality. When Malford Bates accepted the office of Prime Minister after a six year absence from any top position, Dennis had been the first person he approached to serve as his most important aide. He had given Dennis free rein to organize the flow of governmental power and, within a few short weeks, Dennis had firmly established himself as the middleman for any governmental dealings with the Prime Minister. Aidan had become his escape from the pressures—his oasis.

He stretched out on the bed beside Aidan and took the boy's hand to kiss it. "Why won't you marry me, love?"

"Oh, Dennis." Aidan laughed and rolled over against him.

"I mean it, Aidan," he said. "It would make every-one very happy." He ran a line of kisses up the man's muscular shoulder. "Including me, love."

Aidan rose up on his elbows. "Now, Dennis, we've already been over this."

"Apparently not enough."

Aidan sighed. "Baby, we have two careers to build. You have to admit we don't have a whole lot of time to give each other right now."

Aidan had burst in on Dennis' life quite by accident. As the creator of Mrs. Bates' new fashion image, Aidan had been a guest at one of the Bates' diplomatic functions at Downing Street. Because Dennis and Aidan were both Irish, Mrs. Bates had blatantly thrown the two of them together in the hopes that the young and handsome Aidan would introduce Dennis to some equally young and eligible women. She had made a fateful miscalculation. It wasn't long before the two men were living together in what Dennis referred to as the *glories of sin*—much to Ms. Bate's chagrin.

"I'll make time," Dennis assured Aidan. "You know I love you."

"Yes, I know that."

"And . . ." Dennis waited expectantly.

Aidan laughed. "And you know I love you, too." He rested his head on Dennis' chest. "Marriage would be redundant. I'm home when you're home. We go out and have wonderful times. We come home and have even more wonderful times."

Though constantly busy with his boutique, Aidan always tried to be home when Dennis was. He was aggressively monogamous and attributed this trait to the fact that he was an only child. His father was an Irish manufacturing tycoon and apparently had plenty of new money to burn—but Aidan rarely spoke of him. Being seven years younger than Dennis' thirty-five years, Aidan would tease him saying that, to him, Dennis was like the father he never had.

Dennis sat up and ran a hand down Aidan's back. He squeezed a buttock. "Don't you want to be respectable?"

Aidan sat up, too, and laughed. "Mother Mary, no!"

Dennis fell back on the bed and pulled the boy over on top of himself. They wrestled, laughing, while Big Ben, not far away by the river, toned its version of the hour.

"My God!" Dennis jumped up from the bed and grabbed for his watch on the night stand. "What the bloody hell time is it?"

"What difference does it make, baby?" Aidan purred. He reached for Dennis' most vulnerable parts. "Aren't you having fun anymore?"

"Christ, Aidan! I'm going to be late for the fucking State fucking Opening of Parliament." Dennis dropped the watch back on the table and headed for the bathroom. "I'm catching a quick shower." He looked at Aidan hopefully. "It'd really be super if we had some coffee around."

Aidan lay on the bed for a moment listening to the sound of the shower running. He toyed absentmindedly with the nipple of his right breast and gnawed at the manicured thumbnail of his other hand. Finally he got up and walked hesitantly toward the bathroom.

He stopped at the bathroom door. "Dennis, don't go," he said.

The door opened. "What?"

"I said don't go. Stay home with me." Aidan leaned into the doorway.

Dennis laughed at the absurdity. "You're crazy."

"I mean it." Aidan watched his lover lay out various toiletry items on the sink. "It's not like you'd be missed or anything. Everyone and their grandmother will be there."

"It's part of my job, Aidan, you know that." Dennis reached into the shower to turn on the water. "Bates is going to be pushing for some important new legislation and I bloody well need to be there to help twist a few arms." He slipped out of his boxer shorts and stepped into the shower. "Is the kettle on?"

Aidan started to speak, but thought better of it. He loved Dennis, but there were greater, more important things to consider. He thought about getting into the shower with Dennis, sure that he could distract his partner. The thought made him chuckle.

"Aidan?" Dennis called out from the steam. "Are you still there?"

"No, I'm making you coffee," Aidan responded with a laugh and backed up to the door.

"Thanks, darlin'."

Aidan shook his head. What will happen will happen. The day's events were out of his control. It was Dennis' decision. He looked down at his naked toes and flexed them against the cold tile floor. Resigned to the workings of fate, he headed for the kitchen to his appointed task.

2

Dennis broke into a run as the early morning fog began to condense into a cold drizzle. For a moment he lost his balance but quickly regained his stride, as he jumped off the curb onto the icy street that bordered the side of Westminster Palace. Grabbing the front of his wool blazer, he tightened it about himself against the cold. A crowd of reporters had gathered around the members' private entrance to the House of Commons. Dennis pulled at his hat which refused to fully cover the telltale red hair that made him so readily identifiable.

"Hello! It's the Prime Minister's man!" shouted the burley Scotsman from the London Times. "Will they do it, do you think, Perkins?"

"You're guess is as good as mine, McClure," Dennis said. He attempted to push his way through the ring of reporters.

"Come on now, Perkins, give us a wee break, won't you?"

"Give us something, Dennis," said a short woman as she pushed her way up to him. "Does the Prime Minister plan any response to the latest series of demands?"

"I'll give you a statement from the Prime Minister after the Queen's address—but right now, you gentlemen," Dennis nodded solicitously toward the short brunette, "and ladies are getting me soaked to the skin." He pushed his way through the door and a House Guard prevented any attempt by the reporters to follow.

The House Chambers had already emptied save for a small group arguing heatedly as they moved out of the vaulting room. Dennis looked about, disappointed. He always liked the ritual and pomp that accompanied the Lord's invitation to the Commons to attend the Queen for the opening address. He chided himself for his lateness. He removed his hat and shook the rain from it. He paused a moment to straighten his tie and allow his breathing to settle. The many hours spent at his desk over the last year had pulled him down from his usual peak physical condition. He gave himself a quick check in the mirror that covered the south wall of the long corridor fronting the House Chambers.

"Well, how's the Prime Minister's young hatchet man holding up?"

Dennis turned quickly towards the sudden, gruff voice behind him.

"You're pretty enough as it is, my boy!" The voice boomed again. "Come away from that mirror. Her Majesty awaits her loyal subjects."

"Fitzroy." Dennis smiled at the large, fleshy statesman attempting a courtly bow. "What brings you to the House today? Have the pubs closed in honor of the Queen's address?"

Fitzroy laughed heartily. "Why should the pubs stay open as long as Parliament is in session?" He put his arm around the younger man. "Come, come! I'll walk you over. A young Irishman needs a proper English escort these days—especially in the House of Lords!"

Dennis accepted the older man's familiarity. "Guilt by association."

Fitzroy laughed again, slapping Dennis on the back. "Ah, Dennis, you always manage to raise my spirits. Tempers are up today," he said growing somber.

Dennis stopped, studying the older man's face. "You don't think there will actually be any incidents while the Queen is here, do you?"

"Anything could happen. A lot depends on whether or not the Prime Minister can keep Conroe and his bunch in tow." Fitzroy shook his head ruefully. "Conroe." He almost spat. "That man is trouble!"

"He would have to be mad to try anything in the Queen's presence. The voting public would crucify him!"

"Since when has Conroe cared a bloomin' pence for his constituency?" said Fitzroy waving a massive arm. "This Irish thing has made him as fanatical as any IRA terrorist."

"Certainly he could have no significant effect," Dennis ventured. "He's of no real importance in the government anymore."

"Don't fool yourself, Dennis," Fitzroy said. "You of all people know he's been making quite a big stink in the Commons. The Prime Minister has been under considerable pressure from his cronies ever since he resumed negotiations with Sinn Fein." Fitzroy puckered as if the name of the new IRA's political arm left a sour taste in his mouth.

"I know Conroy can't stand me and the feeling is mutual." Dennis ran his fingers through his strawberry-colored hair self-consciously. "Sometimes I feel like the red flag before the bull."

"At least you're not a practicing Roman Catholic, my boy," Fitzroy roared. "God forbid, had you been a loyal Papist!"

The two men stopped outside the massive, ornate doors to the House of Lords. Dennis could hear the rasping voice of the Prime Minister in his preamble to the Queen's address. He caught Fitzroy's hand as it reached out for the brass doorknob.

"Before you go in, Fitzroy, let me ask you this." He stared hard at the old politician. "This latest series of IRA threats—how seriously are you taking them? We negotiated a peace once before."

Fitzroy pulled at one of his chins. "I don't put anything past 'em, Dennis. You know what the government's position has been since the Royal Yacht incident. Every threat is being taken seriously." His face darkened. "Good God! Half the Royal Family was lost in that explosion."

Both men stood silent. A thunderous applause was beginning to settle from within the chambers and the soft, precise voice of the Queen could be heard as she began her annual address to Parliament.

"God bless her!" Fitzroy whispered. His face creased with sadness.

Dennis nodded. "She has recovered bravely."

"Bravely!" Fitzroy's voice echoed down the long marble corridor.

"Where are the Prince of Wales and his wife? Surely they've been sent up to Balmoral for protection."

Fitzroy shook his head. "The Queen will not let them out of her sight."

"Is this wise?"

"Wise or not, it is her wish," Fitzroy added. "As a matter of fact, even as we speak, the Prince and Princess of Wales are seated beside Her Majesty." Fitzroy pulled at the heavy oak doors. As he slipped quietly into the chambers he turned back. "Chin up, Dennis, my boy." A conspiratorial grin flickered across his corpulent face. "I shall spend the better part of this hour giving Conroe the evil eye!" The door closed behind him.

Dennis smiled to himself as he headed for the side stairs that led to the spectators' gallery above. The sound of the Queen's voice stirred his memory as he climbed to the upper level.

"I need an Irishman," the Prime Minister had said at their first meeting just weeks after the fatal bomb blast that ripped through the Royal Yacht. "The assassinations have generated a wave of ill feelings toward any and everyone Irish, and I must demonstrate that this government does not share those feelings."

Dennis also remembered the hostile presence of Gerald Conroe at the meeting. Conroe, his face clouded with hatred, had blatantly refused to shake hands with him. Dennis had shrugged this off at the time. Conroe's wife had been one of the many killed while attending a charity function on board the Queen's yacht. Dennis was able to dismiss the man's behavior on those grounds, thinking it would change with time as the man's grief subsided.

"I can't believe the government's going to allow a filthy, bloody, goddamn IRA lackey to be as highly placed as this," Conroe had screamed at the Prime Minister. "Next thing, you're going to give these bastards the atom bomb!"

Conroe had been dismissed from the cabinet shortly thereafter, much to Dennis' relief. He had never been an IRA sympathizer but understood firsthand the hatred and prejudice his Irishness generated in the average English mind. At one time it was just directed toward the Roman Catholics. Now, you just had to be Irish.

Dennis' fist slammed the stair railing angrily. The IRA had, long ago, ceased to represent the Irish Catholic minority of Northern Ireland and, like all politically insulated movements, its purpose had grown more and more self-serving. The political doctrine it espoused depended on which of its members you were speaking to at the time. Now the general consensus was that they were fighting for Church, doctrine and Pope—at least on the surface. Abortion clinics, gay bars, protestant churches that blessed same-sex unions—hell, protestant churches in general—all had become potential bombing targets. Mostly, as in all things, it was about power and the exercise of it. The Pope had condemned the violent acts, though not with the same vehemence that he had condemned the abominable acts of social progress which were sweeping through all the parliaments of the Commonwealth.

Every political overture for peace from Her Majesty's government was answered with ever bloodier acts of terrorism. The intelligence services fumbled about as if impotent. The moment they seemed to be closing in on the center of IRA command it would vanish like a mirage. No one had managed successfully to infiltrate the movement deep enough to uncover the sources.

Dennis became aware that he was being closely watched as he reached the gallery floor. In point of fact, he had been scrutinized from the moment he had entered the building. Since the Royal Yacht incident the Special Branch had almost tripled its security around the remainder of the Royal Family as well as the Prime Minister. The stone-faced men in dark suits appeared and vanished at every corner, alcove and door. All were exceptionally interested in the redheaded man making his way toward the gallery doors.

Dennis flashed an Irish smile at each, tauntingly. This special attention over the last few weeks had begun to erode his usual reserve. There was an Irish temper in him, to be sure. The government's security services had made a game of harassing him until four of the worst offenders had been suddenly and mercilessly reassigned to protect an offshore oil rig in the middle of the North Sea. Dennis made sure it leaked out that the retaliation had originated from his office.

Dennis secretly dared anyone to step out and confront him as he reached the top of the stairs. Almost as if in response, Dennis found his path blocked by an overdeveloped Welshman with a small, electronic metal detector wand.

"I need to see our identification please, sir," the agent demanded, running the device over Dennis, head to toe.

Dennis drew himself up sharply, trying to control his growing irritation. His smile grew taut but better sense convinced him it was best to keep his mouth shut. Two more security men came up from behind. He reached slowly into his jacket's inside pocket and pulled out his security clearance.

The Welshman studied the plastic I.D. carefully while his two colleagues stood menacingly behind.

Dennis lost his patience. "If you gentlemen," he lingered on the word acidly, "have any serious questions concerning my credentials let's go see the Prime Minister and we'll all have a little chat as to why you choose to harass one of his top aides."

"That won't be necessary, Mr. Perkins," the security man said stepping back with a smile. "It will help if you would keep this clearance badge clipped to your lapel while in the building." He returned the badge to Dennis. "I hope, sir, you'll understand the need for making these security checks from time to time. There's a lot at stake here."

His jaw tightening, Dennis replied, "I understand perfectly." He slipped the badge back in his inside coat pocket. "More than you can possibly imagine."

"Don't bother arresting him, Constable, just shoot the Irish son-of-a-bitch!"

The security agents turned quickly toward the bottom of the stairs. A group of MP's were pushing noisily out into the corridor, walking out on the Queen's speech.

Gerald Conroe waved to his delegation with Shakespearean eloquence. "As I have said repeatedly," he boasted, gesturing to Dennis, "you can't trust any of the bloody bastards!"

The group swept past the stairwell and the open-mouthed secret servicemen.

Dennis, flushed with anger, turned quickly to the Welshman. "I recognized Conroe at the front of that pack, but wasn't that Devon Harper walking beside him?"

"I believe so, sir," said the agent, stepping a short ways down the stairs for a better look. "Leader of the anti-monarchy faction. Can't imagine what those two have in common."

"I'll bloody damn well find out!" Dennis barreled down the stairs in pursuit. The Prime Minister would forgive him this one confrontation, he thought. After all, the men had walked out on the Queen.

When he reached the bottom of the stairs, Dennis spotted the group heading out the side door. He sprinted down the hall, the adrenalin rush feeding his anger. He reached the exit just as they were stepping up on the curb across the street.

Dennis threw open the door. The reporters were gone, having already moved to the press section of the gallery.

"Conroe!" Dennis called out. "You bloody bastard! What the—"

A thunderous explosion ripped through the building behind him, blasting him out of the doorway onto the sidewalk below. Two more explosions rocked the ground simultaneously. The shock waves turned cars in the street over onto their sides.

Stunned, Dennis lay on the sidewalk in the rain, covered with splintered glass and stone. A thick haze of dust fought to stay aloft against the rain, suffusing the air with an acrid, sulphurous odor. Slowly he blinked his eyes open, trying to clear his battered head. Echoes of the explosions continued to pound in his ears and brain. Satisfied that his arms and legs were all still attached and functioning, Dennis pulled himself up out of the rubble into a sitting position, oblivious to the shards of broken glass cutting into his hands.

"What in bloody hell . . ." The words almost choked him. Wiping away a trickle of blood from over his eye, he tried to stand. The pounding in his head began to ease, and for the first time, Dennis could hear the screams and panic-stricken cries for help from the crowd of pedestrians and office workers that surged onto Whitehall Street around the burning pile of stone that a few moments before had housed Parliament.

3

Dennis looked about desperately. The men he had been following were no longer in sight. He turned back to the building. The doorway he had been standing in was now a gaping hole. The upper part of the east wall had caved inward making entry impossible.

Those regiments of the Royal Guard which had accompanied the Queen to Parliament were beginning to recover from the shock as well. Dennis could hear the shouts and orders as the men in their bright red dress uniforms, dripping wet from the rain, did their best to push back the frightened crowd. Large sections of the remaining walls continued to crumble out into the streets providing a warning of their own to the people below. The urgent wail of sirens failed to silence Big Ben's chiming of the hour from the Tower of St. Andrews, one

of the few remaining structures that had once been part
of the now demolished building.

Dennis staggered out into the street. Police and
Scotland Yard officials were swarming in by the carload.
Dennis grabbed at his plastic I.D. card, clipping it onto
the pocket of his mud-splattered blazer. His legs were
regaining their strength and he started for the front of the
building pushing his way through the crowd. A black
police van had parked immediately at the base of what
had been the building's ornately impressive facade.
Standing atop the van was a Scotland Yard Inspector
barking commands into a loudspeaker.

Dennis recognized the man immediately and broke
into a limping run, heading for the van. "Inspector
Harlowe!" he shouted as he reached the van, pounding on
it with his fists. "Chief Inspector!"

The Inspector looked down angrily. "Can't you see
I . . ." The Inspector stared at the muddy, bloodspattered
civilian below. "Dennis Perkins! Christ, man! How . . ."
He scrambled down from atop the van. "Perkins! For
God's sake! Is the Prime Minister—"

"In the building!" Dennis shouted above the noise,
waving an arm at the smoldering rubble. He grabbed at
the Inspector's coat lapels. "He'd have been at the rear, in
the vicinity of the Lord's Chambers. You've got to
concentrate your rescue efforts there!"

The Inspector shouted a few commands to several
officers nearby.

"We have some army detachments as well as some heavy equipment coming to help with the survivor rescue," Harlowe said. He helped Dennis into a nearby car. "Frankly, I can't see how anyone could survive this."

Dennis surveyed the damage from the car window. He held his head as a wave of dizziness swept over him.

"We better have that head looked at, Perkins," the Inspector said. He threw the car into gear with a jolt and began swerving around the barricades and fallen stone toward the rear of the building.

Firemen had arrived and busied themselves battling various pockets of flame that continued to stubbornly burn against the rain. A group of soldiers was already in the process of clearing debris from the VIP entrance which, amazingly, still stood intact.

"The worst part of the damage appears to have been in the center of the building causing it to implode. Perhaps someone may have been able to reach a place of safety here at the side before the roof collapsed," said the Inspector. He swerved the car up onto the curb and jumped out. "Stay in the car, Perkins, and rest up. There's nothing you can do out here right now."

Dennis rolled down the window and leaned back in the seat breathing heavily. The full physical effects of the blast were just beginning to catch up with him. He watched as the soldiers began carrying out anonymous bodies in zippered plastic bags. One by one they were lifted onto a canvas-covered army transport truck. Other military units had moved in and were forcibly evacuating civilians, sealing off the city from the river to Bucking-ham Palace.

Dennis shivered as the wind cut through the open window and his rain-soaked clothing. He wondered about the news reports that, by now, were alarming all of Europe—all of the world. A scramble of activity pulled his attention back to the blown-out building. A small corps of Special Branch had moved suddenly onto the scene yelling orders into microphones hidden up their sleeves while cupping a free hand over small hearing aid-like receivers in their ear.

Dennis stuck his head out the window to see more clearly. A crane was being moved up to the entrance and Inspector Harlowe ran out of the darkened doorway waving the crane into position. Dennis became aware of another figure in the doorway, dominating the shadows within. The tall, gaunt figure stood, grimly watching the flurry of activity in silence. Considering the height of the average Englishman, Major Peter Von Schiffer was a giant of a man. Not just his size, but a shock of sandy hair and granite jaw bespoke his Aryan lineage.

Dennis tried to recall more of the personnel file he had read. A first generation Englishman, the Major's parents had fled Austria in the Second World War. Not only could he claim the Austrian title of Baron, but his mother was a great-great-grandchild of Queen Victoria. These were not the things of which he boasted, for as the Queen's personal Chief of Royal Security, he had all the prestige anyone needed. Dennis watched as the crane hoisted a huge slab of concrete.

"Perkins!" was all the Inspector shouted before rushing back through the door with the Major and several security men close behind.

Dennis climbed stiffly out of the car. He wove through the rubble to the doorway supporting himself there for a moment while he massaged his badly bruised knee. Peeking into the darkened space beyond the doorway, Dennis was amazed to find the inner foyer still intact. He limped through the rock strewn room toward the only light, a magnesium torch. A small group of soldiers worked frantically clearing the pile of broken brick which blocked further progress through the cave-like corridor.

"Perkins! Good." The Inspector pulled Dennis over to the side.

"What's the news?" Dennis coughed. The haze of dust and smoke was unbearable.

"There may be people alive beyond this cave-in. Some of the lads reported hearing voices calling out. This leads to the anteroom directly behind the Speaker's platform."

The men jumped back as a shower of plaster, stone and water struck them from above.

The Inspector removed his hat and shook the dust from it. "If the remainder of this roof holds we may get lucky here." He replaced the hat gingerly.

Dennis nodded in the direction of the Major. "That's a strange fellow. How long has he been here?"

"Major Von Schiffer is personally responsible for the security of the Royal Succession. After we found the bodies of the Prince of Wales and his wife . . ."

"Damn!" Dennis said through clenched teeth. He shook his head at this newest revelation.

"He's waiting for news of the Queen."

The two men stood silently, watching the dig continue.

The Inspector picked away absentmindedly at the crumbling plaster on the wall behind them. "Well, Perkins, as one of the few politically intelligent people left, what do you make of all this?" His eyes did not leave the digging. "My God, what will happen to the government?"

Dennis squatted on the floor leaning back against the wall, obviously exhausted. "That depends on how much is left of it."

"Not much, I would venture," said the Inspector. "Reports from the air are that the top two floors have collapsed directly above the Lords."

"Bloody hell!" Dennis closed his eyes.

"Anyone surviving this would be a miracle."

Dennis tried to take a deep breath. "It's a damn sticky situation to be sure, Inspector. I suppose the military will ensure civil order until elections can be organized again. It will all be so much simpler if the Prime Minister can be found . . . alive."

"That is partially correct, Mr. Perkins." The precise voice of Major Von Schiffer echoed off the stones.

The two men looked up startled.

"I beg your pardon, Major?" Dennis rose to meet the challenging, even stare from the towering Austrian.

"Your explanation is only partially true," the Major repeated with added emphasis.

"Then you know better?" Inspector Harlowe eyed him sternly.

"If the Prime Minister is dead or incapacitated, it is the prerogative of the reigning monarch to appoint a new government." His face did not change expression. "The armed forces will obey the reigning Sovereign as Commander in Chief." The Major turned back to where the soldiers were frantically trying to penetrate the cave-in.

Dennis stepped forward, irritated by the Major's abruptness. "The problem, Major, would seem to be the fact that there is an equal chance of finding the Queen dead as well as the Prime Minister." The Austrian's face grew taut causing Dennis to step back, regretting his accusatory tone.

The Major glared down at him. "That may be true, Mr. Perkins," his voice continued evenly and without emotion, "but the Royal Succession is immediate. When a sovereign falls the Crown is taken up automatically by the heir. The government is in no real danger. That is the distinct advantage of our Monarchy."

A cry from the direction of the dig put an end to further debate. "Inspector, we're breaking through to an open space here!" The young soldier dropped to his knees trying to see into the space beyond the pile of crumbled stone he had just pierced.

"Don't waste time, soldier," Harlowe commanded. "Get that shovel to work and widen this damn hole!" He waved at the other workmen. "Concentrate all your efforts over here. Let's get a man in there."

The men quickened their pace, tearing away at the impacted stones with their pickaxes. A young corporal cried out suddenly. He jumped back and dropped his pickax, eyes wide with fear. The Major was beside him almost instantly. Dennis marveled at how quickly the giant could move.

The small tunnel had widened considerably and the darkness within was finally giving way to the bright light of the magnesium torches. Staring out of the hole like a desperate swimmer were the lifeless eyes of a man, his body pinned down by a massive concrete support column. The body seemed to embrace the pile of stones beneath it.

"It's one of my men," said the Major, his voice controlled, staring into the sightless eyes before him. "Let's get this rubble cleared away." He picked up the dropped pickax and hammered at the wall of stone.

Finally the tunnel was opened enough for one of the soldiers to squeeze through. Another quickly followed and the two strained in the darkness to pull the fallen support beam off the dead man. After a few moments the Major crawled through the hole impatiently. The steel and concrete beam offered little resistance to the giant Austrian as he leaned his weight against it. The beam rolled off the dead man crashing in a cloud of dust on the floor.

Dennis and the Inspector were next through the tunnel. Inspector Harlowe pulled another magnesium torch out of his overcoat and quickly ignited it. The movement of the beam had caused the dead man's body to shift slightly on its bed of rock. An eerie polished gleam caught the light of the torch and flickered from beneath the body. The Inspector moved closer.

The Major raised his hand commandingly. "Stop right there!" His eyes transfixed on the metallic shimmer radiating from the broken rock beneath the corpse.

"Now see here, Von Schiffer..." The Inspector turned angrily.

Major Von Schiffer ignored him and moved quickly to the side of the body, pushing the Inspector aside. With one hand he lifted the body by the shirt collar and tossed it at Dennis' feet. The Major knelt down beside the crumbling pile of stone. Dennis was struck by the open expression of pain that clouded the normally impassive face of the Major. With deliberate, almost reverent precision, Von Schiffer removed the stones one by one from around the shiny object.

Harlowe gasped audibly. He dropped to his knees to bring the light down closer. Sticking up from the chalky mound of dirt and stone were the graceful, golden curves of the Imperial State Crown. The men knelt in silent disbelief.

"Dear God!" Inspector Harlowe barely managed to whisper.

Von Schiffer did not move. He remained on his knees, eyes closed as if he were praying. Inspector Harlowe thrust the torch at Dennis and went to work with both hands clearing away more of the dust and rock. Gradually, like a sculpture taking form, what was once a mound of rubble took on the small, frail figure of the crown's fallen owner, the Queen. The Inspector could not bring himself to go any farther. He stood slowly, for the first time feeling all of his fifty-three years.

"Sir!" the young corporal whispered across the catacomb darkness. "I believe there are others over by that door." He pointed toward the back of the room.

The Inspector inched his way along the wall with Dennis close by, carrying the torchlight.

A soldier was already on the scene inspecting the body. "This one seems to be alive, Inspector!" He felt the man's neck for a pulse.

Dennis felt his own pulse quicken. He hadn't really expected to find anyone alive. A small hope triggered a rush of adrenalin through his fatigued body.

"Looks like one of the Special Branch," said the Inspector, standing over the man. He turned quickly back to the other soldier still standing by the tunnel. "Get some oxygen in here, soldier, and make it quick!"

While the soldier called to his companions on the outside, Inspector Harlowe pulled off his overcoat. Folding it into a tight bundle he slid it under the injured man's head. The soldier returned almost immediately with a canister of oxygen and a breathing mask.

"Light another torch, corporal," the Inspector ordered. "But keep a safe distance from the oxygen." The soldier dutifully obeyed.

While the others worked to revive the man, Dennis explored the surroundings more carefully. Despite the random destruction, he was able to recognize the place as the small anteroom that lay behind the Lords. He peered out into the hallway that connected the room to the Speaker's platform and thrust the torchlight deep into the dusty haze. What had been the opposite end of the hallway was now a mass of solid rock and twisted iron. Dennis bit his lower lip in despair. He turned the light to the other end of the hall squinting his eyes against the glare. The torch had begun to sputter and its light was dimming perceptibly. The hallway towards the speaker's platform was still open, though portions of the upper floor lay in massive chunks all about.

For a split second Dennis' eyes caught what he thought was a slight movement up ahead. Before he could get closer, his light went out. "Damn!" he almost shouted. "Inspector, I need another torch over here!"

"We have enough to worry about right here, Perkins," said the Inspector sharply, as he fumbled with the oxygen mask.

"No! I think I saw something move down here!"

The Inspector motioned to one of the soldiers who tossed another of the magnesium torches to Dennis. After picking at it a moment, Dennis finally managed to get the thing to light. Slowly he made his way down the hallway, stepping carefully through the debris. He held the torch high, sending its light as far as he could, closely watching the shadows at the other end. Moving carefully towards the corner he could barely make out a figure lying on the floor propped up against the wall.

At first Dennis couldn't be sure what it was until the shadow appeared to move slightly when the light hit it. Dennis' heart began to quicken as well as his pace. He heard a gasp for air. "Inspector! I've found someone alive!" The force of his voice shook a volley of plaster from the unstable ceiling.

The Inspector was at the door instantly. "How bad is he?"

Dennis dropped down beside the figure anxiously. The man was cold and still, quite obviously dead. Another body was stretched out on the floor with its head cradled in the man's lap.

Dennis checked for a pulse. "No! He's dead. But I could have sworn . . ."

The other body on the floor twitched and coughed.

"Inspector! Wait!" Dennis brushed the dust from the man's face and pulled the light closer. Dennis froze.

"What is it, man!" the Inspector shouted impatiently stepping into the hallway.

Dennis could not speak. He dropped the torch and took the aging white head in his hands, lifting the man into his arms.

Harlowe thrust his own torchlight into the swirl of surrounding haze. "Is he alive or not?"

Dennis grabbed up the elderly man into his arms. "It's the Prime Minister!"

4

Dennis gripped his overstuffed brief case tightly as the helicopter dropped closer to the rolling hills of pine below. Major Peter Von Schiffer guided the craft effortlessly along the rising and falling contour of the Scottish countryside, oblivious to the discomfort it was causing his passengers. He only seemed concerned with the two RAF transport choppers that followed close alongside and the various reports he was receiving over his radio.

Her Majesty's helicopter was certainly not standard military issue, more resembling a miniature conference room with, so Dennis thought, a rather too sophisticated communications system than should be needed by a symbolic head of state. It was, however, a convenient setup for the moment.

Seated across from Dennis and leaning sideways against a window, was the First Sea Lord, Admiral Martin Sterling, obviously airsick, and not wishing to be bothered. Sir Arthur Leeds, head of British Intelligence, reclined in the chair next to him snoring loudly. Dennis shook his head at the man's ability to sleep, feeling more empathy at the moment with the Admiral's dilemma.

Inspector Harlowe threw down his headset and stepped back away from the communications console. "I'm still unable to reach Special Section at Balmoral." He turned to face the other men.

"How much farther to the Royal estates, Major?" intoned Leeds, his eyes still closed.

Major Von Schiffer gave the controls over to the copilot and moved back to join the others. "We're in the Dee Valley now, Sir Arthur, and will be reaching the outer edges of the estate in about ten minutes." He reached over Dennis to an overhead compartment and pulled out two of the special, military issue, Uzi machine guns.

Dennis visibly stiffened at the sight of the weapons. "Major, surely, you don't think there will be need . . ."

"The detachment of Royal Security at Balmoral isn't answering their coded call, Mr. Perkins. I think we should be prepared to meet the worst." The Major gave Dennis a contemptuous look. "You may remain within the safety of the helicopter if you wish, Mr. Perkins, until we have secured the estate."

"Now see here, Schiffer!" Dennis rose to face the Major, but the blonde giant stood a good head taller even though he had to bend over in the helicopter's confining space. "What are you implying?" Dennis felt like a petulant child.

"Sit down, Perkins!" Harlowe's voice reverberated about the cabin. "We don't have time for this." He cast a hard glance at the Major. "And Schiffer, if you can put your toys aside for a minute, we also have to make preparations in the event that we find a living heir to the Throne."

"I have every confidence that we will, Inspector," said the Major, deliberately sitting down next to Dennis. "There is a special safe room in Balmoral as in all Royal residences that is impenetrable to assault, bomb-proof and fully equipped for outside communication. We monitored an automatic emergency signal earlier so our inability to raise the castle on the radio might only mean that the hidden, exterior transmitters have been found and sabotaged."

"Then with that hope in mind we need to cement a practical strategy for setting the civil government firmly back on its feet." Inspector Harlowe let the importance of his last words settle on each of the men's mind before continuing. "Artie, why don't you read us the agency file on the Heir in case we find him alive. Perhaps if we know a little something about who's going to be in charge we'll know a little more about how to plan."

Sir Arthur sat forward in his chair, the file already opened in his lap. He studied it for a moment before speaking. "Alexis Richard Leopold Windsor, Earl of Ulster; as of his father's death four hours ago, Duke of Kent, now by the grace of God, King of the United Kingdom of Great Britain, and Northern Ireland and of His other Realms and Territories King, Head of the Commonwealth, Defender of the Faith!"

He paused again, nodding at the text before him. "Twenty-seven years of age ... Hmmm ... somewhat young ... attended the usual schools ... interesting ... took advanced degrees in theology from Oxford."

"Theology!" Admiral Sterling stirred queasily in his chair. "Hardly fit training for a King. At least it shows he's not an imbecile like his late cousin, the Prince of Wales. What about military background?"

"Nothing that I can find," said Sir Arthur, knitting his brow. "Unusual for a member of the Royal Family."

Dennis tried to remember if he had ever read anything about this obscure Royal in the tabloids. "Perhaps he just chose differently for himself," Dennis commented with a shrug.

"Younger members of the Royal Family do not choose their studies for themselves," Harlowe replied. "I agree it is rather odd."

"There is a comment under medical history that might shed some light on the matter," continued Sir Arthur. "Apparently some vague childhood condition that kept him out of school sports."

"So, perhaps our young King has a chronic medical problem of some sort," Inspector Harlowe said thoughtfully. "Let's hope this doesn't complicate matters too much."

"Here's a promising note," said Sir Arthur, pulling up a page from the file in his lap.

"Something useful, at last?" Dennis asked, shifting impatiently in his chair.

Sir Arthur glared at Dennis over the rims of his reading glasses. "As I was saying, it seems that the late Duke controlled a rather vast shipping and banking concern over which, for the last four years, his son has assumed increasing responsibilities so that the Duke could give more time to political and Royal concerns in London. The Duke apparently vetoed the son's desire to enter the Church. It seems that the Irish problem had become an obsession with His Lordship since he lost the Duchess in the bombing of the Royal Yacht."

All eyes turned unconsciously toward Dennis.

Dennis bristled and reddened. "Now really, gentlemen!"

"Don't be so sensitive, Dennis." Inspector Harlowe sat forward. "No offense meant."

Sir Arthur coughed, waving the sheet of paper at the group. "So, at least we know His Majesty has some practical experience in administering." He looked up to be sure he had regained everyone's attention. "There are two other brothers, one fourteen and one just turned five."

"A somewhat considerable age span," the Admiral said. He reached for the paper. "Is the King married?"

"There is no mention of such," Sir Arthur said.

"Considering the quality of your records, that's not surprising," Dennis said. He continued before Sir Arthur could reply. "It would seem that our most important consideration for the moment would be possible candidates for the post of Prime Minister to submit to the King."

Sir Arthur nodded in agreement. "What is the word on the Prime Minister's condition?"

"Not good," replied Von Schiffer with little hint of feeling.

"A replacement must be named." Sir Arthur fumbled among his files. "Who would be a realistic possibility?"

"I wonder if enough MP's survived to even compose a cabinet," Dennis said ruefully.

"New elections would be impossible for the next few months," Sir Arthur commented. "This is going to be difficult."

Inspector Harlowe turned again from the communications console. "I'm still unable to raise anyone at Balmoral." He pulled a .45 from inside his coat and checked the clip.

Major Von Schiffer reached for one of the Uzis at his side. "Perhaps, Inspector, you might find one of these more useful in this type of operation."

"Thank you, Major, but I'm rather used to this small, but I assure you, accurate weapon."

"It's been a while," said Sir Arthur, reaching for one of the Uzis, "but I think I still remember how to use one of these."

Major Von Schiffer looked inquiringly at Dennis.

"I've never fired a gun in my life," said Dennis uncomfortably.

"It's a talent that comes easily when your life's at stake, Mr. Perkins," the Major said, slapping a .22 revolver into Dennis' hand. "Put this in your pocket. You may find it handy."

Dennis accepted the gun grudgingly. It was small, light-weight, almost like a toy. He slipped it into his coat pocket.

"We've reached the perimeter of the estate, Major!" called the young lieutenant who was piloting the copter.

The Major moved to the front of the helicopter. "We'll set down on the east ridge above the castle. There's a windbreak of trees between the ridge clearing and the main house that will afford us some cover."

"Well, Perkins," the Inspector said, taking in a long, deep breath. "You've made one narrow escape this morning. Think your luck is still holding?"

Dennis tried to manage a smile. "You know what they say about the Irish and luck, Inspector." He could feel the weight of the gun in his pocket.

Admiral Sterling slid a clip into one of the Uzis. "I think you'll find combat a little easier than political debate, Perkins," he said. He eyed his weapon admiringly. "There's no room for compromise. Just kill or be killed."

"Good Lord, Admiral!" Harlowe shook his head.

"There's nothing more frightening to the sane mind than an old soldier with a gun," Dennis said deliberately.

The Admiral only smiled as he tested the weight of his gun in his hand with childlike enjoyment.

"Sit tight, Gentlemen," the Major called from the pilot's seat. "We're setting down now."

Dennis peered out the window as the helicopter descended. He was unable to make out anything through the billowing dust pulled up from the ground by the churning blades of the three large aircraft.

The Major executed the landing with a hard jolt to his passengers. Dennis' ears tingled as the craft's powerful engines shut off. The monstrous whirling blades dying momentum continued to cut through the air and dust, before finally coming to a stop. The group sat in total silence.

Major Von Schiffer moved back to join them. "Things seem rather quiet outside, Gentlemen." He unlatched the door and swung it open. "I think it's about time we change all that." He leapt from the helicopter into a crouching position and looked about warily.

Dennis reluctantly joined the other men as they stood cautiously at the side of the door. Directly ahead of them grew a tall line of pines cutting along the horizon like a wall. The grassy ridge sloped downward beyond the trees, and in the distance Dennis could make out the fairy tale turrets of Balmoral Castle. He listened for any sign of life, but an occasional bird and the rustling of a breeze through the trees was all he could make out.

Von Schiffer signaled to his men in the other choppers and they jumped out obediently, crouched for a moment, and then ran for the cover of the trees. Dennis counted about twenty men. Inspector Harlowe dropped down beside the Major and the rest of the older men followed. When Dennis hit the ground a sharp pain cut through his left leg. He winced and muffled a cry of pain.

"Take it easy, Perkins," the Inspector whispered, taking his arm.

"Still a bit sore from this morning," Dennis said, massaging his calf.

"All right, gentlemen!" The Major looked at each of them. "You are armed solely for self-protection. You will leave any fighting that needs to be done to my men, and you will stay back at all times."

Admiral sterling bristled. "Now see here, Schiffer, I—"

"Each of you is too important to the government to be playing hero." Von Schiffer interrupted. He grabbed the Admiral's arm tightly. "I am in charge of this operation, Admiral, and I will be obeyed or you will be left in this helicopter under armed guard. Is that understood?"

The Admiral glared at the Major, but nodded his head anyway.

Quickly they all moved into the trees to join the others. The old admiral sprinted youthfully across the heath while Dennis trailed along behind, cursing his injured ankle, feeling like so much useless baggage. The men lay prone on the ground behind the trees watching for any movement on the grounds below. Dennis crawled up behind the Inspector.

Von Schiffer motioned to the young lieutenant from the helicopter, who quickly moved behind the line and knelt down beside them. "What do you make of the situation so far, Toby?" the Major asked.

"No sight or sound yet, sir," the Lieutenant answered. "If anything is going on it's probably happening inside the castle."

"Then our arrival may have gone unnoticed." Von Schiffer eyed the lay of the land. "Too much open ground to cover to the house." He thought a minute. "Time to test the waters, men." The Major carefully studied the house for any sign of surveillance. "Lieutenant! Get the two fastest sprinters we have over here now."

The young soldier hesitated for a minute before signaling to a tall, lanky young corporal who moved quickly to join them.

"Corporal Lydd and I would be the fastest, sir," said the Lieutenant removing his backpack.

"Right," said the Major. He looked hard at each of them. "You men are targets . . . nothing more . . . nothing less. Once you reach the wall of the building you'll be pretty much safe from sniper fire." He paused a moment looking across the grassy expanse of the lawn leading up to the palace. "Keep low and keep moving whatever you do. If you draw any fire don't stop. Any snipers would probably be set in the towers and from that angle, if you lay still on the ground, you'd be a sitting duck."

Inspector Harlowe moved up beside the Major. "If you draw any fire it's best to sprint out in opposite directions," he said. "That'll confuse the sniper momentarily, forcing him to choose a target. You'll get a few precious seconds to maneuver."

"Very good, Inspector." Von Schiffer nodded his approval to the idea. He rose slightly, signaling sharpshooters up to the edge of the trees, covering every strategic aspect of the large house.

Dennis moved up a little closer into a position behind one of the sharpshooters. He scanned each window and tower of the mansion looking for any sign of activity. The surrounding quiet on so large an estate struck Dennis as somewhat unnatural. There were no groundskeepers about, no windows open to let in the crisp fresh air, not even a maid stepping to a door to shake out a rug.

As the Major signaled, the two soldiers sprinted out onto the open lawn, side-by-side. Dennis watched the house closely. As the two soldiers reached the first terraced section of the hill leading up to a row of ornamental hedge, Dennis' eye caught the glint of sunlight on metal coming from the uppermost turret of the fantasy-like castle.

Before Dennis could shout a warning, the Major fired his weapon into the air causing the two runners to suddenly fan out in opposite directions. A blaze of automatic gunfire from the castle turret strafed the grassy slope where only seconds before the two runners were headed. At the same instant, Royal sharpshooters zeroed-in on the sniper and sprayed the tower window with bullets, putting an end to the rain of enemy fire. Dennis watched, relieved, as the two target soldiers reached the safety of the castle walls and flattened themselves against the stone.

Dennis turned to question the Major about the next move but Von Schiffer was already on the run down the hill. Another small detachment of soldiers immediately followed, fanning out across the grounds. Dennis jumped to his feet, cursing to himself, and struggled down the hill in pursuit. The small pistol in his coat pocket bounced heavily against his side, making him feel curiously off balance. The throbbing pain in his ankle ebbed slightly, gradually being replaced by a prickly numbness.

The Major had already reached the castle and was inching along the wall toward one of the many windows. Dennis hobbled up the manicured slope toward the window as best he could.

A rifle shot shattered the window. Dennis froze instantly, paralyzed by the sound of a bullet screaming past his left ear. His perception seemed to shift into slow motion. Unable to move he watched in horror as the muzzle of a semi-automatic was thrust through the window and aimed at his chest.

Von Schiffer spun around to the window and thrust his hand through the broken glass. In one motion the Major pulled the gunman out through the window by the hair and blew the crown of the man's head off with the Uzi he held in his other hand like a pistol. Blood and fragments of bone splattered over Dennis and he felt himself begin to retch.

The Major grabbed Dennis by the collar and threw him to the ground against the wall, crouching over him menacingly. "Bloody, goddamn hell, Perkins! I told you to stay back! What are you doing—trying to get yourself killed?"

Dennis tried to take a deep breath and turned his face from the corpse, whose shattered skull still emptied its contents onto the grass. "Sorry, Major. I wasn't thinking—"

"Well start! We're not playing games here."

"I can see that, Major," Dennis muttered through clenched teeth. He pulled a handkerchief from his back pocket to wipe his face clean.

Von Schiffer signaled to his two sprinters who had moved up to the other side of the window in response to the gunfire. Without warning, Von Schiffer grabbed Dennis by the lapels and lifted him to his feet. Dennis tried to meet the Major's steel-gray eyes but was reminded of the gun barrel he had been staring down moments before and could not suppress a shudder.

"Do not move from this or any spot unless you are told to," the Major commanded. With that he released his hold and Dennis fell back against the wall.

Von Schiffer moved to the edge of the window again and signaled the two soldiers with a nod of his head. He dove through the window like a battering ram and hit the floor of the castle in a roll. In the same instant the two soldiers began to spray the room over his head with covering fire.

Dennis pressed back against the wall with his eyes closed. More gunfire broke out around the castle as other detachments of soldiers penetrated the castle interior. Dennis waited a few moments after the gunfire ceased before opening his eyes. The young lieutenant Von Schiffer called Toby had already followed the Major through the window. Corporal Lydd remained outside for cover. He stood, gun at the ready, his eyes darting about the grounds and back through the smashed window, watching for any sign of trouble.

After a moment, he waved the barrel of his Uzi at Dennis, motioning him into the castle.

5

For a second Dennis considered declining the invitation, but instinct told him that the wisest and safest course would probably be to stick with the Major. He stepped through the broken glass into an oversized room that appeared to be one of the castle's side parlors. Bullet holes speckled the light patina of the paneling along with several old but unimpressive portraits of Royals in various sporting pursuits. Dennis was relieved to find no bodies decorating the Persian carpets. He shuddered, trying to erase the picture he had left outside.

Major Von Schiffer stood at a pair of heavy, oak doors that opened into a large hallway. Dennis started to speak, but was silenced abruptly by Corporal Lydd, hand clasped over his mouth.

The Major signaled Toby to cover the door and motioned the Corporal and Dennis over to him. "The fact that hostile forces are still here indicates that at least some of our objectives are still alive. We'll make directly for the safe room."

The Major snapped out the now spent clip from his weapon and replaced it with a full one from somewhere inside his jacket. Dennis always marveled at how much artillery security people could carry about undetected.

"Mr. Perkins, you will stay here out of harm's way," the Major ordered.

"The hell I will!" answered Dennis. "What's to stop some more of your people from barreling in here and spraying this room with bullets again. Sorry, Major, but I'm sticking with the group." He pulled the small pistol out of his pocket, trying to keep his hand from shaking. "Don't worry about me, Major. I think I can take care of myself."

The Major's stony face almost managed a bemused smirk. "I think, Mr. Perkins, we'd all feel safer if you were unarmed, but suit yourself."

"Go to hell, Major," Dennis said.

"Stick with us, Dennis, and I think you'll find the journey there a little shorter." With that the Major moved quickly out of the room and down the hall.

The two soldiers followed. Corporal Lydd kept back slightly, moving down the hall backwards, covering their rear. Dennis kept close to the wall between them in the hopes that he was out of the line of any potential fire.

Occasional bursts of gunfire could still be heard echoing down the hall from some distant part of the castle. Dennis tightened his grip on the small pistol. He tried to swallow, but an annoying lump had formed in his throat which made it difficult.

He glanced back to the safety of the room he had just left and regret clawed at his stomach. The hallway ended in a large foyer off the main entrance with a vaulted ceiling and a monstrous staircase which rose from its center up to a balconied second floor. The Major stopped suddenly and went down to his knee. Instantly the soldiers followed suit. Corporal Lydd pulled Dennis down with him without a word.

A sound from across the foyer behind the staircase caused Dennis to raise up slightly for a better look. He was instantly wrestled down by the young corporal. One look was enough, however. On the other side of the staircase stood two men in camouflage fatigues similar to those Dennis had seen sported by a lot of the fashion-conscious youth in London. The difference, of course, was that these men had added such accessories as guns, grenades, and fully packed ammunition belts.

Von Schiffer and the Lieutenant crawled out into the room on their stomachs hidden from view by the rising staircase. They began to circle back to a small cloak room that opened underneath the back of the stairs. Such cloakrooms were usually accessed from both sides and Dennis realized they were trying to come up behind the two guards. Corporal Lydd was also on his stomach and had inched up to the doorway.

Dennis' curiosity overwhelmed him. He raised up slightly for another look. And look he did, right into the eyes of one of the guards who quickly pulled his weapon up, catching the attention of his comrade. The gun never fired. In one fluid movement the Major was on him with both arms wrapped about the guard's head. Dennis heard the muffled snap as the man's neck broke.

Before the other guard could shout a warning, Toby sprang up behind him, grabbed him by the hair, pulled his head back, and cleanly cut his throat from ear to ear. Dennis shuddered as the blood boiled out from the man's gaping neck. The only sound heard was the body dropping to the floor. Major Von Schiffer moved out in front of the staircase and signaled to Corporal Lydd and Dennis. Dennis stood up behind Lydd and raised a hand in acknowledgment of the signal.

A shot sounded from the balcony above. The Major was knocked back a step as the bullet slammed into his left shoulder. Stunned for a moment he reached instinctively for his arm. Toby reached up from the floor and grabbed the Major by the belt, at the same time kicking his feet out from under him and pulling him down behind the stair banister.

More bullets singed the air above them. Corporal Lydd threw himself into the middle of the room, his Uzi spraying the balcony with deadly fire. Another body came rolling limply down the stairs. Dennis jumped to his feet and headed across the room to the Major's side.

Two more soldiers burst through the front door, automatic weapons at the ready. Luckily they looked before they shot and quickly moved to position themselves about the room to further secure the area.

Dennis dropped to his knees beside the Major, who was sitting up, leaning against the banister, eyeing his shoulder wound with clinical detachment as Toby tied a make-shift pressure bandage about it. "Are you all right, Major?" asked Dennis. He winced as Toby jerked a knot tight.

"Considering the fact that by all rights I should be dead, I'm doing quite well." The Major tried to move his arm without much luck. "I was careless and nothing more." He shook his head with disdain. Grabbing the banister above his head he pulled himself to his feet. "The library is behind these doors," Von Schiffer said, gesturing with his good arm. "The safe room is a vault hidden behind the library fireplace."

"Do you think the assassins have found it?" asked Dennis.

"I'm positive they have." Von Schiffer snorted. "But they'll find opening it a damn sight more difficult than discovering it." The Major walked out into the middle of the foyer and stared for a moment at the spot where the sniper had stood. He tested his shoulder again, willing it to a greater flexibility, before rejoining the others. "I think we can assume the bastards know we are out here and that they've probably prepared a small welcome for us." He thought for a moment. "Gentlemen, let's take a moment to survey our overall position. Corporal Lydd!"

"Sir!" The young corporal left the group of soldiers he had been conferring with and snapped to attention with a salute to the Major.

"Current status, Corporal?"

"Sir, section leaders report all perimeters have been secured, six enemy dead, one prisoner taken. No casualties on our side . . ." He glanced at the splatter of blood about the Major's shoulder and dropped his eyes to the floor clearing his throat.

"A prisoner." The Major raised an eyebrow. "Let's have a look at him."

Moments later Lydd returned with another corporal, dragging the captured terrorist, who had been neatly bound and gagged. He squirmed about fruitlessly in protest, his eyes glaring fanatically at his captors.

"Feisty little bugger, isn't he," commented Sir Arthur from the doorway.

Admiral Sterling pushed his way in ahead. "A successful assault, Major." He waved his Uzi about with much bravado. "Got off a few shots myself!"

"Admiral!" Von Schiffer almost shouted. "Why aren't you waiting at the helicopter? You were told to stay back."

Sterling blustered, "Well, when you let Perkins follow, naturally I—"

"Enough!" Von Schiffer glared at Dennis who merely shrugged. "We're wasting time."

"Quite right, Major," said Inspector Harlowe slipping up beside Dennis.

"Where in blazes did you come from, Inspector?" Dennis said with a start.

"I manage to get about, Dennis. Never you mind. What's our situation, Major?"

"We were just about to determine that," said Von Schiffer, turning to his writhing prisoner. "Drop his pants."

Immediately Corporal Lydd jerked the man's fatigues down.

"Hold his head and remove the gag."

Toby moved up behind the prisoner and gripped the man's jaw in his hand, ripped off the gag, and held his face toward the Major in a vise-like grip. Von Schiffer slid a jagged-edged knife from a sheath strapped to his leg. He held the gleaming blade up to the man's face and leaned in with cold-blooded purpose.

"Goddamn English—" The man's voice choked off as Toby's grip shifted to his throat, but not before the prisoner managed to butt his head forward into Von Schiffer's injured shoulder.

The Major clamped his teeth against the pain. "You deserve to die Irishman, but you won't make me kill you so quickly." The Major reached down and grabbed the man's foreskin between his thumb and forefinger, pulling it out sharply away from the glans. He smiled maliciously at the man. "I've never seen a circumcised Irishman before." The Major pulled a little harder at the foreskin. The man's eyes widened in fear.

Von Schiffer's knife sliced down with razor precision, cleanly severing the foreskin. Even in Toby's choking grip, the man managed a chilling scream.

Major Von Schiffer stepped back holding up the foreskin for the man to see. Almost blind with pain, the prisoner strained against his captors, kicking spasmodically. Blood poured from the sensitive incision, spattering about the man's torso and legs and onto the floor.

"Jesus Bloody Christ." Dennis clenched his fists, feeling the man's pain. "Is this really necessary?"

Sir Arthur put a restraining hand on Dennis' shoulder. "Don't look if it bothers you that much, boy. Pain is an excellent truth serum."

Von Schiffer ignored them both. Unmoved by the man's screams, he slapped him hard across the face with the back of his hand, jolting the poor wretch back to the moment. The prisoner's body went limp against his captors, all his effort expended. The rhythmic coursing of relentless pain spasmed his body into a pathetic twitching motion. A harsh, gurgling moan erupted from deep in his throat. His eyes, though glazed, stared up into the Major's face.

Von Schiffer leaned into him again. "There, there now. Abraham survived it. So might you." He patted the man's cheek. "After all, you're not really in with these animals all the way, are you?"

The prisoner tried to jerk his face away but the Major gripped his chin and pulled him back.

"You and your . . .comrades did swear an oath not to be taken alive, didn't you?" He smiled at the man again, nudging his face with the palm of his hand. "Didn't you? That's the usual procedure. And here you are, alive and well . . . not at all dead . . . not yet, anyway." The Major nudged the man's face a little harder. "You've failed your mission. That's two marks against you with your friends. Alive and a failure. You were supposed to capture the young Earl unaware, but he made it to the safe room first, didn't he? You Irish shit!" He slapped the man again, hard, baiting him out of the pain. "The Earl's safe and you blew it, didn't you?" Von Schiffer laughed in his face.

The glaze over the man's eyes turned from pain to angry fanaticism. With renewed effort he jerked his head from Toby's grip. "We'll get to him before you do, filthy, motherfu—"

Von Schiffer slapped him silent. "Oh, will you, Irishman? The sum-total of your remaining forces are locked behind those doors. I think my men can clean up this mess in short order."

"Go ahead and try, bloody bastard, go ahead—"

The Major back-handed him again. He sheathed his knife and patted the man's face taunting—laughing.

"Fuck you!" the Irishman rasped.

"You might find that somewhat painful," Von Schiffer said, reaching down to flick the man's still bleeding appendage with a finger.

The prisoner's screams stopped abruptly. With a nod from the Major, Toby snapped the man's head around sharply, breaking his neck and killing him instantly.

"He wasn't supposed to be taken alive," Von Schiffer said coldly. "A man should always keep his promises, Lieutenant."

Toby smiled back at the Major as he let the prisoner's body slide to the floor. "Another martyr to the cause, sir." He kicked the body.

The Major stepped toward the door where Corporal Lydd had attached a small sound amplifier. He crouched under the headphones, eyes closed, his face creased with concentration. "Sounds like they've found the vault door now, Major. I hear drilling." He handed the headset to the Major.

Von Schiffer listened for a second and nodded. "Right. Let's get on with it."

"Get on with it?" said Dennis, pulling away from Sir Arthur. "Get on with what? What have you accomplished so far but cold-blooded murder?"

The Major looked at him calmly. "I have interrogated a prisoner in the field, Mr. Perkins, and had him executed on the basis of that interrogation."

"Interrogation? You didn't learn anything from this man. This was torture and killing simply for the sport of it."

"On the contrary, Dennis," Inspector Harlowe said gently. "We've learned a great deal that we weren't sure of before."

"To be specific," intoned Sir Arthur, standing over the dead man, studying the body like a hunter counting his stag's points, "we know, for a fact, that the Earl is not dead. We also know that he has not been taken prisoner but is safely ensconced in the vault beyond these doors."

Dennis righteous indignation wavered slightly.

Sir Arthur continued, "I believe we may also assume, judging from the prisoner's challenging demeanor at the end, daring us to break in and stop his comrades, that they have established some sort of perimeter defense to stop us."

"Big problem there," Admiral Sterling commented, sliding a new clip into his weapon.

"Very astute, gentlemen," said the Major. He drew himself erect, towering over the small group.

Dennis braced himself and looked directly into the Major's gray-granite stare, refusing to be intimidated.

Von Schiffer spoke without taking his eyes off Dennis. "Your analysis is quite correct, Sir Arthur." His chilling gaze intensified on Dennis. "As for the execution of the prisoner, the directives operating in time of national emergency entitle me to kill anyone I damn well please if I judge them to be a clear and present danger to the Crown." He leaned into Dennis. "Any . . . one."

"Fuck off, Major," Dennis said before he could stop the words. His stomach knotted in anger at having let himself be so easily baited. He glanced at the dead man on the floor. "And it may disappoint you to know, Major, that I've already been circumcised." He met the Major's eyes with a defiant look.

Major Von Schiffer broke out in a loud, uncharacteristic laugh, catching the group, and especially Dennis, totally off guard. "I am disappointed, Dennis," he said, using Dennis' given name for the first time. He cast a lurid glance at Dennis' crotch. "But we'll have to postpone your proving that fact till later." He turned quickly to his men. "Lieutenant! I want that door plastiqued and ready to blow in three minutes."

Toby disconnected the listening device from the door and reached into a pocket on his pants leg for the clay-like sticks of plastic explosive.

Dennis followed Inspector Harlowe, Sterling and Sir Arthur to a safe distance behind the stairway. He pulled at Sir Arthur's sleeve. "What about their perimeter defenses?"

"The whole bloody thing's a joke, Dennis. These people aren't professional soldiers. They're terrorists who act only for the moment because they don't care if they survive. They're here to kill or be killed and now they've got themselves boxed in with no way out. Their only perimeter is these doors with probably a couple of machine guns trained on them."

"Hell, lad, we're not going to break in shooting!" the Admiral said. "We'll blow the bloody room up and everyone in it." His face was red with excitement and he clapped his hands together relishing the image.

"But the Earl . . ." worried Dennis.

"That's the beauty of it, Dennis," Sir Arthur responded. "Their only hope was to have him as hostage. But he's in the vault—a bomb-proof vault. We could blow the whole damn castle up and he'd still be all right."

6

"Jesus." Dennis squatted down behind the railing watching the blur of activity as the special forces unit went about its deadly business.

A massive marble-topped buffet had been pulled to the center of the room facing the door some distance away. Cushions and pillows from furniture in the surrounding room had been stacked up against it forming a barricade against the explosion to come. The Major had stationed four soldiers behind the barricade while Toby set a small radio relay into the plastique. When the fuse was set he pulled a small, palm-sized transmitter from his jacket and extended its delicate antennae. On a signal from the Major, he moved over behind the staircase next to Dennis.

Von Schiffer cast a momentary glance at the government delegation. Assuring himself of their safety, he paced the distance from the barricade to the door for the soldiers. "All right, men. Two grenades each. Get one into the room immediately after the door's blown. The second round should go in immediately after the first has detonated." He moved behind the barricade and bent down behind his men as they readied two grenades each in front of them. "Heads down, gentlemen!"

Toby pressed the button. The room lit up in a bright flash as the doors were blown from their hinges. Before the smoke could clear the four soldiers lobbed their first round of grenades with practiced expertise through the doorway into the target room. At the same time, Dennis could hear machine gun fire spit from behind the cloud of smoke. He pressed himself closer to the stairwell. A spray of plaster showered from the wall behind him as the high velocity bullets impacted. The grenade explosions seemed more powerful than the plastique to Dennis. The floor shook under him as the little bombs released their deadly shrapnel. Dennis thought he heard a scream as the explosion sounded.

Again the soldiers lobbed a second round into the room. When the shaking was over, Dennis unstopped his ears and shifted his position slightly to try and get a better look. The only sound coming from the room was the occasional splintering of glass or wood as pieces fell from the wall and ceiling.

Von Schiffer leapt from behind the barricade flattening himself against the wall next to the open doorway. The soldiers now had their guns at ready, watching for any movement in the room as the dust and smoke from the successive explosions began to settle. The Major inched around the corner into the room. His eyes narrowed, cutting through the haze as he surveyed the debris beyond. He signaled to the men, who quickly moved from the barricade and followed him into the room. Toby motioned to Dennis and the three older men to stay put and then crossed into the room.

Admiral Sterling stood up for a better vantage. "I shouldn't think we'll be hearing any more resistance from these buggers."

Sir Arthur stood up as well. "Shame about that room. I remember an excellent Matisse hanging over the mantle."

Inspector Harlowe pulled Dennis up by the sleeve as Toby waved his gun from the doorway. "Come on, lads," Harlowe said. "Looks like the coast is clear."

"Laid waste would be more accurate," said Dennis, following behind tentatively.

Dennis' nostrils stung as he stepped into the pungent swirl of plaster and gunpowder. The room itself was not as large as he had imagined. The remains of a heavy mahogany desk, apparently used to barricade the door, lay splintered just to the left as they entered. The space was probably used as a small study, Dennis thought, noticing the bookcases just ahead. Most of the shelves had been blown away, but a few books remained. The floors, however, told another story. Mangled corpses and their unidentifiable pieces littered among the remains of books, papers, and furniture.

Dennis felt strangely detached. Gone were his earlier feelings of revulsion and horror, replaced with a numbing magnetism that seemed to draw his eyes to each gruesome detail. The only shock to his system was the sudden realization of his own morbid curiosity.

"Mind your feet, boy!" warned the Inspector.

Instinctively Dennis threw his weight sideways, his shoe barely missing an anonymous lump of viscera in his path. The sudden shift in his momentum took away his balance.

Inspector Harlowe caught him under the arm, preventing him from falling on top of it. "Careful there, Perkins." The Inspector's eyes reflected a certain understanding. "You're handling all this a bit better as the day goes on."

"Thank you, Inspector," said Dennis, righting himself. "Though I don't know if better is the word for it."

"Ah! There we are," Harlowe said. "Vault's over here."

Dennis followed the Inspector across the room, this time stepping carefully through the wreckage. The fireplace, hearth and all, was swung away from the wall revealing the mirrored surface of a stainless steel door just large enough for one person to squeeze through. Several soldiers worked at dragging various bits of ceiling, furniture, and human remains from in front. The Major knelt before the small but formidable door, inspecting a small punch-pad with numbered keys.

"Dreadfully botched affair," commented the Admiral standing over a steaming corpse in the center of the rubble. "Couldn't have been more than six men in here."

"How the hell can you tell?" Dennis asked forcing himself to look about at the piecemeal gore. "Bloody Christ, it would take an army of pathologists to put this mess back together." He began to grow less steady on his feet.

"Over here, gentlemen," called the Major, standing impatiently. "The locking mechanism appears to be unharmed." He ran his hands over several freshly drilled holes along the vault door's side. A half dozen sticks of dynamite and blasting caps lay at his feet, miraculously unexploded. He fingered the holes in disgust. "The fools would've never made it through this door," the Major said. "The whole operation should have been aborted when they realized the Earl had made it into the safe room."

Dennis caught his breath as the Major kicked disdainfully at the pile of explosive. He looked for a place to take cover, but there was none. "Let's hurry and get it opened then, Major," Dennis said nervously. "We've a lot to do."

"Open it?" Von Schiffer raised an eyebrow. "We don't open it, Dennis. This door can now only be released from the inside."

The Major knelt beside the punch-key mechanism again. "We can, however, with a prearranged, numbered code, signal to whoever's inside that everything out here is secure." He pointed to a small red light flashing above the keys. "If the message is accepted the light will turn green and the door will open."

Sir Arthur moved up behind him for a closer look. "Of course that's assuming the people inside know what the codes are."

"We can only try, Sir Arthur," said Von Schiffer impatiently. He began to slowly key in a series of numbers and each key responded with a beep of varying pitches.

All eyes kept a steady train on the red warning light and patiently waited as it blinked methodically. Moments passed in silence, punctuated by the little red eye flashing against its background of polished stainless steel.

"It's still red," said the Admiral, breaking the silence.

The Major turned slowly to him, not even attempting to hide the sarcasm in his voice. "Thank you, Admiral. We noticed."

Sterling turned away from the Major's cold stare and coughed self-consciously. Again the Major entered the numerical pattern into the keyboard. His eyes fastened on the light as if he could will it to turn green. The seconds passed with each blink of the light.

"Bloody hell!" cursed the Major under his breath.

Inspector Harlowe moved up behind him, "Give them a minute to think about it, Major," he said softly. "Even if they don't know the code they might figure out what you're trying to do."

Von Schiffer nodded impatiently and reached to punch in the numbers a third time.

"There!" Dennis pointed excitedly.

The light was flashing green. Everyone backed away as the door began to vibrate to a whir of sounds as its internal mechanisms engaged. With a whisper of air, the door swung outward. The Major ducked his head low. Because of his height he almost had to crawl through the cave-like corridor of concrete and steel. Dennis quickly ducked in behind him.

He heard the Major draw in a sharp breath. Dennis looked up quickly. Von Schiffer was standing motionless, hunched over at the end of the short corridor. The twin barrels of a shotgun were shoved up against his forehead. Dennis heard the gun cock.

"Sir," said a strong treble voice, speaking without a hint of fear. "If you so much as breathe, I'll blow your brains out your ass!"

Von Schiffer stared down the barrels calmly. "Sir, if I don't breathe, you won't have to kill me."

The boy at the end of the gun looked quizzically at the Major. Dennis guessed his age to be somewhere near the beginning of puberty. He held the heavy gun with an experienced ease. Bright hazel eyes flashed with deadly purpose through bangs of light brown hair as he sighted down the heavy gun at Von Schiffer.

His ruddy cheeks dimpled as he considered the Major's words. "Very well. You may breathe ... slowly. Drop your weapons, please."

The boy took a step back into the vault while Von Schiffer set his pistol carefully on the floor.

"Hands up ... all of you. Palms open and facing me." The boy motioned his prisoners in with the barrel tip. "Quickly now!"

The small group filed in slowly, hands held above their heads. Dennis glanced over his shoulder for one of the armed soldiers but they were back in the room out of sight.

Dennis stepped a little closer to the Major. "Where are the soldiers?" he whispered.

"Soldiers?" asked the boy sharply. He moved quickly to the side of the door, his gun cocked and ready. "What soldiers?" His voice rose, ringing off the steel walls.

Von Schiffer looked calmly down at the boy, bowing slightly. "A detachment of Royal Marines, sir—Special Forces Unit. They'll be standing guard outside to assure your safety."

The boy cocked his head to one side, eyeing the Major with suspicion. His fingers tightened slightly around the gun.

"Papa." He looked back into the vault behind his captives. "They claim to be Royal Marines, sir. They don't look like Royal Marines to me." The gun barrel turned ominously toward the Major.

"Put the gun down, Nicky," came a voice from the room beyond.

Dennis restrained himself from turning around. The voice was oddly pitched somewhere between tenor and contralto. Its resonance was more like a hoarse whisper, but with enough depth and intensity to carry about the room.

"Nicky." It was a quiet voice, accustomed to being obeyed.

"All right, Papa. But we'd best keep an eye on them." The boy lowered his gun to one side and walked haughtily around the men in the direction of the voice.

The group turned as he moved.

The vault was long and narrow, spreading out perpendicular to the door. In the shadow at the end of the room Dennis could make out a small writing table and chair, from which rose a frail figure not much taller than the boy.

He stood slowly with the aid of a silver-tipped, ebony walking stick. His hair was so blonde as to be almost white, causing Dennis at first to think he was an old man. But the face was hairless and unwrinkled, the skin almost translucent. Electric blue eyes seemed to command the whole room with their gaze. Seated on the floor against the wall were several liveried persons, obviously house servants. They sat in silence, shifting about nervously.

As the young man stepped forward, Dennis caught a glimpse of a small child, possibly four or five years of age clinging to the figure's pant legs from behind.

"Gentlemen." The young man's eyes seemed to fasten on each one of them simultaneously, the voice calm and commanding. "We thank God you've come. Nicky is an excellent shot but, I regret to say, we were in such a rush to find safety here that he neglected to bring any ammunition."

The boy with the gun smirked at the Major, who only cocked one eyebrow.

"I am Alexis Windsor, Earl of Ulster," said the frail young man standing in the shadow. "My brother, Nicholas you've already met, and this," he nodded to the small child at his feet, "is our little brother, Bertie."

"Albert," a small voice whispered up at him.

"Oh, yes . . . Albert. Bertie is a family nickname."

"Brothers?" Admiral Sterling whispered loudly to Sir Arthur. "I thought the other boy called him papa."

"Also a family nickname," the young Earl answered. He rested a hand on the small child's head reassuringly. "They're special names which only we use." He smiled down at the little boy peeking out from behind his legs, eyes wide more with curiosity than fear.

"Sir." The Major stepped forward bowing deeply. "I am Major Peter Von Schiffer, special secret service detachment, Royal Security. I have the honor to introduce the First Sea Lord, Admiral Martin Sterling; Sir Arthur Leeds, Intelligence Service; Chief Inspector Macklin

Harlowe, Secret Service, Scotland Yard, and Mr. Dennis Perkins, Chief of Staff to the Prime Minister."

Each one stepped out in turn, bowing.

"What's the word from London, Major?" asked the Earl. Before our radio was sabotaged, we were getting some rather bad news. Is our father all right?"

Von Schiffer dropped his eyes a moment, then spoke. "Sir, your father, the Duke, is dead, killed when a bomb was set off underneath the Lord's Chambers of Parliament."

"Father!" Nicholas dropped the shotgun and rushed to the side of his brother. He stared for a moment at the Major in disbelief, then buried his face against his older brother's shoulder.

The littlest child clung tighter to his brother's pants leg, looking up at him, not quite comprehending.

The Earl's eyes did not waver. He stood motionless supporting his younger siblings. "What about the Queen?"

This time Von Schiffer did not hesitate. "The Queen is dead, sir. Killed in the same explosion."

"The Prince of Wales?"

"Dead, sir, as well as the Princess." The vault reverberated with the finality of Von Schiffer's words.

Slowly the Major went down on one knee, as did the others in the room. For a moment the brothers stared at the men kneeling before them in the ancient symbol. Suddenly Nicholas pulled away from his older brother, falling to his knee beside Von Schiffer, his face pale with the recognition of what had occurred.

He held out his hands to his little brother. "Bertie!"

The little boy rushed across into his brother's arms looking back at his former protector in confusion. Their older brother stood alone in front of them, leaning heavily on his cane. He closed his eyes, raising his head as if to pray some great weight off his shoulders.

"Your Majesty," Von Schiffer said softly.

"God save you, sir," the new Prince Nicholas whispered beside him.

7

"Well it's about bloody good time!" Dennis slammed down the phone receiver. He stared at the television screen unblinking, exhausted.

An endless panorama of helicopter views of the bomb destruction, peppered with the usual interviews with one of the thousands of eyewitnesses played against the constant government announcements that everything was all right—everything was under control. Dennis felt everything but under control. He continued to undress while keeping an ear to the reports. As yet he had heard nothing about the mess at Balmoral, and even more disconcerting was the lack of any information or announcements concerning the fate of the Prime Minister or of the Queen.

"Did you finally get through," Aidan asked from the end of the bed.

"They won't give out any information over the phone," Dennis said. He reached up to unbutton his shirt. "But at least a meeting has been scheduled at Buckingham Palace in an hour for surviving members of the government."

"That was quick."

"Not quick enough as far as I'm concerned." He fumbled with the shirt buttons.

Aidan pushed his partner's sore fingers aside and continued unbuttoning his shirt despite his protests. "You look the mess, don't you?" he said.

"Politics is bloody hell, love," Dennis said, trying to laugh. He dropped his hands to his side wearily and smiled down at Aidan. Tired as he was, the sight of the beautiful young man standing naked except for his boxers, assured Dennis there was still life below the belt.

"A hot shower and a good night's sleep will take care of you, Mr. Hotshot Politician," Aidan said. He kissed his partner's bruised shoulder.

Dennis sighed. "No sleep for me, Aidan. I've got a meeting in an hour at the Palace. I've just got time for a quick shower and a shave."

"A meeting this late, Dennis? What for?" Aidan pouted seductively.

"Jesus, Aidan," Dennis said hugging the boy tightly. "Don't you ever watch television? Your favorite Irishman almost got vaporized this morning."

"Which makes it all the more silly to go running back into that madness." Aidan stroked Dennis' cheek lightly. "Can't the PM run things for a little while without you just this once."

Dennis hugged Aidan again and then released him. "I'm needed at the Palace," he said. "God willing, I won't be too late getting back tonight." He headed for the shower.

"You've never had a meeting at the Palace before," Aidan followed him. "Why aren't you meeting at Downing Street?"

"Because the meeting is at the Palace," Dennis answered. He slipped off his underwear and stepped into the shower.

Aidan leaned against the bathroom door. "Are you meeting with the Queen? Is that it? Has something happened to the Prime Minister?" He heard Dennis jump as the water went on in the shower.

"Shit! What takes the hot water so goddamn bloody long?"

"Well?" Aidan persisted.

Dennis stuck his head out of the shower. "What, Aidan? I'm sorry, I couldn't hear you."

"I was just asking if your meeting was with the Queen."

"It's just a meeting, love. Like a thousand others I've been to."

"Yes, but not at the Palace." His voice was growing thin. "I don't understand why you can't give me a straight answer?"

Dennis was aware of a tone in Aidan's voice he had never heard before. He stuck his head out again, puzzled. "What's the problem, Aidan. You're asking more questions than a barrister at a rape trial."

Aidan's demeanor changed abruptly. "I don't mean to be a pest," he said, tousling Dennis' wet hair. "I'm just worried is all. Like everyone else."

"Everything is just fine," Dennis said, echoing the television reports as he leaned out to kiss the boy lightly. "Now stop worrying."

"That's hard to do, Dennis." Aidan smiled coyly. "There's been nothing on the BBC about either the Queen or the Prime Minister. Everyone's frightened." He tapped on the shower door. "Now, what's the use of having a lover who's best buddies with the PM if you can't get a little inside gossip once in a while?"

"I'm sure the BBC will tell all that needs to be told as the information becomes available, Aidan. Now be a good boy and go put on some tea. I need more than a little caffeine tonight." He closed the shower door. "Ah, hot water at last."

Aidan stood outside the shower for a moment. In one graceful motion the boxers slid down his legs and onto the floor. Opening the shower door, he stepped naked into the steaming mist behind Dennis.

Dennis turned to him, startled. "Aidan, I don't..."

Aidan put a hand over his mouth. "I don't want to be a good boy," he said, curling his tongue about his lips. He reached around Dennis, digging his fingers into the man's thighs, pulling him up against his own taut body. They kissed hard. Dennis' tongue forced its way past Aidan's, hungrily exploring. A sound welled up deep in Aidan's throat, exciting Dennis even more. Aidan ran his hands over him, sliding his fingers down between their wet bodies, weaving together Dennis' silky pubic hair with his.

Dennis felt himself swell up against Aidan's stomach. His engorged penis slowly arched up following the thin line of hair snaking up Aidan's groin to his belly button. Dennis caught his breath and began a slow gyration against Aidan's wet torso, kneading his fingers into the pliant cushion of the boy's buttocks in rhythm.

"I'm gonna be late," Dennis protested weakly.

Aidan moaned happily as his tongue played with the sparse red curls around Dennis' right nipple. Dennis backed the younger man up against the cold tile wall and drew his arms up around Aidan's neck. He reached down and grasped his partner's buttocks, spinning him around. Aidan braced himself against the tile, arching his back and grinding his buttocks against Dennis's erection. Aidan cried out as Dennis slowly slid into him. The boy leaned back holding onto his partner's supporting arms to allow his lover's mouth access to his own.

Before Dennis could begin to move inside him, Aidan contracted his sphincter about Dennis' manhood, sending a rippling spasm of pleasure and pain through Dennis, almost causing him to pull out. A doubtful prospect considering the peculiar hold Aidan had on him.

8

Dennis wasted no time on the elevator but bounded up the side stairs toward one of the state reception rooms at Buckingham Palace. He cursed himself silently. He was late . . . very late. Still, at least he felt a little rejuvenated. He could thank Aidan for that. He paused for a moment at the top of the stairs to catch his breath and straighten his tie. He opened the door and stepped out onto the crimson carpet blanketing the ancient marble hallway that ran the course of the state rooms. Priceless paintings hung in equally priceless frames on the hand-painted, gold and silver damask walls.

Dennis could remember being in the Palace only once for a reception the Queen had sponsored for cabinet officials and their aides. He recalled finding it unimaginable at the time that anyone could live comfortably in such a gargantuan, cold, museum of a house. He had assumed, though, that the private quarters of the Royal Family were probably smaller and more "lived-in" than those parts of the Palace that served for public functions.

He moved quickly down the hallway mentally calculating the millions of pounds sterling that comprised the personal art collection hanging about him. So much for the "lived-in" look. A footman met him halfway down the corridor and directed him to the double, dark walnut doors which opened into the mirrored reception hall. It was already somewhat crowded. Dennis politely elbowed his way through.

"Over here, Dennis. We were beginning to wonder," a voice called out.

"Sorry I'm late, Sir Arthur," Dennis said. He made his way to the large conference table stretched across the far corner. "I was a bit delayed."

"Apparently the gods are with you, my boy. You're late, but then, so is the King."

Dennis breathed a sigh of relief. "Smashing. A moment to catch my breath then."

"If His Majesty doesn't arrive soon there will be a few fist fights," Sir Arthur noted dryly.

"What's been happening?" Dennis raised an eyebrow.

"Oh, the usual political maneuvering, power plays, and various factions caucusing for support. This group blaming that group for this and that and vice versa."

"A bit premature, don't you think? The King must appoint a Prime Minister first."

"I'd say those decisions will probably already be made before the King arrives," Sir Arthur answered with a bemused glance about the room.

"I'm curious to see how he'll deal with that."

"If he's smart he'll probably give in to the majority opinion," counseled Sir Arthur wisely. "Royals are very good at calculating the odds and coming out survivors."

"Have you heard anything further on the condition of the Prime Minister?" Dennis asked. "The television hasn't said a thing and I can't get through the security to find out a bloody thing."

"Curious thing," Sir Arthur said. He pursed his lips. "The new King has ordered him brought here to the Palace infirmary."

"What?"

"As yet no one has been allowed to see him." Sir Arthur leaned in conspiratorially. "Security has been very tight."

"Dennis, lad!" A thick and heavy hand slapped down on Dennis' back almost sending him to the floor.

Dennis turned sharply. "Fitzroy! You old walrus. You're alive! How in bloody . . ."

"Not enough TNT in the world to blow all this away." The older man laughed, patting his swollen belly.

Dennis cast a worried glance at the bandage capping Fitzroy's grey head.

"Nothing to worry about, lad," Fitzroy said, noting his worry. "Just a good bump on the noggin."

"Christ, Fitzroy! How did you get out?"

"I was already on my way out, Dennis. When I saw that socialist scum, Conroe and Harper, storm out in the middle of everything, I slipped out the back to try and head the buggers off."

"An Irish and a Scots both saved by pride and bad tempers." Dennis laughed.

"Try to keep this good humor," Sir Arthur interrupted. "I noticed your two esteemed colleagues are present this evening."

Dennis turned sharply. "Where?" he demanded.

"They're here all right," Fitzroy said acidly.

"How dare they show up here." Dennis scoured the room for them.

"Keep a cool head, Dennis," Sir Arthur said. "We've more to worry about right now than personal prejudices."

"Personal prejudices?" Dennis stammered. "Tell me, Sir Arthur. Don't you think it's a bit odd that only seconds after these two left the building the whole place blew?"

"The same could be said about you, Dennis," Inspector Harlowe said from behind him. He casually stuffed a pipe.

"Inspector."

"I've already spoken to the gentlemen in question," Harlowe continued. "I can think of no motive or reason to link either of them to this affair more than anyone else."

"No motive!" Dennis bristled.

The Inspector raised his hand. "Before you go too far, remember. There is no evidence whatsoever to suggest their reasons for leaving the House when they did was anything other than what they said—a protest."

"Very convenient," Dennis said. He folded his arms, shaking his head. "The timing couldn't have been better."

"Until there's evidence to the contrary, the Yard will continue to investigate all possible suspects," the Inspector said. He smiled up at Dennis from his pipe. "*All* suspects."

"Gentlemen," whispered Sir Arthur sharply. "The play is about to begin."

A footman was standing at the door, rigid and formal. "His Majesty, the King!" he called out loudly before moving stiffly to one side.

Talking stopped abruptly and all eyes turned to the door.

Major Von Schiffer stood first in the doorway, commanding the entrance completely. He eyed the room like a school master coming upon a rowdy class. An ominous stare across the room toward the conference table instantly cleared a path as people pushed to get out of his way. The Major nodded his head several times, his Teutonic mind satisfied at order restored, and stepped back into the hall.

Alexis Richard Leopold Windsor entered the room slowly, taking deliberate steps with the support of his walking stick at the left and his right hand on the Major's arm. His eyes were fixed on the floor ahead of him and he made no effort to acknowledge the presence of anyone in the room by looking up. Dennis watched from the side of the conference table, wondering if the new King was aware of the various groups and factions instantly sizing him up at this moment, preparing to make their stand for power.

Von Schiffer led the King around the table to a chair at the center, then stood at attention directly behind him. The King sat back in the chair for a moment as another aide opened a large portfolio of briefs in front of him. The King then motioned to the various government leaders about him at the table to be seated as well. For the first time he looked up at the formidable assemblage, smiling—a smile that dared contradiction.

He spoke without preamble. "The remaining majority of the Privy Council, with my consent, has prepared and issued to the world press and to the people, a statement confirming the death of the Queen and the Prince and Princess of Wales, as well as my father, the Duke of Kent, and affirming myself as the rightful King of the realm."

He paused, allowing the greater meanings to be understood. "Of my family names, I have chosen to be called Richard IV. This being done, and having now assumed the mantle of government, I am prepared to revive and restore right and competent government to this nation."

The Right Honorables looked at each other with uncertainty.

The King continued. "To you Members of Parliament not directly participating in the present government of Prime Minister Bates, I thank you for attending this meeting. I would ask that for the days to come you would offer every assistance and cooperation to these ministers as they seek to restore order and security to our land. Replacements for those ministers killed or incapacitated have already been named in the news release now being given you."

One of the aides busily distributed the list throughout the room.

"I would ask," the King continued, "that those not already seated at this table to find their place, as We will require cabinet ministers and heads of the armed forces and the security services to remain for a short meeting. The rest of you may go."

A confused paralysis struck the dumfounded politicians about the room. No one moved except to look at one another incredulously.

"Sir!" Gerald Conroe protested. He pushed his way to the front of the table.

The King sat back in his chair wearily. The aide dutifully whispered a name in his ear.

"Mr. Conroe. You have a question?" the King asked.

Conroe looked about the room as if seeking some sign that he was not in a dream alone. He faced the King squarely. "Sir. We were under the impression that Prime Minister Bates was severely injured ... incapacitated ... comatose." He looked back to his supporters who stirred in agreement. "Surely it behooves this assembly to make sure a competent man is chosen to replace him as demanded by the constitution. I myself have offered—"

"Mr. Conroe," the King interrupted sharply. "The Prime Minister is presently being cared for here in the Palace Infirmary. He has indeed been injured, but, having seen and spoken with him, We have judged him to be competent to continue as Our Prime Minister." The transition to the royal first person added a solemn authority to his words. "We, as King, decide who administers Our government. That is Our constitutional prerogative and not the prerogative of any other person or assembly of persons. Is that quite clear, Mr. Conroe?"

His eyes cut down over the bridge of his nose right through Conroe and the assembly behind him. "It is too important for Our people and for the world that this government appears stable and ready to act on the problems we face. There is no time to waste changing the hands of government or worrying about new elections at this time. And furthermore it is not necessary."

The sudden furrowing of the King's brow betrayed his growing irritation. "This government shall stand as it is so long as We are assured that Prime Minister Bates is capable of directing this cabinet, at least until the present fears are calmed. It is enough that Our people must deal with the death," his eyes hardened at Conroe, "the cold-blooded assassination of a beloved Queen. There will be time for you to make personal political gains at a later date. For now, We insist that you set these aside for the sake of the nation."

The edge to his voice grew even sharper as he stood slowly to face them. "A state of national emergency has been declared for the next seventy-two hours," said the King. The entire room jumped to its feet. "We trust that you ladies and gentlemen will see to it that your public personas are kept in line with Our government's policy during this time." A chill fell over the room. "We should not like to see any of you arrested for inciting disorder." The King looked pointedly at Conroe. He waved his hand in dismissal and regained his seat.

Major Von Schiffer moved from behind to ensure that the room was cleared as the King had ordered. He shut the doors and positioned himself in front of them at attention. The noise level in the cathedralesque corridor beyond grew to a roar as the crowd of MP's was escorted unceremoniously out of the Palace.

For a long time the King sat silently, studying various reports in front of him. Dennis raised his eyes to Fitzroy sitting across from him. Fitzroy looked at the King, then back at Dennis and merely shrugged his shoulders. At last the aide began to distribute stacks of the briefs out to the appropriate ministers. Sir Arthur nudged Dennis. He slid one of the papers over to Dennis and pointed a finger at the signature. Dennis recognized the signature instantly as that of Prime Minister Bates.

The King spoke. "Gentlemen. Now in front of you are various emergency directives this government has drawn up in an effort to contain the problems that now or soon will be confronting us. We charge you to implement and administer these directives to the best of your abilities." He looked at each one of them, underlining what he was about to say. "We will serve Our own purpose in steadying the reins of power, and the government, being you gentlemen, will obey the directives which Our Prime Minister initiates."

The ministers' eyes met.

"It must not be known to anyone beyond this room that We, the King, are participating in the power of government in any way," King Richard said. He smiled disarmingly. "This is at best a temporary situation and We act only in the best interest of this nation. It must appear that all decisions emanate from you, the Cabinet, and from the Prime Minister . . . as they most assuredly do." His smile disappeared as quickly as it came. "Is that understood?"

Heads began to nod hesitantly.

"The commanders of the armed forces and security agencies will report to me directly as King and Commander in Chief. I will personally keep the Prime Minister informed and discuss the making of policy with him. His strength is limited, which is why I'm sure you gentlemen will respect Our limiting access to him to his doctors, nurses, and myself." The King closed the folder in front of him. "Thank you for coming. We will meet again in the morning at ten at which time I will welcome your comments and ideas concerning the directives before you. Good evening."

The men stood as if on cue, grabbed their papers, and with a look from Major Von Schiffer, headed quickly for the door. Dennis followed behind Fitzroy, who was chuckling contentedly to himself.

Fitzroy turned slyly to Dennis and whispered, "The scrambled phone lines are certainly going to be hot this particular night, lad."

"Mr. Perkins?" Dennis felt a tap on his shoulder and turned to the liveried footman. "His Majesty wishes to confer with you before you leave." The footman stepped to one side and nodded to the reception room.

Fitzroy looked at Dennis under his drooping eyelids. "Into the fray, lad. Good luck." Humming softly, he headed out the door with the other ministers.

Dennis followed the footman back to the conference table. The King continued reading reports in front of him for a moment before acknowledging Dennis' presence.

Dennis stood facing the young King. When the King looked up, Dennis bowed slightly. "You wanted to see me, sir?"

"Yes, Dennis," the King said. "Thank you for staying after. The Prime Minister speaks highly of you."

Dennis nodded for lack of anything better.

"I have spoken to the Prime Minister about you, to be sure, and I have a personal favor to ask of you."

Dennis stood puzzled for a moment before responding. "Sir?"

"The Prime Minister is, as I have said, unable to receive unnecessary visitors at this time. As such, you would be rather useless to him."

Dennis winced at the idea he was considered an unnecessary visitor. "Yes, sir. I have already anticipated being out of things for a while. That isn't a problem though. I could use a few weeks off."

The King studied him for a moment and then smiled. "Nonsense, Dennis. You're dying to get into the middle of all this."

Dennis shuffled his feet slightly, beginning to feel even more uncomfortable.

The King continued. "Though you might be useless to the Prime Minister, you could be invaluable to me."

Dennis raised his head, surprised. "Sir?"

"I want you to take on the role of my Private Secretary. You will serve me much the same as you served the Prime Minister with the small exception that there is always more attention to ceremony and protocol."

"But, Your Majesty," Dennis protested. "I know very little about Royal Protocol. Surely you could find—"

"I've found what I'm looking for, Dennis, in you. I'm not offering you this job lightly. You've already got connections and expertise in dealing with the various government agencies. I'd choose you for the same reasons the Prime Minister chose you."

"Because I'm Irish." Dennis frowned, unable to hide his feelings like a bad taste.

The King smiled up at him. "That and the fact that you are more than competent." He paused and settled back in the chair. "I am the King, Dennis. I'm offering you the distinct honor to serve me as Private Secretary. That honor is doubly distinct as We are personally asking you. Will you do so?"

Dennis stared at the desk for a moment, thinking. What else was he going to do? And, he was curious, damn curious. "Very well, sir," Dennis said at last. "I'll accept the position." He bit his lip, knowing it was now too late to retract. "Will I be allowed to see the PM?"

"Not just yet," the King said. "But not to worry. He has plenty of assistance to help deal with the duties of his office. You will, in essence, still be working for him. The only difference is that I will act as . . . a middle man, so to speak."

Dennis shook his head at the whole idea. "Sir, I have to tell you that this is politically a very dangerous thing for both the Prime Minister and the monarchy to do."

"These are dangerous times, Dennis," the King responded.

"If the home press even suggests that a Royal is involved in government decision making . . . the constitutional prohibitions alone—"

"The press will not be a problem, Dennis, and neither will the Constitution." The King's demeanor hardened. "The Prime Minister is still the head of this government, Mr. Perkins. We are merely exercising Our prerogative to be informed and to advise. I don't think the Constitution or you should have a problem with that."

Dennis shuffled his feet. "Sir, I wasn't meaning to—"

The King raised a hand. "I'll see you at seven in the morning, Dennis. We'll have a lot of work to catch up on." He nodded his dismissal and returned his attention to the papers before him.

Dennis bowed again, turning to leave. Suddenly a soft bed at home had taken on all the national importance he could think of.

The Major shut the door behind him and continued to guard it at attention. He watched Dennis quick retreat down the immense corridor. A slight smile broke across the Major's face.

9

The King leaned forward onto the desk, cradling his head in his hands. Major Von Schiffer studied him closely, noting the beads of perspiration forming on the monarch's brow. The face remained a mask of concentrated calm, but the Major could tell from the position in which he held himself, that the King's every joint was throbbing with arthritic-like pain. There was a stiffness about his shoulders and an occasional, almost imperceptible tremor of the head.

Von Schiffer moved quietly to the King's side. With an economy of motion that was almost predatory, he wrapped his fingers about the base of the King's neck. King Richard stiffened for a moment, then gradually relaxed, folding his arms on the desk and laying his head down. The Major gently pressed the fingers of one hand into the King's back at the shoulder blades and carefully massaged downward to the lower back.

Von Schiffer could feel the swelling at the base of the spine, markedly warmer to the touch. The King's breathing deepened and the knotted muscles gave way to the Major's gentle ministrations. He blotted the King's pale features with a napkin from the desk. It was a Royal affliction and only the Major and the King's doctors knew the horrible consequences it also carried. The thought that this was the way it should be, excited Von Schiffer in a way he had never experienced before. He knew the young King's life was wholly and completely in his hands, totally trusting and given over to his protection. Someone so frail could die so easily, in so many different ways.

The Major picked the now sleeping form up from the chair in one smooth, effortless lift. He carried the King out of the study and into the bedroom, carefully laying him on the oversized bed. For the Major, his ambition was totally fulfilled. Now he served a sovereign who ruled as well as reigned—one on whose very life the fate of the nation depended.

Von Schiffer flexed his fingers, marveling at the power they now possessed. In one bone crushing squeeze he could alter all of history. He knelt beside the bed and stared in open adoration at the one in whom he would finally discover ultimate redemption and salvation. Perhaps his own peculiar calling had, of late, become too mechanical. Killing no longer needed a moral or political justification. Any excuse for bloodshed and the fear it produced would do.

He reached out to remove the King's shoes with a deliberate slowness, as if he were handling a religious relic of great importance. Watching this one die would be hard the Major knew, but he had his orders. He covered the sleeping King with a quilt and watched him for a moment. On an impulse he raised the quilt up slightly and lifted the King's hand out, resting it gently on the edge of the bed. He stroked the thin, pale, porcelain skin, tracing each vein with his fingers.

The King was in a deep sleep and Von Schiffer grew more bold when Richard did not stir at his touch. He turned the delicate hand over, spreading the long fingers. He bent slowly and lightly kissed the King's palm, shivering at the thought of how much power these hands, too, now held. For a brief moment he was so overcome with emotion he thought he might weep actual tears—but that was no longer possible. It was enough to feel alive again—to know his purpose more clearly. He lay his head on the King's hand and tried to remember the number of times he had put his own gun to his mouth and tried to force enough purpose into his finger to pull the trigger. Now he knew the reason he had not succeeded. The fragile life lying on the bed before him would justify everything he had ever done. If he could complete the great mission that was his, God would forgive everything. In that one moment he broke free of the guilt, the fear of living he had harbored for so long.

Von Schiffer rose from his knees, breathing in deeply like a bloodhound trying to memorize a scent. He would have stayed on his knees like that until the King awoke but there was another need he felt now, a more familiar addiction that could not be allowed to desecrate so holy a sacrificial altar as this surely was.

The Major moved quietly out of the Royal Apartments and into the cavernous hallway. He made his way to his own quarters in the side wing. A sense of continuity and history seemed to possess him with each breath he took, calling back to his mind the first day he had set foot in the Palace. He felt so alive his skin prickled.

Entering his bedroom he quickly undressed, laying his clothes out on a side chair. He was too elated to sleep. The renewed assurance in his own power and purpose for living infused him with a sense of excitement he had almost forgotten. He reached down and grasped the mammoth erection he had been sustaining for some time. The sexual tension in him was overwhelming.

He sat down on the edge of the bed, masturbating slowly. "Toby, are you awake?" he asked.

A sandy patch of hair stirred from under the covers next to him. Von Schiffer threw the covers back hungrily. The young lieutenant stretched out sleepily on his bed. The momentary tightening of his round, muscular buttocks inflamed the Major even more.

"Wake up, Toby!"

"Not now, Peter, please. I'm too tired," yawned Toby. He hugged the pillow under him.

The Major climbed onto the bed behind him, grabbing the Lieutenant's hips and raising his buttocks into the air. "Now, Toby!" he gasped and thrust himself into the young officer.

10

Aidan burst into the pub with his usual flair, pulling his dripping umbrella closed. He paused for a moment in the bright light of the open door to give everyone a good look. It wasn't really vanity on his part—well it was a little—but mostly it was in his nature to please others—and he was very good at pleasing his own kind. He let the door swing shut and shed his suede waistcoat so that the other men could admire his well-honed build and the fit of his couture shirt and jeans. His appearance was by no means overdone. He was gay—but he had good taste and a body that displayed his good taste . . . in the best of taste. He waved to a few acquaintances who seemed to take in his beaming smile like a personal validation of their own self-worth. Aidan wasn't a big fan of the gay pub scene, but it had its uses, and today, he needed the attention of others to achieve his own agenda. He slipped into the booth, settled back into the taut, cushioned leather and signaled to a black leather-clad waiter.

The boy, who had noted with undisguised dislike the attention Aidan had received, sashayed haughtily to Aidan's table. "Somethin' to drink, Miss?" he asked with mock solicitude.

Aidan resisted a smirk. "Gin and tonic," he said. "I'm meeting someone."

The waiter sauntered off in the direction of the bar, annoyed that he was no longer receiving the appreciative notice he was used to.

Dennis lunged through the heavy door out of the cold rain. He reached for his hat to shake off any clinging droplets but then thought better of it. Instead he unbuttoned his overcoat and glanced about the small bistro for Aidan. His younger lover stood and waved to him from the booth across from the bar.

Dennis stopped in his tracks at the sight of him. He raised an eyebrow at the tight . . . very tight, low-cut jeans and half-unbuttoned shirt that revealed an expertly manscaped hint of chest hair. He was immediately conscious of the looks Aidan was drawing from the other male patrons and Dennis wasn't sure whether or not to be proud or jealous. He realized that they were going to be the center of attention no matter what he did so he pulled the hat off his head dramatically and bent over to kiss his trophy.

"Show-off," Aidan teased, reaching up to tousle his red curls.

"Me?" Dennis threw his coat and hat to the back of the booth. "Why is it when I first saw you a moment ago, the word *hot* popped into my head?"

Aidan laughed and gave his shoulders a slight shimmy. "Does that mean you actually looked at me?"

"Me and every other fey bloke in the place." Dennis pushed in beside Aidan and gave the boy's knee a playful squeeze.

The waiter delivered Aidan's gin and tonic to the table. "Somethin' for the gen'leman?" he cooed with an appreciative wink at Dennis.

"A whisky and soda, please, love, and a couple of your cold cut plates." He returned the wink.

The waiter tittered and pulled at his leather pants. "Righ' away, sir." He threw Aidan a victorious glance before floating off to the kitchen.

Aidan reached under the table to give Dennis a pinch on his inner thigh.

"Ow!"

"Serves you right," Aidan admonished, flexing his biceps.

"Can't a bloke have a little play now and then?" Dennis asked eyeing the clear impression of Aidan's nipples against through taut, silken shirt.

"Only last night you told me you were too tired to play."

"That was last night."

Aidan smiled at him again and snuggled closer. "Well, maybe we ought to run by the flat before you charge back off the Palace."

"No, no. Don't even suggest it. I've been late once too often this week, as it is, because of that."

Aidan leaned back chuckling, causing the full contents of his jeans to bulge even further upward.

Dennis noted the movement appreciatively. "Don't you think you ought to cover that up? I'm having unclean thoughts and, after all, I've just come from church."

"Church?" Aidan almost choked on his gin. "What in, pardon the expression, Christ's name were you doing in church? What church?"

Dennis laughed. "Just a little meeting over at the Abbey."

"About the noontime funeral service for the Queen, next Wednesday?"

"Oh, this and that," Dennis responded noncommittally. "Where's that waiter?"

"Don't you change the subject," Aidan pouted. "I don't see you anymore. You're always off playing politics somewhere."

"I know, baby, I know." Dennis' sigh was audible. "Things will slow down before too much longer. The government's getting things back under control. It's all just been madness since the bombing."

Aidan refused to be mollified. "You're falling into the old English school chap trap. You get a few of them together and it's all slaps on the back and crotch scratching. You forget about such things as love."

Dennis exploded with a laugh. "I promise you, nothing of the sort happens. When they're in a group, the opposite sex and their various attributes are all the boys talk about."

Aidan eyed him suggestively. "And what about you? What do you talk about?"

"I mostly just smile a lot and think about the fact that those old boys don't know what they're missing."

"And how about what you're missing?

"Oh, I think about that a lot, too . . . an awful lot." Dennis resisted the urge to pull Aidan up on top of the table and prove it.

The waiter arrived and removed the temptation by setting the table with their plates of food and Dennis' drink.

Dennis took a quick sip and nodded his approval. "Six more of these and I might be able to face going back to the office."

The waiter shook out a napkin and placed it in Dennis' lap for him.

Aidan all but giggled. He took his hand out from under Dennis' napkin to take a sip of his gin and ignored the waiter's dithering. "Thank you, dear," Aidan said with a sniff. "Everything looks delicious." He reached for the thin-sliced rye bread and began piling on the pale orange, smoked salmon. "That will be all."

The waiter retreated to the bar stammering under his breath. His heated whisperings increased in volume and velocity as he grabbed the bartender's ear. The bartender only smiled and gave Dennis a knowing nod.

"I guess that's probably the last time we'll be able to come here for lunch," Dennis said. He shook his head at an unrepentant Aidan.

"You'd probably be too busy anyway," Aidan responded, biting into his sandwich.

Dennis began to construct his own, beginning with a spread of coarse mustard on an onion roll. "Speaking of busy, how'd you manage to get away from that bloody shop of yours for this little rendezvous?"

"Cameron managed not to be sick today."

"He must of had an usually good horoscope in the Old Londoner this morning then." Dennis bit ravenously into the slab of ham and roll.

Aidan tried not to laugh with his mouth full of salmon. He took a sip of gin to clear his throat. "So, how's the PM treating you these days?" he managed, reaching for a crumb on his chin with his agile tongue.

Dennis wiped it away with his napkin. "Let's just say that if I have to deal with any aspect of another state funeral, they'll be laying me to rest."

"That's all that's been on the BBC this week." Aidan shook his head. "It must have made a mountain of work for you."

"That's a mountain I don't ever want to have to climb again." Dennis took another bite. "It's all pretty much been handled now, though."

"How's Bates . . . the PM holding up?"

Dennis paused in his chewing. "As well as can be expected, I suppose."

"You suppose?" Aidan turned to face him. "What do you mean by that?"

"Well, very few people are really allowed access to him. He has to conserve his strength."

"Conserve his strength? The latest news was that he was doing well and carrying on his duties. Haven't you, of all people seen him?"

"Well, I have other responsibilities to deal with right now," Dennis said. He put his sandwich down.

"Other responsibilities?" Aidan's voice kept rising. "You're his top aide. What other responsibilities could you possibly have above that?"

Dennis turned to him. "The situation is quite different now than before. Christ's blood, Aidan, we just lost the majority of this country's elected government. I've also had to help the new King get his act up and running." He hoped that would explain his previous slip.

Aidan turned back to his sandwich thoughtfully. "No wonder you have no time. They're spreading you way to thin as usual."

Dennis patted the almost visible handles at his waist. "Don't worry. There's still a little of me left to spread." He squeezed Aidan's hand. "I'm not working any harder than any of the cabinet ministers. I don't think Hughen Fitzroy ever goes home even to sleep. Bloody hell! I'm the youngest one in the group. It'd be a sad thing, for sure, if I let all the old men outclass me."

"Not much chance of that," said Aidan, reviving his seductive smile. "What's the new King like?"

"King Richard?"

Aidan slapped his arm. "No stupid, Henry VIII."

"What makes you think I've even met him?" Dennis laughed.

"Well, I find it hard to believe you skulk about Buckingham Palace all day and most of the night and don't even see him."

"Okay, I've seen him."

"That's more than the rest of the country can say."

Dennis swallowed the last of his sandwich. "It goes without saying that security has been a major concern. No one felt it wise to throw the new King out for a public viewing before things were a little calmer."

"You speak in the past tense," Aidan responded quickly. "Does that mean they're finally going to show him off?"

Dennis sighed. "You're worse than a Fleet Street scandal hound."

"But Dennis, this is exciting news. You government people are so jaded."

Dennis wanted to respond, but his mouth was full.

"People need to see the King," Aidan continued. "Everyone will feel better after that." He put a hand to his mouth. "Oh dear, I've got to figure out what I did with that little television set at the shop. I want to be sure and have it out for Wednesday."

Dennis swallowed quickly. "Now, I didn't say there was anything definite. You're jumping to a lot of conclusions."

"Yeah, yeah . . . right," Aidan said, waving a hand in the air.

"Aidan . . ."

"Don't worry so much." Aidan patted his lover's hand. "You know I won't breathe a word to anyone."

"I haven't told you anything to breathe," Dennis said. "Can we please change the subject?"

"Well excuse me for expressing an interest in public affairs." Aidan scooted around the booth, putting a little space between himself and Dennis.

"Now don't start." Dennis reached an arm around the boy. "You know I have to be careful about the things I say in public."

"Oh, so I'm the public now."

"If those jeans get any more revealing, you'll be about as public as a person can get."

Aidan gave him a half-smile. "I suppose I should be relieved. I thought you were getting too high up on your white horse to notice my little gifts."

"I'm sure the view would be plenty visible from up on a horse," Dennis commented. "And your gifts are not exactly . . . little." He leaned over to nuzzle Aidan's cheek with his nose.

Aidan buried a hand in Dennis' curls and nipped at his ear. "Why don't you come back to the flat with me for an hour? It's not every day Cameron can cover for me."

Dennis growled at him. "Stop tempting me to treasonous acts." He studied the nape of Aidan's neck hungrily. "You know I'd like nothing better."

"Then why don't you?"

Dennis leaned back into the cushioned leather miserably. "It'll take me most of the afternoon to reschedule the King's appointments for next week."

"Next week?" Aidan paused. "You mean next Wednesday?"

Dennis threw his head back and rolled his eyes. "Don't be such a nosy-Nelly."

Aidan smiled and made a grab for his partner's crotch under the table. Dennis jumped ramming the table with his knee and upsetting Aidan's gin and tonic.

"There you've gone and done it." Dennis grabbed for a napkin before the spill reached the table edge.

"It's nice to see you can still feel . . . something." Aidan put his hand on Dennis' and helped guide the cleanup.

Dennis wanted the boy so badly he was almost willing to risk it. Instead he dug into his pocket for his money clip and pulled off a few notes to toss on the table. "I know I'm gonna hate myself, but I've got to get back to the office," he said.

"Come back home with me," Aidan pleaded. He pulled down on Dennis' shoulder holding him in the booth and leaned in to his ear. "This table's not the only thing that's wet and hard."

"Christ, you're killing me!" Dennis moaned and pulled away from the boy to grab his overcoat and hat. "I'll see you tonight." He gave Aidan a meaningful look of his own.

"A lot of good you'll be then," Aidan teased.

"You just wait and see." Dennis threw on his overcoat and hat and waved to his lover. He tossed the waiter another wink before heading back out into the rain.

Aidan finished off his gin and tonic and glared down at his half eaten sandwich, no longer interested. He eyed the unoccupied payphone next to the bar and pulled a few coins from his pocket. When the waiter came to clear the table, Aidan made his way to the phone. He turned his back to the bar and dropped in his coins.

Sure that no one could see his hand he dialed a number and stood waiting. A voice he recognized answered. "Wednesday at noon," Aidan said softly into the receiver. "The memorial service at the Abbey." He hung the receiver up.

11

"Christ, bloody God Almighty!" Dennis cried out, slamming the phone down on the receiver. He pushed back from the desk in his chair and tried to stretch the annoying crick out of his neck. No sooner had he worked the stiffness out than the intercom buzzed on his phone. "What now, Agnes?" He tried not to growl.

"I'm sorry, Mr. Perkins," came the haggard female voice. "It's Tompkins from the *National Reporter.*"

"Oh, Agnes, please. I can't talk to any more of these damn reporters. Tell any others who call that an information packet has been prepared and is available through the Press Office. I'm in conference for the rest of the day as far as reporters are concerned."

"Whatever you say, Mr. Perkins." The intercom light flashed off.

Dennis stared down at the papers in front of him trying to remember where he had left off before the latest interruption. The din of clacking typewriters in the adjoining offices staffed by a legion of stenographers and secretarial assistants was getting to be too much for him. He propelled himself across the floor in his swivel chair to shut the doors on either side of him, dampening the noise to a tolerable level. Finally able to concentrate, he turned his attention back to the rough draft of the King's itinerary for the afternoon.

He had been over it twice already, trying to prune away all but the most essential meetings—those that could not wait another day. As it stood, the schedule was impossible. Over the last week the demands on the King's time had escalated almost out of control and, though at first the pace had been exciting, Dennis was beginning to weary of eighteen hour work days.

He marveled at the stamina King Richard was displaying through it all despite the obvious frailty of his health. The young King's example only served to make the other members of his staff work longer and harder, and even Dennis admitted to feeling a pang of guilt each night when he would finally break away to go home, even though the King continued working.

He thought about Aidan, who had done nothing but complain since Dennis had begun keeping such long hours. Still, nothing made him relax and lose the tension of a hard day better than Aidan. Every night Aidan would be all over him like a starved animal, and he felt rather smug about the fact that, of late, he had been able to perform no matter how exhausted he came home. Aidan could make a coma patient horny.

He laughed at the idea, rubbing his overworked eyes. A red light began to flash on his phone, signaling a call coming in on his private line from the King's study. Dennis jerked up his notes quickly in a conditioned reflex shared by all other members of the King's staff. Everyone else buzzed each other on the intercom for attention, but the staff had learned to sense the little red light flashing even with their backs turned. King Richard refused to speak on the telephone to anyone. Dennis knew that when the King signaled, His Majesty wanted to see you that moment.

Dennis made a dash out the door and down the stairs—the elevators were much too slow—hoping that he had everything he needed. He reasoned that the staff, though officially deskbound, were being kept in excellent physical shape running up and down, back and forth, between office and King. He was certain the carpet would have to be replaced in another six months.

King Richard had dispensed with the traditional suite of Royal offices, having the large private study adjoining his bedroom converted into an office and conference room. This, owing to the fact that a considerable portion of his work was done from his bed in order to conserve his strength. Only those functions not dealing directly with his personal staff were conducted in the study. His Majesty insisted on correct appearances.

The expansive hallway outside the King's study had been, of necessity, put to use as an anteroom receiving area, where the endless assortment of bureaucrats and officials sat patiently on cushioned benches, waiting their turn to have audience with the King. Two small desks flanked the double doorway into the study from which two of Dennis' assistants attempted to keep a tight rein on the appointment schedule as well as the incoming and outgoing traffic. Dennis breezed past them all without even a nod and slipped in through the door, shutting it quickly behind him.

King Richard was lying back in the cushions of his chair behind an oversized desk, listening wearily to the debate ensuing among the group of ministers seated in a circle about him. Major Von Schiffer stood between the King and the window behind, glaring at the uncomfortable bureaucrats with hostile impatience.

Upon catching sight of Dennis, the King sat up quickly and motioned to him to approach. "Dennis, at last," said the King, instantly silencing the group. "We need your assistance." He gestured to a chair at the corner of the desk to his right, which Dennis occupied immediately. "Gentlemen," continued the King. "The plan We have outlined to you is a necessary step in the revitalization of the economy here at home. Such open immigration as we have experienced in the past must stop. This island can hold only so many people. The past policies have been nothing but disastrous."

One of the ministers coughed noisily.

"Yes, Mr. Allen," said the King ominously. "You have a comment?"

"Sir, if I may," began the minister. "Of course we agree, and public opinion supports ending open immigration from the Commonwealth nations, but we must consider these added directives, for what will amount to mass deportations, as another matter altogether."

"Mr. Allen," the King responded in withering tones. "The citizens of these isles will no longer be called upon to offer free room and board to anyone who can beg, borrow, or steal passage to get here. The welfare rolls and housing shortages are unbearable and intolerable. The end to open immigration and the deportation of unemployed non-natives is imperative to our survival."

"Yes, Your Majesty, but—"

"We are not debating with you, Mr. Allen, We are directing you to carry out the policies handed down by Our government."

The whole building seemed to grow silent for an instant and the errant minister cowered back into his chair.

"We understand the problems you will have with regard to manpower when attempting to enforce these directives," continued the King, "and We sympathize with you. Dennis, if you will please draw up orders for the defense department to place idle regiments at the disposal of Mr. Allen's department."

"Yes, sir," Dennis answered, already mentally composing the directive. He jotted a note on his pad.

The King leaned back wearily. "Now if you gentlemen have no further questions, We dismiss you to your duties. You have one week to get underway." He tapped a hidden pressure pad under the desk with his foot which signaled one of the aides outside into action.

Immediately the door flew open and the ministers were quickly ushered out without another word. It was always a source of great mystery and wonder to visitors at the Palace exactly how the staff always knew when an audience with the King was over, even without his saying a word or lifting a hand.

King Richard turned his head to Dennis. "While there is a moment, what do you have for Us, Dennis?"

"Several things which require your signature, sir." Dennis rummaged through his briefs producing several documents which he put on the desk in front of the King. "This is your proclamation officially dissolving Parliament and naming Prime Minister Bates to continue as head of a caretaker government until new elections can be organized."

King Richard quickly scanned the document. "A ridiculous redundancy considering the fact that there isn't a Parliament left to dissolve," said the King. He signed the document quickly, pushing it back to Dennis.

"This, sir," Dennis motioned to another page, "is a list of suggestions from the Privy Council with regard to your coronation. As a possible date they suggest—"

The King pushed the paper away. "Our Council need not concern themselves with this."

"Very good, sir." Dennis hurriedly retrieved the paper and slipped it back into his brief. "I'll have the rough draft of this latest directive to you immediately." He started to leave.

"There is no rush, Dennis. I have one other matter I want you to look into." He pressed the floor button again and instantly one of the aides responded. "What is my next appointment?"

"The Foreign Secretary, Your Majesty, concerning the trade embargoes."

The King raised an eyebrow, a sure sign of displeasure. "Reschedule him."

The aide was out the door in a wink.

Richard collapsed back into his chair again, his face creased with pain. Dennis studied the King with concern. His Majesty dropped appearances only in front of the closest members of his inner circle. It was a show of trust that created a powerful bond of loyalty between the select few and the King, a bond which Dennis had grown to feel very strongly. No one, however, dared to offer the King any sort of personal aid. This was strictly the territory of Major Von Schiffer, who guarded that right with uncompromising savagery.

"Let me lie down for a few minutes," said the King through clenched teeth.

Instantly the Major reached down, lifting the King effortlessly from the chair. Dennis moved ahead of him to open the bedroom door. Von Schiffer carried the King into the room as if he were a large doll and set him down on the bed with the utmost care. King Richard pulled a pillow down to his chest and rolled over onto it with excruciating slowness and lay panting for a moment.

Dennis stood uncomfortably at the end of the bed, feeling like an interloper as he watched the Major gingerly raise the back of the King's coat and shirt and laid his hand over the swelling at the base of the spine.

Von Schiffer caught Dennis eye and nodded toward the small refrigerator nestled under a marble-topped commode to the side of the bed. "Bring me some ice in a towel," He ordered, lightly massaging his fingers over the King's back.

Though Dennis generally grew annoyed at the Major's highhanded manner, he did what he was told this time, rationalizing the command into a request in his own mind. He broke the tray of ice into one of the white, hand towels that sat stacked on top of the commode and brought it over to the Major. Von Schiffer lightly rolled the cold compress over the inflamed area.

The King gasped softly, but the Major continued his ministrations. Try as he might Dennis could not assimilate the violent, cold-blooded nature of the giant Austrian with the seeming devotion and tenderness that characterized his behavior with the King. Seeing it with his own eyes, however, was still not enough to fully erase the distrust he intuitively felt for the man.

"Dennis," called the King, his voice a little stronger. "Please bring a chair around where I can see you."

Dennis obeyed, pulling one over beside the bed from the window.

The King managed to smile at him. "I want the benefit of your particular political acumen with several other measures I . . . the Prime Minister wants to enact quickly."

"Any way I can be of help, sir," responded Dennis genuinely.

"We believe the time is right to aggressively attack the Irish problem, since we don't have the factional pettiness of a Parliament to stand in the way." The King closed his eyes, relaxing a little more into the pillow.

"What does your Majesty propose?"

"A threefold plan, basically. It should begin with a display of military force in order to remind and assure the people of Northern Ireland that they are still very much under this government's protection."

"Your Majesty is, of course, aware that such a move would be construed as an invitation to violence by the new IRA."

"It is my feeling that just the opposite will be true," said the King with a slight smile. "We will proceed under the assumption that these extremist rebels will no longer be such a problem to us. Our main concern is to unify the support of the people behind Us as the only solution to the problems and prejudices that exist. This so-called IRA must be finally and completely discredited in the eyes of the Irish people, including the Roman Catholics."

"I'm not quite sure what Your Majesty is suggesting," said Dennis tentatively.

"Yes you are, Dennis. I want a plan—truth or fiction—drugs, treason, sex scandal, I don't care, but something that will give the Papists pause."

Dennis nodded his head thoughtfully. He knew exactly what the King was after. "I think it's always best to begin with at least a grain of truth, just for the sake of making things a little easier."

"You have an idea then?" The King's eyes sharpened.

"Well, of course, the most defensible excuse western democracies find for political suppression is in finding some link to world-wide terrorism."

"Very good, Dennis. I knew you would be helpful."

Dennis began to make several notes on his blotter.

"Go on," insisted the King.

"There has been, in the past, some covert support and manipulation of the new IRA via Palestinian/Arab extremists, especially the Al Qaeda connection. Nothing, however, that could be safely brought to light in the media."

"You are then suggesting that we create and plant a story of extensive outside terrorist involvement in IRA affairs."

"It would make NATO and the Common Market nations less likely to condemn any extreme measures

Your Majesty might consider necessary." Dennis couldn't believe his own words.

King Richard considered the problem quietly, unmindful of the Major's continued massaging. Dennis fidgeted in his chair, wondering what plan was hatching in the King's fertile brain.

"Dennis," the King began, "I want a directive for the Admiralty to begin extensive military maneuvers along the upper coast of Northern Ireland. I want them ready to begin in one week."

"Yes, sir. But that won't be giving much time for proper planning."

"That is unimportant. The nature of the exercises is irrelevant. I want a display of military force and preparedness on that coast line in one week."

"Yes, sir." Dennis jotted a few more quick notes.

"Then I want a proclamation of law, drawn up."

"Without consent of Parliament?"

"This will be an exercise of the Prime Minister's special powers in time of national emergency."

"The Prime Minister is able to sign it?"

The King's visage darkened. "The only signature that is of importance to law in this kingdom, Dennis, is mine."

"Yes, sir," said Dennis quickly. "I only meant to inquire about the Prime Minister's health."

Dennis could feel the heat of his ear lobes flushing under the King's scrutinizing stare. He wondered if his thoughts were being read.

"Our Prime Minister's condition has not changed," said the King levelly. "He continues, however, to serve Us to Our satisfaction."

"Yes, thank you, sir," Dennis stammered.

The King's visual cross-examination of Dennis continued a moment longer. "Let's keep our minds on the matters at hand," the King said finally, punctuating with a raised eyebrow.

"Yes, sir." Dennis made a fruitless attempt to look unflustered.

"This proclamation," continued the King pointing to the notes Dennis was jotting down, "will serve as an amendment to the Act of Settlement of 1701."

Dennis sat forward in his chair at the mention of this.

The King noted his sudden intensification of interest with a half smile. "I'm sure you recall, Dennis, that this act excludes Roman Catholics from Crown and government. In the interest of peace and justice, I wish to change this principle, or shall we say, make it a little more specific."

"In what way, Sir?" Dennis asked looking up from his writing.

"I wish to allow a limited form of representation for this minority. I want the voting district realigned to assure the election of a proportionate number of Roman Catholic parliamentarians. They will, however, be barred from voting on issues dealing directly with the Monarchy or the Church of England. They must also be willing to swear an oath of allegiance to the King and Crown above all others."

"Your Majesty must recall that a similar plan was considered by several past administrations but none could find the support in Parliament needed for passage."

"Yes," said the King, unconcerned, "but by the wisdom of God, a King is not limited by the will of the parliamentarians, but acts only for the good of the people as a whole. We shall accomplish by proclamation what Our ministers have been unable to do in open forum."

Dennis took in a deep breath. Such exercises of power were dizzying especially to anyone who truly understood the historical consequences. "I will pull out the old records and drafts," he said, "and have something put together for you to work with by morning, sir."

"We'll leave it in your capable hands then."

Dennis stood to leave.

"One other idea, Dennis."

"Yes, sir."

"I would like an analysis from M-5's think tank, but this request must in no way appear to come from the Palace."

"That would be no problem, sir," answered Dennis, trying to recall the names of the men he had routed previous requests of this nature through, so as to cover their point of origin for the Prime Minister.

"It will be in the nature of a cost/benefit analysis of a hypothetical situation, whereby, along with the previous directives I have given you, the Roman Catholic

Hierarchy of Northern Ireland becomes implicated in this terrorist scandal."

Dennis' heart hit the floor. "Sir, is it your plan to manufacture a connection between the bishops of Northern Ireland, the IRA, <u>and</u> Al Qaeda?"

The King considered Dennis' question. "Dennis, I rather doubt that it will make any difference to this analysis whether or not this connection is created or discovered." He raised an eyebrow again. "If there are no further questions, that will be all."

Dennis wondered which King Richard was more interested in stamping out in the kingdom—the IRA or Roman Catholicism. He gave a terse nod to the King and retreated from the room, heading back to his office with a new load of work. His day's labor had certainly lost its tedium. If the King's Machiavellian designs were soon realized, a new era of peace and prosperity could conceivably be ushered in. But at what cost Dennis wondered. If, on the other hand, the plan were to fail, tensions could well escalate beyond the ability of the government, or even such a charismatic leader as King Richard, to contain them.

"Mr. Perkins," a voice called out from one of the other offices.

Dennis stopped at his door. "Make it quick, Agnes, I'm carrying a headache with me this morning," Dennis responded, nodding to the load of briefs and papers he was toting.

The older woman smiled primly as she approached him, waving another piece of paper in his face. "Phone message for you, sir, from the Yard."

"The Yard?" Dennis grabbed at the paper with his free hand. "Who, in particular?"

"An Inspector Harlowe. I've jotted the number down there." She stood looking at him over her reading glasses as if waiting for a reward.

"Did he say what he wanted?"

"Lunch, I believe."

"Lunch!" Dennis almost shouted. "He has time to take lunch?"

Agnes turned and headed back down the hall. "Just delivering the message, I'm sure," she said.

Dennis sighed with exasperation. "Sorry, Agnes," he called after her. "It's been a hell of a morning." His tone was more soothing and she slowed her charging retreat. Dennis smiled at her. "Did he happen to say when and where?"

"The Tower Hill Bistro in an hour," answered Agnes. "It's all there in the message." She smoothed out her skirt self-consciously. "Shall I phone back for you and confirm?"

"Please, Agnes. You're a love." He flashed her his best model of a sensuous smile and watched her flutter away, petted and purring, before stealing relieved into his office.

Dennis tossed the papers down on his desk and dropped back into his chair. The morning was only three quarters over and already he felt overwhelmed with an unassailable mountain of details to deal with. He sorted the various documents which the King had just signed among the appropriate out boxes lining the front of his desk. He grabbed his note pad and sat trying to form a mental outline for the various drafts of legislation the King had asked for. Though Dennis couldn't remember a simple phone number from one minute to the next, there wasn't a law, a memo, or a speech he had worked on that he could not remember in detail.

He began to pull up similar pieces of material from his subconscious files that had been previously rejected by parliamentary referendum and jotted their useful parts in among the current notes he had taken from the King. A subtle stirring of the surrounding air rustled the papers on his desk slightly and disturbed the fine red hairs on the back of his hands. He looked up automatically for the source of the offending breeze.

He stifled a gasp. "Major Von Schiffer!" Surprised he stared up at the hulking, blonde giant looming over his desk.

"Mr. Perkins, a word if I may," said Von Schiffer, showing rows of strong, gleaming white teeth.

"Major," Dennis coughed, trying to regain his composure. "You startled me." He tried to make his demeanor more stern. "I didn't hear you knock."

"I would like to look at the afternoon's agenda for his Majesty," said the Major, ignoring Mr. Perkins' subtle rebuke.

"Certainly, Major, though it's not complete by any means. I'm still whittling at it." Dennis plowed through the papers on his desk, looking for the right folder.

"A rough idea will do," said the Major, moving around the desk to stand over Dennis' shoulder. "I want to be sure the security is sufficient."

"As far as I know there are no scheduled outings." Dennis pulled the folder out and laid it open on the desk. "The entire afternoon is taken by endless appointments and meetings here at the Palace."

Von Schiffer put his hands lightly on Dennis' shoulders and leaned over him. He brought his face down within inches of Dennis' own as if to study the folder's contents more closely—too closely for Dennis' comfort. Dennis tried to shift his chair to the side but he felt the Major's vise-like grip dig more tightly into his shoulders.

"Don't let me disturb you, Mr. Perkins," the Major said softly into Dennis' ear. "I'll only be a moment."

Dennis tried to stand but Von Schiffer held him down.

Dennis twisted his shoulders to the side to break the Major's grip, stiffening visibly. "If you like, Major, I'll make you a copy of the agenda and you can take it with you."

Von Schiffer smiled down at him cannily. "That won't be necessary, Dennis." He straightened, releasing his hold. "I've seen all I need to."

"You have a nice body, Dennis." The Major strolled back around the desk towards the door. "A little small and soft, but with possibilities. Find some time to come down to the gymnasium and I'll put you on a program that'll have you in shape in no time."

"Thank you, Major." Dennis kept his eyes down on the folder, trying not to appear too uneasy. "But I get enough exercise running back and forth between my office and the King's. And as for time . . ." He shrugged his shoulders.

"Understandable," the Major echoed, ducking under the doorway. "It's a pity, though, to waste what God has given you." He shut the door behind him without a sound.

Dennis let out his breath and tried to relax. "What the hell was that all about," he muttered to himself. He glared at the door. It almost seemed as if the Major had been baiting him . . . hoping that Dennis would react to his suggestive taunting and give him some worthless reason to discredit Dennis. From the window behind him he could hear the great chimes of Big Ben toning the hour and checked his own watch out of habit. He fidgeted for a moment in his chair. It was still early yet, but he had an overwhelming urge to get out of the office. He shuffled all the papers into a pile at the center of his desk.

Dennis punched the intercom button. "Agnes," he said and pushed away from his desk.

"Yes, Mr. Perkins," came the immediate reply.

"I'm going out for the next hour or so and then off to lunch. If anyone calls or wants me say I'm in a meeting."

"But, Mr. Perkins, we haven't typed out the agenda for this afternoon yet—"

"It's on top of my desk, Agnes. You know how to do it." Dennis released the intercom and grabbed for his coat.

"But sir, what about these other news releases. Don't forget we still . . ."

Dennis headed out the door, leaving her talking to the empty air.

12

The tube tunneling beneath Victoria Station rumbled as the subway pulled away and burrowed into the labyrinth network of track that was the London Underground. The hour was late and the few passengers that disembarked scurried to the exits to escape the gloom pressing against the dim light cast by the few, working fluorescent bulbs overhead.

A lone traveler stood at the edge of the track and waited till the last of the passengers had made their getaway. He adjusted the shoulder strap which bore the weight of a long slender bag slung from his back. It appeared to hold a pair of cross country skis, if the attached ski poles were any indication. A more knowledgeable observer, however, might wonder at the apparent contradiction between the heavy pull of the bag upon the shoulder strap and what should have been light-weight skis.

The man pulled at his woolen cap before thrusting his hands into the insulated parka he wore. His dark eyes scanned the terminal for any signs of life and his nostrils seemed to flair at the surrounding air. His face shadowed at every point of its sharply defined bones giving him a gaunt, drawn look under the strobing, overhead light.

Without warning, a fit of coughing racked his body making him unstable on his feet for a moment. He let his burden slide off his shoulder and used the bag as a prop to lean on. When he was finally able to get his breath again, his coloring had gone from yellow to dark grey. He waited for the pain to go away, mentally ticking the seconds off as if timing the interval between thunder clap and lightening strike.

After a moment, he straightened and tried to take in a deep breath—but there was little room left in his ravaged lungs for air. He spat a mouthful of loose secretions onto the rail tracks and dug a hand into the parka for his pill bottle. Hoisting the ski bag back onto his shoulder, he twisted the cap from the bottle and extracted one of the large caplets. He smirked at the white narcotic. Before it was the bottle of whiskey—now this was the only friend he could truly count on. He could handle the pain. He just liked the way this medicine kept him from worrying about the inevitable.

A scuffling of gravel caught his attention in the subway tunnel beyond and he turned sharply. A short, stocky figure was ambling along the edge of the track toward him, stumbling as if drunk. Again he put a hand into his parka and let it rest on the powerful pistol holstered under his arm. Better safe than sorry. He shifted the weight pulling at his shoulder, and reached into his breast pocket with his free hand for a cigarette. With experienced inattention, he clamped a filterless smoke between his lips and fired up a cheap, plastic lighter. His eyes never left the stumbling figure in the tattered, soiled clothes slowly approaching him, nor did his other hand leave the pistol.

"Ah, lad," spoke the figure in a thick Irish brogue. "You're a stroke of good fortune, to be sure."

The gaunt man eyed the squat figure silently.

The tattered figure reached a dirty hand out. "Might you have another one of those for a fellow trav'ler, then?"

The man pulled the ski bag from his shoulder and rested it on end in front of him. "We're alone, O'Dell. You can cut the theatrics," he said in a rasping voice.

The man called O'Dell looked about the terminal before offering the other a toothy smile. "So we are, so we are. And how might you be feeling, Mikey?"

"I have good days and bad," the man responded, offering O'Dell a smoke.

"Good day?" O'Dell inquired, accepting a light.

"Bad." The man fought for another shallow and labored breath.

"Will you be up to this job then?" O'Dell stared up into the man's haggard face.

The man managed a wan smile. "I'm looking forward to it."

O'Dell took the man's hands and studied them for any sign of tremor.

"Don't trouble yourself, O'Dell." The man started to laugh, but instead suppressed a crackling cough. "There's nothing wrong with my eyes or my aim. I just can't run away anymore."

"It's sad to see you lookin' this way, Michael Bannion," O'Dell said. He gave Bannion the once over and shook his head sadly. "I guess I shouldn't be one to talk, though." He gave his corpulent belly a pat. "I'm not exactly the picture of manly beauty meself these days."

Bannion shrugged. "We had our time."

"Ah, Mikey, that we did." O'Dell stretched his back. "Some of us will end up outliving our usefulness, though."

"And some of us won't." Bannion managed a smile at this.

O'Dell pursed his lips. "I'm sorry this has fallen on you, me boy, but Shane says you're the best."

"Shane exaggerates everything. I was picked because I've already got one foot in the grave." Bannion's eyes caught the dim light and seemed to flash for a second. "One cancer's plenty. I can't do much about this one, but I can damn sure take the other one out."

O'Dell nodded his understanding. "We expect you'll be killed."

Bannion's lips spread into a thin line. "I'm counting on that." He squeezed the bag in front of him tightly. "I'll take a gun to myself before I go out puking and blubbering in some hospital ward, being eaten alive from the inside."

O'Dell reached up to squeeze the man's shoulders. "You'll die a hero, Mikey."

"Dead is dead." Bannion dropped his cigarette butt to the floor and stepped on it. "When and where?"

O'Dell felt a slight trembling in the ground beneath his feet. "Train's coming." He looked up into the dying man's eyes. "You look like a man who needs to pray a while, Michael Bannion."

Bannion raised a tortured eyebrow. "Where would you suggest?"

"The Abbey at Westminster. There's a loft . . . the pipe organ chamber . . . above the choir . . . it'll be quiet there."

The man shouldered his burden once more and started up the steps to the street. "And when can I expect my prayers to be answered."

O'Dell folded his hands like a priest.. "Only God knows that, lad."

Bannion turned back with a sigh.

O'Dell smiled. "But, with a little faith, by noon tomorrow, I'd say," he added, quickly.

Bannion stepped out onto the street above. O'Dell stood, listening to the man's labored steps until they faded away. He felt the rumbling in the floor below him growing in intensity and looked down the tracks into the darkness for any sign of the impending train. A look at his watch assured him he would get out on time. Out of habit, he studied his surroundings, noting the most efficient sites to place explosives, possible hiding places for sharp shooters, and storing that information in the back of his memory for future reference.

He stared at the burning cigarette in his hand and let it drop to the gravel. O'Dell crushed it out with his foot. "Nasty things, these." He blew the last of the smoke from his lungs and headed back into the tunnel.

13

Dennis strode briskly across the grass through St. James Park, still stewing over his run in with the Major. He pulled at his ever-present hat and shook the incident from his mind. He couldn't help but feel rather conspicuous in his poor attempt at disguise, and wished he had left the overcoat back at the office. Since his royal appointment and his seeming defection from the Commons to the Lords, he was an even more delicious target for any hungry reporter or paparazzi lurking about.

The sky was amazingly clear with an occasional peek of sunlight. All about him conservative business men lay on the grass, stripped to the waist, trying to absorb what rays they could during lunch. Only occasionally would one or two look up from their sleepy repast at the still obviously redheaded man bobbing past them covered like an albino at the beach.

Dennis caught a cab at Whitehall and barely escaped the scrutiny of a television crew filming in the bombed-out area. In the safety of the cab he pulled his cap off and opened his coat, cracking the window a bit to let in some fresh air. The cab wound around the cordoned-off area about the Parliament buildings where work crews had already cleared most of the rubble in the search for bodies. Now, only the building's shell remained precariously braced like an old world war ruin. Damn pity, thought Dennis. Another piece of history blown away by stupidity.

Returning to the scene of his near demise made him even more uneasy about his meeting with Harlowe. What was it the Inspector's message had said about a "lead to a lead?" Dennis shook his head, still feeling a little rattled by the morning.

Yet, any lead to the bombing was enough to bring him running. The King had left specific instructions that any information related to the bombing uncovered by the staff was to be relayed to him instantly. It was, after all, an unbelievable breach of what was supposed to be impenetrable security. Scotland Yard higher ups were facing the public as well as the royal chopping block.

Dennis' curiosity flickered to the surface again. Now even the idea of this luncheon meeting with Harlowe sounded peculiarly off key. How was it the Inspector could spare the time for such an informal meeting? Even more peculiar, why would the Inspector want to meet with him?

The cab dropped Dennis at the tourist's approach to the old Tower of London. He broke through the line of sight-seers queued up to ogle the Crown Jewels, ignoring the ugly looks and multi-lingual putdowns. It was all he could do to keep from running down the ancient cobble stone lane which circled around the Tower and along the bank of the Thames.

Through the crowd of tourists, Dennis spotted the small, outdoor bistro butted up against the base of the Tower Bridge, which Inspector Harlowe had directed him to. The Inspector was not seated at any of the tables and Dennis was beginning to think Agnes had gotten another message wrong. A movement caught his eye and Dennis turned to find Inspector Harlowe waving at him from a small bench above the esplanade overlooking the river.

Dennis angled his way over to the small grassy knoll. "Inspector?"

"There you are, Perkins. Have a seat."

"It seems an awful long way to go just for lunch, Inspector," Dennis said. He sat stiffly on the bench.

"Sure, my boy, but what a lovely spot to relax a moment. Can't let the tourists have it all now, can we?"

Dennis reached to remove his cap, though not without looking about first for reporters.

"Go on and relax, Perkins," the Inspector said. "No self-respecting journalist chap would be caught dead around here. Tourist spots are the perfect get-a-way for the wanted politician." Harlowe produced a large paper sack, from which he extracted a squat, silver thermos and proceeded to pour them each a cup of tea. "Hope you don't mind. The food here is really not fit for us natives, so I took the liberty of packing a little something for us to chat over."

"Anything is fine, Inspector, thank you. After the morning I've just had, my digestion is a bit off."

"Nonsense, my boy. Never let the pressure of state and foreign intrigue ruin the prospect of a good lunch. Let's see . . ." He rustled about in the sack a moment. "Perfect. Marriage is a delightful thing, Perkins . . . especially if she keeps a small kitchen garden, too. Cucumber and cheese sandwiches?"

"Sounds delicious, Inspector," said Dennis, assuming an air of boredom. He accepted one of the sandwiches. "I'll enjoy this even more if you'll tell me what this little meeting is all about."

"About, Perkins?"

"Come now, Inspector. My morning was bad, but yours must have been positively radioactive." Dennis took a bite of the sandwich. "Well?"

The Inspector was dutifully inspecting the contents of his sandwich. "It's not so much what I can tell you, Perkins, as what you can tell me."

"I don't understand."

"Very simply, Perkins, I want to know about the Prime Minister."

"The Prime Minister?" Dennis put down the sandwich. "What can I tell you that you don't already know?"

"Oh, I don't know. Something. Perhaps nothing. But you're certainly closer to the situation than I."

"Inspector, you know everything I know. Exactly what His Majesty told everyone. I know it's slightly irregular . . . highly irregular, but I don't understand Scotland Yard's interest. I should think you would have more important things to worry about."

The Inspector stared out over the water for a moment. "We've captured one of the bomb terrorists."

"You've what?" Dennis almost spilt tea in his lap.

The Inspector smiled at the reaction he had gotten.

"Don't play games with me, Inspector," Dennis said. "Who is it? Let's have it."

"Perkins, Perkins." The Inspector took another bite of his sandwich. "It's customary in these situations, that is, somewhat a tradition, Perkins, to agree on an exchange of ideas, a trading of information." He glanced out over the river, chewing contentedly.

A tour boat churned by them loaded with sightseers and cameras, its loudspeaker blaring a canned speech about the Traitors' Gate entrance to the Tower from the river—at one time a gateway from which no one exited.

Dennis smiled at the Inspector. "Not meaning to contradict you, Harlowe, I believe the actual tradition involves the right of His Majesty to be informed by all branches of government. I don't believe there's ever been a precedent where the King was required to share that information among the various departments."

"Indeed?" The Inspector tried not to laugh for fear of choking on his food. "I rather think this is not the best of times for the King to fall back on constitutional precedent considering his current, and I might add, illegal involvement in government."

"Illegal? Now Inspector. How can the King do anything illegal. That's like saying God sins."

"Quite!" The Inspector laughed heartily. "Quite. Well, if not illegal, then at least unconstitutional, you must admit."

"A natural debater, Inspector. My compliments. Surely your talents would be better used in Parliament."

"Perhaps you could arrange for me to see the Prime Minister and I'll persuade him for an appointment," said Harlowe.

Dennis finished off his tea and returned the cup to the Inspector. "Frankly, Inspector," he said, growing more serious, "I don't see how any improprieties the King might be accused of are any of your business. Such matters are Parliament's concern, not Scotland Yard's."

Harlowe turned to face him pointedly. "I'm investigating the most heinous crime ever committed in our nation, Perkins. Anything which concerns this crime is my business."

"All well and good, Inspector," Dennis nodded, "but you have as yet to explain exactly what the King has to do with all this, other than his place in the Royal Succession."

Harlowe's eyebrows rode up his brow. He sat back on the bench, slowly sipping his tea, staring down into his cup as if to read his fortune at the bottom. "The terrorist we captured . . ."

Dennis looked at him expectantly. "Yes, go on."

"Very curious." Harlowe sipped his tea.

"In what way?"

"There has been some question as to whether he was really a terrorist at all."

"What?" Dennis' mouth gaped.

"Yes, very curious."

"Do quit stringing me along, Inspector and get to the point."

"Well, it's just that, up until about a year ago, the man was part of a covert Royal security detachment."

"A traitor?"

"Well, that goes without saying." The Inspector pulled out his pipe. "Do you mind?"

"Get on with it, Inspector."

"Certainly, my boy. The security detachment in question is under the personal command of one Major Peter Von Schiffer."

"Schiffer?" Dennis thought a moment. "I doubt there's any way the Major could be implicated in any crime against the Crown. Honestly, I think he would favor the death penalty for even the smallest breech of Royal protocol."

"Yes, a very zealous man, I agree."

Dennis thought the Inspector's words lacked sincerity. "What's the full story on this terrorist, Inspector? What is your reason for keeping this from the King? Has Von Schiffer offered any explanation?"

"I doubt he even knows we have the man, Perkins. I've kept a pretty tight lid on this. Still, the Major has his sources."

"I don't understand. Surely the Major would be the best source of information about this man's history."

"We have our sources, too, Perkins. Every branch of security has its watchdogs among the others. This particular man was set up as a mole in the IRA underground near Banbridge. A termination file was turned in on him to the Home Office six months ago with a rather terse account of his death at the hands of IRA nationalists after his cover was blown. The file alleges a body was recovered and buried with full honors."

Dennis sat stunned for a moment, going over the facts in his head. "Still, Inspector, I don't see any link between this man and the Palace except by past association. It sounds more like Von Schiffer's mole turned on him without his knowing about it."

"Could be, could be." The Inspector puffed at his pipe. "We have, however, made at least one significant breakthrough." He pulled a small, folded piece of linen paper from his breast pocket and handed it to Dennis.

Dennis took the paper and opened it carefully. It was an inexpensive piece of stationery, plain, white, and containing no letterhead. The only writing on it was a matrix of numbers. There wasn't a signature in the proper sense of the word. Only a small green ink seal stamped at the bottom—a rather filigreed representation of a shamrock.

"Code?" asked Dennis studying the matrix.

"Undoubtedly." The Inspector moved closer tapping the seal at the bottom. "This, however, is the most significant part of the note for us. The code, itself is unbreakable, using a one-time-only number key. This seal, however, unmistakably identifies this as an extremely important communication coming from the highest command in the IRA. We've had only brief eyewitness accounts of this seal and notes like this. They're always destroyed after being read. Curious that our man still had this with him."

Dennis studied the seal more closely. "So, a link to the top dogs," he said. "Any ideas?"

"The Leprechaun."

"You're joking, of course." Dennis shook his head.

"I know it's a bit cliché but that's the bugger's code name. The IRA is known for creative killing, not writing."

"Have you discovered any leads to this . . . so-called Leprechaun that you can follow through on?"

"Well, we're not even sure the Leprechaun is one man," Harlowe said. "This could be a pseudonym for some sort of central committee. Still we've begun the tedious process of trying to run down the comings and goings of our terrorist captive for the last few months, clarifying his personal history a little more."

"He's talking?" asked Dennis.

"He was." Harlowe's eyes narrowed.

"Was?"

"He was found hanging in his holding cell shortly before three this morning."

"Suicide?" Dennis met the Inspector's eyes.

"It would appear so."

"But you're not convinced."

"The incident is under investigation," Harlowe said mechanically. "Let's just say that all the facts in the incident don't agree."

Dennis shook his head. "I would think you have enough problems, Inspector, without making new ones. I don't see how I can help your investigation along. I'm not a detective."

"No, of course not . . . but, Perkins, my boy, you do have, shall we say, a very pronounced curiosity streak." Harlowe breathed in deeply. "The Prime Minister is a victim of this crime, and I am being thwarted in my efforts to interview him. If the King would let me speak to the Prime Minister, it would settle various questions I have."

"What questions?"

"I should like some firsthand assurance that the Prime Minister is indeed still alive. There are various crucial directives we are required to implement in the event of a Prime Minister's assassination. The King's machinations in government don't interest me. As far as I'm concerned he has proven himself very good at it. Events have been brought under control miraculously fast. You would almost think he had been planning his moves for months. Still, as you have pointed out, he will have to answer to a Parliamentary review of all this, not to me."

"I still don't see what help I can be," persisted Dennis. "The King has made it clear that no one but the medical staff, select aides, and he may have access to the Prime Minister."

"Talk to him, Perkins. Make him understand the reasonableness of my request."

"I really doubt he will listen."

"Well, Perkins, in that event, any information you might uncover on your own would be welcome. You are, after all, in the Palace, and you might have occasion to accidentally peek into the infirmary."

"Now look here, Inspector." Dennis stood, bristling. "I have no intention of spying on the King or his affairs for you or anyone. You're way out of line in even suggesting I betray the trust of my position at the Palace."

"Relax, my boy, relax." Harlowe gave Dennis' shoulder a pat. "I'm not asking you to do anything of the sort. I merely want you to keep your eyes and ears open privately. There may come a time when you will witness something that you believe I should know. I'm not saying it will have anything to do with the King. There are possibly others in the Palace I'm interested in."

Dennis straightened, looking down at the Inspector for some sign that perhaps Harlowe wasn't really serious. The Inspector sucked on his pipe stem, quietly contemplating the traffic along the river.

Dennis pulled at his watch with growing agitation. "If you'll excuse me, Inspector, I have to be getting back."

"You'll speak to the King, then?"

"His Majesty has been in meetings with his ministers all morning. What with all the catching up to do this afternoon, I doubt there will be any time. Perhaps tomorrow."

"Tomorrow, then," the Inspector said, standing to shake Dennis' hand. "I'll look forward to hearing from you, Perkins." He smiled broadly. "God save the King."

Dennis walked briskly away, ignoring him, and headed back up toward Tower Hill to catch a cab. He wasn't quite sure what to make of his conversation with the Inspector. He was more than a little curious, himself, about Prime Minister Bates and had on more than one occasion seriously considered trying to sneak into the underground infirmary below Buckingham Palace and have a look for himself. But this was mere fantasy.

14

The meeting with Harlowe had so disturbed him, Dennis was halfway down the Victoria Embankment before he realized he was in a cab. He knew that the Major was capable of almost anything but, still, it was obvious he was totally loyal and totally committed to the King. Dennis could think of no way Von Schiffer could be involved, and as far as the King was concerned, it was unthinkable.

The road was blocked at the Westminster Bridge by a detachment of Royal Marines just in front of the old Scotland Yard. Dennis produced his special pass, but the cab was waved through without stopping. The cabby noticed his puzzlement in the rearview mirror.

"No problems today, sir. With the old Queen, God bless her, and her family laid out at the Abbey, they're letting people through again. No private autos though."

Dennis nodded his head. The cab turned onto Victoria Street which ran alongside Westminster Abbey. As they rounded Parliament Square past St. Margaret's, the way became blocked by a sea of people, standing patiently, as far as one could see. The cabby stopped for a moment surveying the situation. Along with the usual lines of police, Dennis noticed a regiment of sharpshooters on the roofs of the surrounding buildings.

"You'd think they'd queue people in a more orderly fashion through the Abbey," Dennis said offhand. "This is a mess."

"Wouldn't do no good today, sir," said the cabby. "Heard it on the radio. The new King's come to pay his respects. Everyone's come out at once to try to get a look at him." He shifted the cab into reverse. "Looks like we'll have to go back and take it down Whitehall, Sir."

"No," Dennis said, reaching for the door. "I'll get out here please."

"Whatever you say, mate." The cabby held out his hand.

Dennis paid the man and pushed his way through the crowd. There was to be a private service, by invitation only, in one of the chapels of Westminster. The King was scheduled to attend, and it wasn't supposed to be a public event. Dennis clipped the plastic security pass to his pocket and threaded his way through the barricades into the Abbey.

The high, fluted tones of the boys' choir rode the sweet mist of incense into the vaulting ceiling where they echoed back in an eerie antiphony onto the crowd of mourners, tourists, and the curious below. The people were all kneeling quietly, giving Dennis a clear vantage of the proceedings.

Before the ancient altar of the Abbey a black draped catafalque had been placed, upon which rested the coffin containing the remains of the fallen queen. At its foot, knelt King Richard in prayer. Lined up on either side were coffins containing the remains of the Prince and Princess of Wales. The positioning of the central catafalque, however, was different from what Dennis remembered in past royal funerals. It was set unusually close to the altar, he assumed, in order to give the people a better view.

Television crews manned their cameras from up in the loft as live remote units broadcast the first public act of the new King instantaneously into the homes of the people. Dennis noted the presence of both the King's brothers in the royal pews, which was also unusual, as recently instituted security precautions specifically forbade both heirs and monarch from being at the same public function at the same time.

Were it not for a difference in dress, the entire scene could have been lifted from one of the medieval plays Dennis recalled from his school days. He considered religion in general to be something of an anachronism and hadn't practiced his mother's Roman Catholicism since he was twelve. In his beginning days of government service he had considered converting to the Church of England but found it easier to plead neutrality.

It was a marvel to him that the history and racial conscience of his people could still be so forcefully influenced by the old rituals and ways. It struck him as odd that in the twenty-first century, the monarchy could still hold such sway and not just from the standpoint of pageantry. The mystical aura of a sovereign anointed by both church and state continued to function as a unifying, sacred symbol despite the socialist humanism that was so prevalent.

The last notes of the choir's benediction lingered in the scented air and the people, still on their knees, watched the King reach down for his cane and begin to pull himself to his feet. Prince Nicholas moved quickly to his brother's side, offering his arm for support. Young Bertie ran from his chair to join his brothers, grabbing hold of the King's pant leg. The lens housing of the television cameras telescoped to close-up for the viewers at home as Richard IV slowly turned with the help of his brothers to face the crowd.

Outside, the sun broke through the cloud cover for just a moment. As if on some divine cue, its beams prismed through the ancient rose window of the Abbey, throwing its jeweled light in a corona about the catafalque and the three Royals. The King's pale countenance glowed with an iridescent halo in the color show, drawing gasps from the mesmerized congregation.

From the side aisle a young woman stood up from her wheelchair sobbing. The crowd buzzed excitedly. A young soldier wearing dark glasses and carrying a white cane suddenly threw off the glasses and blinked his eyes into the window's light. The once reverent assembly was now a cacophony of voices, talking in chorus about the apparent miracles.

The King stood perfectly still and straight, his eyes closed against the brightness. People began to stand and move out into the aisle toward him with hands outstretched, causing the security people about the altar to move down to the main floor in a tight line. Dennis could feel his stomach begin to knot against some unknown fear. He looked about nervously for some sign of Von Schiffer. The Major stood quietly in the shadows behind the massive wooden lectern near the altar.

Dennis began to inch his way along the wall toward him, trying to catch his eye. The Major's attention had shifted from the King to somewhere beyond the television crews in the loft. The nave was quickly bathed in darkness again as the sun moved back behind the clouds. Straining his eyes into the shadow, trying to adjust to the sudden drop in luminescence, Dennis thought he saw Von Schiffer nod slightly up at the loft.

As Dennis turned to look up, a high-powered rifle fired. Its cracking shot was amplified by the stone walls into a small explosion. People dropped back to the floor screaming, pushing Dennis back against the wall. He watched, helpless, as the King's body slammed back against the coffin and crumpled to the Abbey floor. Security agents raced to the altar, throwing themselves in front of the King.

Before the assassin could take aim again, Prince Nicholas ripped a Mossberg shotgun from the inside holster of one of the security men and unloaded both barrels into the loft. The gunman toppled over the railing, catching a foot in the grid work. His torn body hung limply from the rail high above the people below. Blood poured from the gaping wound in his chest and flowed in a steady stream down his arm onto the ancient, slate floor, and anyone who could not get out of the way quickly enough.

The television crews scurried about frantically, trying to obey the volley of orders coming in over their headsets. Camera angles were reset instantly, trying to capture both the action in the loft as well as the tragedy at the altar. The people's panic began to be replaced by shock and grief. Few attempted to rise up from the floor which allowed the security agents to deal with the greater problem of people outside the Abbey who were fighting to get in.

Dennis pushed his way fiercely down the side aisle. He could see the Major, who by that time had made it to the altar. He was standing over the King's body, looking down at him quietly. Dennis caught his eye for a moment and did not try to conceal his hatred. The Major merely raised an eyebrow at Dennis, stonily returning his attention to the King. Two of the Special Branch agents grabbed a defiant Nicholas and carried him, kicking and screaming, behind the altar to safety and out the rear of the Abbey.

The television cameras panned from the scene back to the foot of the altar. In the midst of the chaos of people crying, security shouting orders into walkie-talkies and people fighting to get inside, the little prince, Bertie knelt quietly, cradling the King's head in his lap. His small hands were clasped together under his chin, his eyes were closed and his lips moved as he prayed quietly for his fallen brother.

The cameras moved in, preserving the moment for all time. The little Prince's action moved the crowd profoundly as individual after individual began to follow his example, kneeling in prayer, even out into the street, leaving the security service standing about staring at themselves.

"Bastard!" Dennis said softly under his breath as he watched Von Schiffer standing by.

Without warning, the Major bent down and gathered the King up in his arms. "He's alive!" He shouted over the crowd. "The King lives!" Von Schiffer turned and carried the King out in the same direction as Prince Nicholas had been taken, followed by another security man carrying Prince Albert.

The news hit the crowd like a lightning bolt. Word flowed through the Abbey like a wave out to the people in the street. The police did not even attempt to contain the crowd as it poured across Victoria Street toward the Mall in front of Buckingham Palace.

Dennis followed the remaining security men out the back way, but the King's armored Rolls was already plowing past its police escort toward the Palace. Flashing his security pass, Dennis jumped into one of the follow-up cars, barely getting his door closed before the driver spun out in pursuit. He closed his eyes and held onto his seat as the car swerved at high speed through the crowd. Had he actually seen the Major nodding a signal up to the loft? There was something unreal about the whole business. He could not believe that the Major had simply stood by and allowed the King to be assassinated and it was impossible to imagine that anyone as frail of body as the King could have survived such an attempt.

15

The black Jaguar careened through the open Palace gates. Dennis could see the Royal limousine ahead of him already parked in the interior courtyard. There was no sign of the King or Major Von Schiffer. Several of the Special Branch paced nervously about the car, eyeing the new arrivals and bringing their machine guns to ready. Dennis ignored them. He jumped from the car and ran up the steps into the Palace. A small group of the staff had gathered in the foyer beyond, talking excitedly among themselves.

"Where have they taken him?" Dennis shouted at them breathlessly.

One of the footmen pointed up and Dennis headed towards the stairs to the private apartments. Anxiously he threw open the door to the second floor. The hall was strangely quiet, not at all the bustle of activity Dennis expected. His eyes narrowed. Looming in front of the door to the King's apartment stood Major Von Schiffer. Dennis could feel the anger rising in him again. He walked slowly up to the Major, intending to ignore him and walk through the door. But Von Schiffer fully blocked any passage into the King's rooms. Dennis stood several steps back, staring coldly up at him. The Major did not move but continued gazing ahead at attention, ignoring Dennis as well.

Dennis' annoyance got the best of him. "If you don't mind, Major," he protested acidly.

"Mr. Perkins." The Major slowly turned his head in Dennis' direction, raised an eyebrow and looked down at him imperiously.

"You're blocking my way, Schiffer."

"Am I?"

Dennis glared at him accusingly. "It seems you're everywhere but where you should be."

Von Schiffer turned around fully to face him. His features clouded in an almost feral mask. "Mr. Perkins, the King is not in need of your services at this time. Go home." He straightened as if to emphasize his words. "You will be notified when His Majesty requires you."

"That's not for you to say," Dennis said sharply. "You're a security grunt, Major, and nothing more. I work for the King personally. There is no one in between. Now step aside."

The Major made no effort to move. He smiled, baring his teeth in warning. "Anything and everything which concerns the King, concerns me, little man."

Dennis stepped back slowly. He was too angry to hide his suspicions any longer. "I would be interested to know, Major, just where that concern was this afternoon?"

Von Schiffer eyed him warily. "What are you talking about?"

"Only that while the King was being shot down you didn't seem to do much of anything but watch."

"You're babbling about things you do not understand and which do not concern you." The Major grabbed Dennis by the coat and almost lifted him off the floor. "Go home, Dennis, while you can."

"Goddamn you, Major," Dennis sputtered, trying to pull free.

The Major released him suddenly, returning to attention. Dennis heard the voices coming around the corner at the other end of the hall just in time to straighten his jacket. Prince Nicholas was racing towards them with several security men in tow.

The Prince turned angrily on his pursuers. "I said go away!"

Von Schiffer waved them off.

The Prince's face was flushed with anger and he trembled noticeably. His eyes darted about looking for something on which to vent his emotions. He turned on the Major. "Where is my brother?" He was almost shouting.

Von Schiffer bowed slightly. "Just inside, Your Highness," he said calmly.

Nicholas tensed visibly. He covered his face with his hands and then relaxed, the anger drained from him. "Highness . . . then it's true . . . I'm not . . . He's alive." Relief gripped him. Tears began in his eyes, but he wiped them away immediately, steeling himself against any further display of emotion. "How is the King?" the Prince asked, more controlled.

"Resting, sir."

Dennis stepped forward, seizing the opportunity. "I was just going in to see him," he said quickly. "Perhaps I could accompany Your Highness?"

The Major started to speak, but the Prince raised a hand, interrupting. "Yes, certainly, Mr. Perkins, come with me. Major?" Von Schiffer stepped aside, opening the door.

Dennis could not resist a sharp sniff in his direction which the Major stonily ignored.

They found King Richard fully conscious, attached to several intravenous tubes and pouches, propped up in bed on pillows. Bertie was sleeping soundly next to him. His Majesty's personal physician was concentrating his attention on a large, ugly bruise that had spread over the King's sternum. He stepped back as Prince Nicholas approached.

"Papa," Nicholas knelt beside the bed and took the King's hand. "Thank God you're alive!"

"And thanks to your good shooting, little brother," the King said shakily, reaching out to embrace him.

Dennis moved closer to the bed. The King seemed to be even paler, if that were possible, his eyes drawn back into dark sockets, his movements halting.

Richard caught his look and smiled weakly. "Don't be so amazed, Dennis. Inspector Harlowe was kind enough to insist that I wear a rather heavy and uncomfortable armored vest before entering the Abbey." He gestured to Major Von Schiffer who stood silently at the doorway. "I was trying to console Peter who won't forgive himself for not having thought of it himself."

"The Major is very conscientious," Dennis replied.

Von Schiffer returned his icy glare.

"Yes," the King said drawing out the word as he studied the two of them. "The bullet did not go through, but the impact alone almost did me in."

The doctor moved in to examine his patient again. "A small miracle to say the least, sir," he commented solicitously. "The clotting factor has brought the hemophilia under control but, considering your deteriorating immune condition, I think it—"

"Thank you, Doctor." The King's look told the doctor that he had said too much. "That will be all. Unhook me from these things and take them with you. We shall call if We need you."

The doctor hesitated a moment before carefully removing the IV and applying a pressure bandage. Grabbing his bag, he bowed and left the room.

HIV—it was an unthinkable idea—but it all made sense to Dennis now . . . the constant weakness . . . the emaciated appearance . . . and the hemophilia. Before the problem was known, many hemophiliacs were accidentally infected by contaminated clotting factors needed to prevent them from bleeding to death from the slightest injury. Dennis despaired at the devastating effects the nature of the King's illness would have, should it become public.

"What is all that noise?" the King asked settling back into the pillows.

Nicholas looked out the window facing the Mall circle about the Victoria Monument. "I've never seen so many people in one place," he said excitedly. "They're everywhere."

"People?" The King waved at Von Schiffer. "What is happening, Major?"

"The people are concerned for Your Majesty. They're waiting for word on your condition."

"There must be thousands, Papa," said Prince Nicholas, pulling back the curtains a little more, "Tens of thousands!"

The King closed his eyes, breathing deeply for a moment. "Then We must show them I'm okay." He struggled to a sitting position.

The Major moved quickly to help him. "Your Majesty . . . sir, there is no need for you to get up." He glared at Dennis from the corner of his eyes. "Your Secretary can issue a statement on your condition."

The King considered a moment. "No, the people must be reassured We are well. Their seeing Us is the quickest way to ensure calm." He slid his legs over the side of the bed, gasping. "Help me, Nicky."

Nicholas sat on the bed beside his brother and with great care helped him back into his shirt. Dennis had never seen the King when he was not fully dressed. He was shocked at how thin he was.

"Are you sure this is wise, sir?" Dennis asked. "If I read what the doctor said correctly—"

The King stopped him with a look. "My dress uniform, Major," he commanded, sinking back against his brother from the effort.

Von Schiffer returned from the dressing room carrying the King's scarlet wool jacket, encrusted with an array of medals and ribbons.

Richard sat limply on the edge of the bed and let the Prince and the Major dress him. "Dear God, why do We have to be covered with so many heavy trinkets?"

"Tools of the trade, My Lord," answered Nicholas lightly.

Richard noticed Dennis' look of concern and tried to shrug. "Let them do all the work." He laughed weakly. "I have to save my strength for standing."

The bed shook from all the activity and Bertie began to rouse. He sat up on his knees, rubbing his eyes. "Papa?"

Nicholas picked him up and placed him on the King's lap. Richard kissed the sleep from both his eyes and nibbled at the little boy's neck. Bertie squirmed and giggled at the tickling, but did not release his hold about the King's neck.

"Are you feeling better, Papa?" the little Prince asked, snuggling in close against the King's chest.

Richard winced slightly.

"Careful, Bertie," Nicholas cautioned.

"I'm perfectly all right," the King said, kissing Bertie playfully. "Well, let's see if the King's legs will obey him today."

Prince Albert hopped to the floor and the Major lifted the King easily to his feet. Richard stood shakily for a moment, inwardly trying to adjust his balance, forcing wasted muscles to steady.

Dennis could not help smiling as he watched little Bertie grab hold of the King's leg. Before, Dennis had assumed that, like all small children, Prince Albert held onto his older brother's leg for comfort. Only now did he realize that the Prince was doing what he considered to be his part in helping the King to stand.

"Dennis, do you see my cane anywhere?" the King asked.

Dennis looked about in vain. "It must have been left at the Abbey, Sir."

"Oh dear, it was my favorite." Richard's brow creased with annoyance. "Will you get me the walnut one out of the stand in the study, please. The one with the scrolled end in brass."

Dennis fetched the cane dutifully.

The King accepted it with some disappointment and tested it with little satisfaction. "It'll have to do." He took several steps forward, with Nicholas and the Major still on each arm, and Bertie guiding a leg from below. The King paused for a moment, breathing heavily. "This, Dennis, is what is known as guiding the ship of state."

Dennis could not resist laughing. He moved ahead of them into the large reception parlor and unlocked the bullet-proof glass doors that opened onto the large balcony, from which many generations of monarchs have shown themselves to their people.

The King's progress was slow and painful with many stops to catch his breath. He pointedly refused the Major's attempts to carry him the short distance and stopped a few feet from the door one last time to catch his breath. "All right, everyone," he said, releasing his hold on them. "I'll take it from here."

Reluctantly Prince Nicholas and the Major released their hold on him and moved aside. Bertie clung for a moment longer before running to stand by the door to peek out. The crowd outside had become even more restless when they saw the balcony doors being opened. The din turned into a roar of cheers as the King became visible in the doorway. He inched his way forward till he could brace himself against the front rail.

The deafening excitement of the crowd below seemed to infuse him with new strength and he raised a hand to wave. He motioned to his two brothers to join him. Prince Nicholas swept Bertie up in his arms and carried him out onto the balcony. With the quiet aplomb born of generations of breeding, the three accepted the adulation of what Dennis estimated to be close to a hundred thousand, gathered across the Mall below them.

Dennis watched from the doorway. He shook his head, mentally picturing how the three would be treated in the next day's headlines in the *Times*—"The Miracle Monarch, the Hero Prince, and the Little Cherub who prayed a king back to life." He wasn't sure which bothered him more, tomorrow's headlines, or the fact that he could feel the Major breathing down his neck.

PART II

We do not know very much of the future
Except that from generation to generation
The same things happen again and again.
Men learn little from others' experience.
But in the life of one man, never
The same time returns. Sever
The cord, shed the scale. Only
The fool, fixed in his folly, may think
He can turn the wheel on which he turns.

T. S. Eliot

1

Abernathy's Pub had the distinction of being the single most beloved spot on the British Isles for the Right Honorable members of Parliament. More legislation and acts of historical consequence were created and cemented among its walnut encircled booths and tables than on the floor of the Commons itself. MP's of longstanding have, ever since the pub's inception, occupied various spots among the polished, wooden dividers as offices away from the office.

When Parliament was in session, Enzio Bulgherini, Abernathy's owner, could always be seen standing proudly behind his bar with a smile. But Bulgherini had not smiled since the explosion down the road had crushed the majority of both the nation's leadership and his own profit margin. The displaced Italian had already sacrificed the use of his own proud family name to make his pub English enough for the English. Now there weren't enough English to fill it.

Dennis found the lack of hustle and bustle a little disconcerting as well. He shifted further over in the booth to make more room for the abundance of Hughen Fitzroy, who seemed to swell a little more with each pint of dark lager he downed. Dennis sat nursing his own tumbler of gin and tonic, blinking his eyes wonderingly at the connoisseur next to him. Business at the Palace had slacked off a little as matters were brought more and more under control allowing Dennis to escape his chains, every so often, in the middle of the afternoon for a moment's relaxation.

"No, Conroe and Harper have been pretty quiet of late," boomed Fitzroy. He seemed unconcerned that someone might overhear him. "First sign of intelligence either has ever shown. I think they are wisely taking the King's threats seriously this time."

Dennis might have laughed had they not been talking about Gerald Conroe. "But what do you really think, Fitzroy?" Dennis leaned closer. "Their timely exit before the bomb went off was a little bit more than suspicious. Do you think they're connected to it all?"

"Sorry, my boy, but I can't speak without prejudice. The question is whether or not such a connection can be proved. What annoys me is to think that I might owe them my life."

"Preposterous!" Dennis gestured angrily with the hand holding his drink, sloshing a little gin over into his lap. "Bloody hell!" He reached quickly for the small napkin he was using for a coaster. "How could you even think such a thing?"

Fitzroy laughed, reached over and slammed one of his ham-sized paws onto Dennis' shoulder, causing a little more gin to spill over onto Dennis. "Imagine," said Fitzroy, "if it weren't for my extreme dislike for those two muckrakers I might not be alive today." His eyes twinkled at Dennis. "The same might be said for you."

"I still say Scotland Yard should be concentrating its efforts on those two and their cronies."

"Maybe so, but there are quite a few other avenues of possibility to consider. I'm sure the Yard knows what's best." Fitzroy signaled to a barmaid for another round. "So, lad, what do you think about the latest miracles?"

"Latest what" Dennis asked, preoccupied with the football match playing on the television above the ar..

"Pay attention, boy!" Fitzroy guffawed. He reached over and jovially pounded Dennis to attention again.

"I'm sorry," Dennis stammered, wondering how many of his teeth had been knocked loose. "What were you saying?"

"The miracles, Dennis, lad, the miracles?" Fitzroy accepted his newly filled pint from the waitress. "What position is the Palace taking on the latest reported divine manifestations?"

"I'm sorry, Fitzroy, but I still don't know what you're talking about. What divine manifestations?"

Fitzroy stared at Dennis incredulously over his beer. "You can't be serious, Dennis. Careful, or the Trades will be saying Palace officials are truly out of touch with current events."

"All right, Fitzroy, you have my undivided attention. Enough filibustering. What miracles?"

"Why the King's cane, the miracle walking stick, the new Excalibur, our latest legend. It's been in all the papers."

"Apparently not the reputable ones read at the Palace," Dennis said, sniffing with mock disdain.

"I see this is going to take some time." Fitzroy smacked his lips. "We'd best order another round to see us through."

"Another round? Christ, Fitzroy, we just had one!" Dennis looked from Fitzroy's empty glass to his full one.

"Don't begrudge me, lad." Fitzroy waved a fleshy hand at the barmaid. "A man's got to have a hobby."

"Order for yourself," Dennis said and took a sip of his gin. "It wouldn't be seemly for me to be seen crawling back to work. Now get on with it. You've got my curiosity aroused."

Fitzroy smiled with satisfaction as the barmaid set his fresh drink in front of him. "I suppose the Palace has read about the attempted assassination of the King at the Abbey several days ago," he said sarcastically, giving Dennis a wink.

Dennis sighed. "I was there, remember?"

"Yes, indeed, you were, weren't you. Amazing that you haven't heard about the healings . . . the miraculous, seemingly divinely ordained healings that resulted from the King's apparent resurrection."

"Oh, certainly I've heard about that, Fitzroy. Such things are always reported following incidents of mass hysteria, as this most assuredly was."

"Don't be too quick to judge, lad." Fitzroy took a long swallow, humming softly to himself. "The situation did not end at the Abbey. An item of His Majesty's personal wardrobe was inadvertently left behind."

"His walking stick." Dennis stated the fact in a bored monotone. He wondered how Fitzroy was aware of the fact.

"Indeed! The walking stick," Fitzroy continued, enjoying the build-up. "But no ordinary walking stick."

"I don't get it."

"Think of it, lad." Fitzroy's eyes grew large with honest enthusiasm as the barmaid laid a platter of cold cuts and bread before him on the table. "This . . . walking stick, as you call it, was present at a rare moment of divine intervention—display of heavenly power—a sign, if you will."

"Good God, Fitzroy!" Dennis laughed aloud. "You do like to embellish. No one can actually be serious about all this."

"Deadly serious, lad," said Fitzroy, assuming his most theatrical look of severity. "It isn't wise to disparage a man's religion."

"Get on," Dennis said, shaking his head in disbelief.

"Events become sketchy at best here. The yellow sheets report that one of the priests picked up the cane with the innocent intention of seeing it returned to the King. This priest, who was suffering from . . . shingles, I believe it was, at the time, found himself suddenly and miraculously cured."

"I can't believe people are giving credence to this," Dennis said. He downed the rest of his drink with some difficulty due to his inability to stop laughing.

"This is just the beginning, Dennis."

"Oh, Jesus!"

"The priest, it seems, took this cane along with him on his rounds to the War Veterans Hospital where it was reported the old and infirm residents of that distressing place were perplexingly rejuvenated—restored in the presence of this now famous relic."

Dennis put his head in his hands, not wanting to believe that Fitzroy might even be half-serious in his story telling.

"From there," Fitzroy continued, chewing lustily on a piece of ham, "the cane was returned to the Abbey and its mystical powers were reported to the proper hierarchy and discussed in deep theological contexts. The papers got hold of the story in due course and the legend has done nothing but blossom ever since."

"That I'm sure of," Dennis replied, wondering if the slight dizziness he was feeling was too much gin or too much Fitzroyan eloquence. "Where is the cane now?"

Fitzroy raised his eyebrows, a mammoth feat considering their size, and stared at Dennis out of the corners of his eyes for effect.

"Well?" Dennis almost demanded.

Fitzroy's jowls retracted in a half moon smile. "The holy object lies encased in glass in a side chapel of the Abbey where the faithful may approach it, kneel and pray for their own divine visitation."

"You're joking!"

Fitzroy's fleshy features wrinkled slyly. "Go and see for yourself, lad. New miracles are reported every day." His face contorted in laughter. "I hear the Pope is so jealous and angry, he shit a gold brick in retaliation." Fitzroy roared.

Dennis laughed in spite of himself. It was all too ludicrous. Religion was fine in its place, but Dennis never felt comfortable around hysterical charismatics. He was relieved to see that, despite his grandstanding, Fitzroy was as much a skeptic as he was.

"What's it all coming to, Fitzroy? As a nation we used to be so civilized."

Fitzroy inhaled another beer to restore his strength from the effort of so much laughing. His face radiated color like a ripe apple. "The country is in crisis, Dennis. If nothing else, the Church of England does serve to pull us through such times with our conscience intact."

"Perhaps, but I can't envision someone as deeply religious and, at the same time, intellectual as the King putting up with such obvious exploitation. I doubt he's even aware of what's going on."

"Don't be too sure, lad."

Fitzroy began to assemble a sandwich from the makings in front of him. Dennis joined in, feeling the need for a little solid food to offset the new drink being set in front of him.

"Hughen . . . Dennis . . . What a pleasant surprise," whined the effete voice standing over them. Devon Harper struck a patrician pose in front of their table, belying his socialist facade. "Taking a break from the toils of government, I see."

"Harper!" Fitzroy's stomach rumbled ominously. "What do you want?"

Dennis stood, slamming his tumbler onto the table. "I'm surprised you'd show your face in public," he snapped.

Harper ignored their hostility with saccharine finesse. "What are you gentlemen so upset about?"

Dennis sat down in disgust. "Go to bloody hell, Harper!"

"Precipitously," added Fitzroy in agreement.

"Gentlemen, gentlemen," Harper soothed. "We should lay aside our petty political differences for the sake of the country."

"I doubt that the sake of the country has ever been any concern of his," Dennis said loudly to Fitzroy.

"Please, please, Mr. Perkins. The Irish do have such hot tempers," Harper chided.

"And socialists are such bloody bores," retorted Dennis, to Fitzroy's immense pleasure.

"Hear! Hear!" the old man bellowed.

"Hughen!" Harper piped, approaching the soprano range. "I gave you more credit than this."

His tone was obviously mocking, and Fitzroy puffed up in an intimidating display of bulk.

"I merely wanted to come by and pay my respects," Harper continued unaffected. "When I saw you sitting here it seemed the proper thing to do."

"And so you've done it," Dennis said. He turned his back on the ferret-like man. "Now if you would bother respecting our privacy a little more."

Harper demurred graciously. "Of course, dear boy, but before I go I should like to inquire about the Prime Minister."

Dennis' guard went up immediately.

"I'm curious," Harper continued, "to know how he's feeling, what with all the work he must have been doing." Harper moved closer to the table. "I mean, military exercises, mass deportations, economic reforms ... the man must have made a miraculous recovery."

Dennis ignored him.

Harper grew more insistent. "Funny how no one is yet able to get an appointment with him. Damn odd way to run a government."

"I'll see to it your concern is conveyed to Prime Minister Bates. Now if you'll excuse—"

"It's just that one hears these rumors," Harper interrupted with oily impertinence.

"Rumors?" intoned Fitzroy, filling the pub with his quavering voice. "You mean to say that there are rumors about, which you have not personally composed?" His voice punctuated the air with Shakespearean precision.

Harper looked about self-consciously, face flushed, apparently relieved by the relative emptiness of the room. His features hardened. "There is a conspiracy afoot, gentlemen, and you know it," he said in a loud whisper. "I don't as yet know what this Richard is up to, but my people will find out. For your sakes, I hope you are not too deeply involved."

"Who the bloody hell do you think you are?" Dennis pushed up violently out of the booth, tipping his drink over completely.

"Easy lad!" Fitzroy reached out for Dennis arm to restrain him.

Dennis pulled away from him and faced Harper squarely. "The only person in this room who'd better watch his step is you, Harper." His voice, though not as rich as Fitzroy's, filled the room amply. "Perhaps you'd like to begin explaining a few things. Perhaps you'd like to let everyone know how it is that you and that traitorous slime, Conroe, just happened to walk out on the opening of Parliament just seconds before the bomb blast." He pushed Harper angrily back from the table. "Perhaps you'd like to clear up that little matter of convenience!"

Harper staggered back, grabbing for his glasses before they fell completely off his nose. Fitzroy slammed a beefy fist down on the table. The sound echoed off the paneled walls.

"Gentlemen!" he boomed. "That's enough!"

Dennis turned back to his seat and sat sullenly, breathing hard.

Harper was shaking. "I suggest you learn to control—"

"Not another word, sir!" Fitzroy interrupted, waving an imperious hand. "Now off with you!"

Harper repositioned his glasses over his small thin nose and huffed off, embarrassed by the tittering of the barmaids watching from the corner of the bar.

"Devilishly unlikable man," Fitzroy commented. He tried to settle his delicate digestion with another swallow of the dark, bitter lager.

"Still, he's an angel next to Conroe," Dennis said. He regained his composure, relieved at the lack of rebuke from Fitzroy concerning his behavior.

"The two of them shall sow their own destruction, Dennis, lad, with no help from us."

"Still it would give me the greatest of pleasure to have a hand in it," said Dennis lightly.

Fitzroy laughed, slapping Dennis on the shoulder again. "He's right about one thing, Dennis."

"Oh?" Dennis laid a napkin over his spilled drink.

"You do have a temper."

"I don't know what you mean." Dennis smiled and stood to leave.

Fitzroy's booming laughter rebounded off the walls.

Dennis left him and started for the door, though, not before signaling the waitress to send another round over to the Fallstaffian statesman, still chortling over his empty glass.

2

The Papal Delegation consisted of a small army of clerics, high and low. They were augmented by various primates of the Roman Church in the British Isles who fought tooth and nail to be a part of so auspicious an occasion. The Delegation was headed by none other than the much respected Cardinal Botticelli, still riding the wings of his latest diplomatic success in mediating a small, but much publicized, Palestinian skirmish. Ever since Richard IV's ascension, the Vatican had been making overtures for such a Royal audience and when a request was finally granted all stops were pulled out. The Pope had immediately appointed Botticelli as his emissary and a date was agreed upon between Palace and Vatican with astonishing speed.

But Botticelli was not in the best of moods. There had been no fanfare to greet his arrival at the airport, and very little, if any, press coverage of the pending summit. True, things had been put together rather hastily, but this was no excuse. It was all he could do to keep from chewing up and spitting out the subordinate English-Catholic priests and bishops who had met him. Advance work for the meeting had been their responsibility.

Boticelli had dealt with the Church of England before and knew first hand of its adherents distrust of anything remotely related to the Church of Rome. They were heretics. There was no debating that, and English monarchs were the worst of the lot—self-styled, imitation popes. He stared out the window as the limousine turned into the gilt gates of Buckingham Palace. Big, but hardly as inspiring as the Vatican courts, he mused.

Watching the train of cars pulling through the gates, Dennis tugged at the morning coat such occasions required and gave a last inspection of the liveried footmen standing in attendance. Other than the King, he was the only other person in the world who knew the true purpose of this meeting. He hoped Cardinal Botticelli was in a good mood.

"Welcome, sir," Dennis said as the rotund Cardinal pulled himself out of the limousine. "I'm Dennis Perkins, the King's Private Secretary."

Botticelli studied Dennis a moment. "You are Irish?"

Dennis smiled. "As a matter of fact yes, sir."

"Church of Rome?" The Cardinal was hopeful.

"Anglo-Catholic," Dennis lied. The sudden drop in Botticelli's countenance made the small prevarication worth it. "Won't you follow me, sir. His Majesty is expecting you."

The procession down the entry hall to the audience chamber was a solemn march. Little small talk, let alone real conversation, was entertained and, judging by the Cardinal's grim demeanor, Dennis declined even to attempt it. He signaled to the footman to open the doors into the Blue Room of State in which the King had chosen to receive them. Of course, the King would not be there yet. Dennis knew His Majesty would uncharacteristically make the Cardinal wait before making his own appearance.

Dennis had originally dreaded being the one left to deal with the group while they were made to wait—but, as Dennis showed Botticelli to the smaller of only two chairs in the room, he was beginning to relish the prospect. The rest of the Cardinal's entourage was left to stand about in the back of the room while all faced the slightly elevated throne the King would soon be occupying. The Cardinal sat sullenly while several of his clerical aides fussed over him, filling his lap with notes.

He waved them off with impatient aggravation and glared at Dennis down the cascading bridge of his Roman nose. "Will King Richard keep us waiting long?" Botticelli inquired. He rolled the "r" with added stress.

"No longer than necessary, sir," Dennis replied. His purposeful failure to address the Cardinal as "Eminence" was having its desired effect.

The Cardinal pursed his lips in annoyance. He drummed his fingers on the side of the chair and stared at Dennis with undisguised anger. Dennis merely stood by, smiling cherubically, and counting the crystals in the chandelier overhead.

"Perhaps the King would prefer we come at a more opportune time," said the Cardinal in a voice that made the priests in the back of the room quake.

"No, no. His Majesty is expecting your delegation," Dennis answered cheerily.

One of the English bishops of Rome stepped forward to try and smooth things over. "I'm sure the King appreciates Your Eminence being so patient." He narrowed his eyes at Dennis. "His Majesty is probably being held up in a meeting with his ministers. Isn't that true, Mr. Perkins?"

"He has been very busy this morning," agreed Dennis. "I think he's finishing up with brunch now. But I'm sure he won't be much longer."

"Brunch!" Botticelli thundered. The chandelier crystals tinkled with sympathetic vibration.

The doors to the audience chamber were thrown open again before Dennis could respond.

"His Majesty, the King!" announced the footman from the doorway.

King Richard stopped at the door and reviewed the delegation coolly. Cardinal Botticelli stood up from his chair slowly. A professional smile had replaced the earlier grimace and he bowed diplomatically as the King made his way to the throne, followed by various ministers and assistants. Dennis accepted a sheaf of papers from one of his aides and took his own place to the side and slightly behind the King.

"Cardinal Botticelli," said the King without expression. He nodded to the Cardinal, acknowledging his presence.

"Your Majesty," replied Botticelli with equal coolness. "We trust your brunch was satisfactory."

"My brunch?" puzzled the King with a raised eyebrow.

Dennis admired the chandeliers again as the King inclined his gaze at him briefly.

"It was quite satisfactory, thank you," said the King without missing a beat. He returned his attention to the Cardinal and gestured that he be seated.

"His Holiness, the Pope sends his warmest regards to Your Majesty and his prayers for the success of this meeting," Botticelli intoned regaining his seat.

"We share in those sentiments," the King replied. "Now let us talk frankly and candidly together while your fellow delegates are entertained elsewhere."

The doors were opened again.

"It will be an honor, Your Majesty," the Cardinal said, used to such personal communication with heads of state. He waved his entourage out the door.

The King pointedly ignored Botticelli while the room cleared. As the Cardinal sat silently stewing, Richard engaged in a brief discussion of the rest of the days schedule with Dennis.

Finally he acknowledged the Cardinal again. "We are pleased the Vatican agreed so readily to this meeting," commented the King.

"As I am sure your Majesty is aware, His Holiness has made overtures to your government on numerous occasions for such a meeting and we were more than pleased to get matters underway quickly."

"Has he?" The King's hand fondled the end of his cane as if it were a trigger. "We are concerned in this meeting about overtures from the Vatican to governments hostile to our own. Overtures to terrorists, assassins, and murderers."

Botticelli sat stunned. He had assumed the meeting would focus on establishing diplomatic relations or on issues common to the Church at Rome and the Church of England.

"Sir, you have me at a disadvantage." Botticelli sat forward, regaining some of his composure. "I'm not quite sure what you mean." The Italian inflection increased in his voice.

"We are speaking, Cardinal, of the documented relationship between the Roman Catholic clergy of

Northern Ireland, the new IRA, and known world terrorist organizations linked to the Middle East."

Botticelli's head reeled. "Again, Your Majesty, I repeat, I don't know what you mean."

The Cardinal's diplomatic persona was slipping precariously. Dennis resisted the urge to smile as he handed the King one of several expertly forged documents.

"We would like to believe," said the King with a chilling stare, "that our brother, the Pope is unaware of these facts. But considering the substantial funds that are being rerouted from these churches to IRA strongholds, we would find that hard to accept."

He handed the paper to Dennis who immediately transferred it to Botticelli who studied it in horror.

King Richard glared down at the dithering church prelate. "As you can see, Cardinal, it is doubtful at best that such substantial investments in terrorism could be overlooked by Vatican auditors." The King paused to let these words sink in. "And still there is more."

The King gestured for Dennis to give the Cardinal another document. "Our intelligence community has traced these funds back to their source—all known fronts for Palestinian terrorists." He leaned forward, balancing on his cane. "Your church is financing a movement against Our sovereign and legal government by a band of terrorists."

Botticelli was speechless.

"You may take this evidence to your pontiff. But we suggest that you hurry lest he read these facts in the morning editions of the world press before you return."

Botticelli recovered his voice. "Surely Your Majesty will give us time to review these accusations and reply to them before leaking such potentially damaging and possibly erroneous news to the press."

"The facts speak for themselves, Cardinal." The King's voice fell to a frigid whisper. "We do not have time to waste on waiting. Our government is fighting to survive a terrorist inspired and Roman Catholic financed insurrection. We will not tolerate any more!" The King hammered the floor with his cane. "We are ordering the confiscation of these Northern Irish and English churches of Rome—all property, records, and bank accounts. We have also ordered the arrest of their clergy pending a full investigation and possible trial for treason. We are also ordering a complete and total freeze on all other assets the Vatican holds in this kingdom, to investigate further illegal financing of terrorist activities."

The color drained from Botticelli's face only to be replaced by a tinge of grayish-green ill-humor. Dennis became concerned the stalwart churchman might fall off his chair. He attempted to hand the Cardinal the remainder of his manufactured evidence but Botticelli seemed unable to move. Instead, Dennis slid them under the Cardinal's hand, trembling uncontrollably on his knee.

Botticelli's voice finally returned in rasps. "Sir . . . I must protest these . . . actions . . ."

"Really!" The King sniffed. "We suggest you save such protestations for the Vatican's explanation to the families of all those murdered by IRA terrorists, financed by your church's collection plate and its Al Qaeda patrons."

The King pushed himself up from his throne with the cane and a helping hand from Dennis. He crossed to the door with a flourish, pausing for a moment in the door before delivering his finale.

"We too send Our regards to this pope," the King said. "If he wishes to retain even the semblance of a church in this land he will do all in his power to suppress, condemn, and remove his clergy's roll in this mockery of Christianity. Either that or We will suppress and remove here, as a threat to Our security, all that speaks of papist apostasy."

The King's eyes drilled into Botticelli who still sat in his chair, totally flustered and unable to voice any defense.

"In this country, sir," said the King as if he were reprimanding a child, "one is expected to stand when a King has risen." He left the room before the Cardinal could stumble to his feet apologetically.

Dennis remained behind to help pick up the pieces. Considering what he had read about the man, Dennis was surprised Botticelli had not found more to say. Judging by the Cardinal's cardinal color, however, it was obvious that the King's surprise attack had worked better than expected. The Pope would most certainly be getting an earful later. In the face of world condemnation, the Vatican would have to take some sort of positive action long before the complicated evidence British Intelligence had concocted could, if it were possible, be unraveled.

"Would the Cardinal like to join his fellow delegates in the courtyard for some refreshment?" Dennis inquired with an air of innocent detachment.

Botticelli looked as if Dennis were insane. He stared down at the papers in his hand for a moment before storming past Dennis and out the door growling like a cornered lion. "Send my car around!" he boomed, flying down the corridor like a red flame.

Dennis signaled to a footman to let the other delegates know it was time to leave before running down the hall to catch up with the angry prelate.

Botticelli raged in the doorway as he waited for his car. "Outrageous!" he sputtered several times. "Complete lies!"

Dennis knew better than to argue with him, preferring to stand by wringing his hands in the perfect imitation of a distraught government lackey.

Tired of waiting, the Cardinal flung the doors aside and headed out onto the drive to meet his limousine as it turned into the main gate. It would have made an interesting picture for the tabloids if a photographer had been handy. The red-faced Cardinal, red cape fluttering in the stiff breeze, hurling various Italian and Latin curses over his shoulder.

Dennis rushed up beside the fuming Botticelli to open the car door for him. "I hope you have a pleasant flight back to Rome, sir," Dennis said matter-of-factly.

With a growl, Botticelli slammed the car door shut and pounded the back of the front seat with his fist for the driver to go.

Dennis stood in the drive for a moment watching the procession of confused clergy assemble in their various limousines and set out after the Cardinal in hot pursuit. Dennis considered sending them off with a one-finger salute but he decided with a laugh that it was beneath the dignity of his position.

As he turned to head back to his office a figure in an upstairs window caught his eye, making him glad he had not given the delegates his spontaneous send-off. Even from the distance, Dennis could tell the King was pleased with the outcome. He acknowledged Dennis with a nod before solemnly crossing himself and disappearing from the window.

Dennis looked back at the line of limousines barreling down the Mall at high speed. Power was almost as much pleasure as sex, he thought. Still, he'd have to give Aidan another chance. He laughed and headed back into the Palace.

3

Prince Nicholas stood at the rear of the King's ornate private chapel at Buckingham Palace, biting his lip and watching his older brother praying before the ancient stone altar. The King wore a heavy silk dressing gown which seemed to engulf his wraith-like features. A faint hint of moonlight pulled the colors of the stained glass windows down to the marbled floors where they played in a kaleidoscope oblivious to the King's frail, still form bent in silent prayer.

As he watched, a greater fear seemed to overtake the young prince. Trembling from the cold surrounding the tomb-like chapel and from his own inner battle with fate, the Prince edged his way down the aisle to kneel beside his brother. The stone floors were like ice and he inched closer to the King for both warmth and comfort.

Nicholas bowed his head and tried in vain to pray. He looked to his older brother's calm and peaceful countenance and tried to draw strength from it.

After a moment the King's eyes fluttered open. A slight shiver from the cold went through him as the reality of his surroundings broke through his meditation. He drew an arm up around his younger brother and pulled him closer, closing his eyes again as if to add a codicil to the prayer just delivered.

"It's late, Nicky," the King said.

The younger boy was unable to speak.

The King kissed him softly on the forehead. "What's wrong? You seem fearful of something."

The Prince reached up to touch his brother's face. "Papa, I can't help it." He looked away unable to meet the King's gaze. "They almost killed you. I don't understand. I'm afraid for you—for all of us."

"God is watching over us, Nicky," said the King, stroking his brother's hair. "He is in control of these events and has a plan that will bring about good. Your day will be easier than mine."

The Prince looked up at him, puzzled. "Sir, what do you mean *my* day?"

The King kissed him again and smiled. "Help me stand."

The Prince supported his older brother, who stood stiffly from the cold floor and sat on one of the short, padded pews.

"Nicky, we are doing what we were born to do—what God has ordained for us."

The Prince looked at his brother, frowning and said, "But Papa, surely we've ended up here by accident. We weren't supposed to be in this place. We were never prepared for this. Why did things have to change?" His eyes watered but he would not let the tears come.

"Nicky," said the King, pulling his younger brother to him. He smiled down at the trembling, yet stubborn set of the Prince's jaw.

They were more like father and son together rather than brothers. Both the time span of their ages and the distancing of their father from them in the last few years of his life had made it so. The Duke had immersed himself in the political problems of the country, serving as one of the late Queen's closest advisors at the expense of his family, marriage, and business.

Richard sacrificed his own dream of entering the church to straighten out his father's estate and business problems, as well as seeing to it his younger brothers were properly raised. As a result of the natural evolution of their relationship, Nicholas and Albert began to refer to their older brother as "Papa," reserving the more formal "Father" for their actual progenitor.

"No one can be truly prepared for these responsibilities," Richard said gently. "Only with God's help and guidance can any man presume to sit on a throne in judgment over others."

"Half the time, I don't know what to say or do—how to behave." Nicholas wrung his hands anxiously.

"You have studied the examples of history, Nicky. You have been well taught both by your teachers at school and at home by me. All you need keep first in your mind is that your moral example is your greatest asset."

"But Papa, surely not all things done in the name of the Crown can be considered moral. I'm not a little school boy anymore, and you've never tried to shelter me from the realities of our situation."

The King sighed and shook his head. He reached out to caress the Prince's cheek. "No, you cannot be considered a child anymore. You've seen and been through too much." He straightened, holding his brother's eyes with his own. "You are old enough now to understand the basic dichotomy in being a Royal."

The Prince's face clouded with confusion.

"A king can be said to be two different entities," Richard continued. "First there is the man, that part which is most visible to the people. A king has the responsibility to stand as a moral example to his people. Though he is neither divine nor perfect, he must strive to appear to be. There are too many laying in wait to pull him down."

Nicholas thought hard on this. "How far should a prince go to preserve this . . . this image?" he asked.

"As far as is necessary," replied the King. "That image, as you call it, is as important to the people as it is to a king. He stands as a symbol to all those things which the people hold sacred, and they have the right and privilege to show their pride and respect for these ideals through their king, whom they, with God's help, have placed high upon a throne for all to see."

"Who'd want to be a king, anyway?" Nicholas asked, shaking his head, wondering.

"It is not a matter of choice. It is ordained in higher places." King Richard held his brother's face up to him. "A king is also given the prerogative to speak on behalf of his people as when We speak of Ourself in the plural. It is the right to judge, to proclaim, to command, to exalt, or to condemn. A king can hold the sway of life and death."

Prince Nicholas stirred uneasily. "But these aren't prerogatives a King has used in the last hundred years," he said. "Constitutionally they have been turned over to the elected government."

"That would appear to be true," Richard said softly. "But every act the government commits is done in the name of the King. These prerogatives have wisely been sublimated to the elected government but it can never be said they have been given up. Elected governments are a product of the modern world and certainly serve it well."

Richard squeezed the boy's shoulder. "Still there is no guarantee that even these institutions will always function for the good of the people, and the King's prerogative to judge and dissolve that government is a crucial check against the tyranny of the self-serving. And if, in time of crisis, there is no stable government to rule, the King, with his prerogatives intact, is always there to insure the orderly transition of power. Not even his death can change that fact as long as the Succession is preserved."

"But still, I have to wonder about the morality of certain acts," Nicholas persisted.

Richard smiled at him. "It is said that the good of the people is the supreme law. The government, and therefore the king, does not act on the basis of personal morality but by virtue of a divine warrant, under God."

"Can a man do this?" asked the young prince.

"Collectively that right has been divinely sanctioned and is found repeatedly in the scriptures. It is an ideal, to be sure. But it can also be done practically with the proper checks and balances."

"I could never make those kinds of decisions," Prince Nicholas said, turning away from his brother.

The King put a hand on his shoulder. "Why would you say that?"

"I don't even know how to be a prince, much less a king."

"What more is there to know? One is but an extension of the other. It's merely a lifelong commitment to one thing. A commitment which you can easily make if it is important to you. Admittedly, living with that commitment is not an easy task, but making it is only a step of trust, and faith, and service."

"I just don't know if I can!" The Prince's voice ascended in a wail. Distraught, he knelt on the cold floor in front of the King, sobbing with his head in his brother's lap.

The King sat quietly waiting, stroking his brother's head as Nicholas expended the store of fear and confusion that had been slowly building up in him. When the Prince's tears subsided, King Richard took the boy's hands between his and sat him up sharply.

"That's enough crying." Richard's tone was markedly different, harder.

Nicholas stopped the tears instantly. He looked down at his hands folded as if in prayer, held tightly between his brother's and immediately recognized the archaic symbolism this gesture held.

"You *are* a prince!" King Richard admonished. His voice echoed off the walls. "There is no changing that. The question is whether or not you will accept the responsibilities of your station and serve as you were born to serve. You are old enough to decide this now. Can you make this commitment, swear to it before God, and your King?"

Nicholas trembled in the cold. He looked about the chapel as if he were seeking help, but he was suddenly alone. He looked to his brother, but it wasn't his brother's hands which were holding his. There was no one there except his King, who was now strangely distant and out of reach.

"Papa," he said weakly. "Tell me what to do."

"You know the oath?"

"I know it," answered Nicholas, his voice reduced to a whisper.

"Say it only if you mean it," the King commanded. "Here, in this holy place. Say it to Us and to God."

The Prince swallowed, trying to find his voice. He moistened his lips, searching his memory for the ancient words that would turn over his life and soul into the hands that held his.

"My Lord."

He felt the King's grip tighten.

"I do solemnly swear to become your liege man of life and limb and of earthly worship ," Nicholas looked his brother in the eye, confident in what he was saying and doing, "and faith and truth I will bear unto you, to live and die, against all manner of folks. So help me God."

The King released his hold and stood, leaning on his cane. He turned his back to the Prince and hobbled slowly to the altar, staring up at the heavy, silvered crucifix that dominated the medieval table.

"Your job has now been simplified," the King said tremulously. "You will never . . . ever have to wonder what that responsibility is again." He kept his back to the Prince. "How you discharge that responsibility will depend on you, your talents and abilities." King Richard's gaze remained fixed, mesmerized by the glittering cross.

Prince Nicholas, still kneeling on the marble floor, watched him anxiously, unable to tell if it was anger or some new and uncomfortable turn in their relationship that had so hardened his brother's tone towards him.

"Answer me quickly." The King's whisper was like a knife.

"Sir?" The Prince's voice cracked.

"Whom do you serve in all things. Whom do you serve even with your very life above all others."

"My King," answered Nicholas without hesitation.

"And if you were King?"

The Prince looked up at his brother, stunned by the question. "If I were King?"

"Answer me!" The King tried to straighten.

Prince Nicholas reached out to his brother, pleading. "Sir, how can I—"

"Answer me now. Whom would you serve?"

Vainly, Nicholas tried to calm himself so he could think. He looked to his brother again. The answer had to be there. Whom *did* the King serve. He thought of the cross. Was it the people—frail, fallible, inconstant? Was it God? It all seemed too easy. There must be more. Could God condone the wars waged by Kings, each one claiming God's protection? Under what circumstances would God forgive such acts? Why was his brother making so much of this?

"The people!" he blurted out wiping the remnant of tears from his eyes. "The King must serve the people." It was too late to take the words back now. "Sir, is this the right answer? The King serves the people?"

King Richard turned back to him slowly, his face betraying neither anger nor approval. "Come here, child."

Prince Nicholas sprang from the floor and threw his arms around his brother, relieved the ordeal was over. The fear was gone and he thought only of his brother. He looked up at Richard's face for any sign of anger or disappointment but found only exhaustion. "Papa, you must rest."

"We must all get some rest, Nicky," the King said, leaning against him for support. "Where is our Bertie?"

"He's sleeping without a care as usual," Nicholas said.

"Go and get ready for bed and then bring your brother to my room. I think I shall like both of you with me tonight."

"Let me take you upstairs first."

"I'll be along shortly," Richard assured him. "Where is Peter?"

"Standing just outside the door, Papa. Shall I get him."

"Send him in to me on your way out."

Prince Nicholas held on to his brother for a moment longer before leaving the King alone.

Richard stood quietly before the chapel altar, his head turned to the floor. Within a moment the shadow of Major Von Schiffer blotted out the myriad colors dancing at his feet, reflected from the windows about him.

"My Lord," Von Schiffer said, going down on one knee. Still he was tall enough almost to look the King in the eye and was forced to hide his own expression of growing impatience.

He sensed something different about the King. The lines of pain that usually framed his sovereign's eyes were curiously absent, erased, putting the King's countenance more at peace.

"My Lord," he repeated.

The King's eyes seemed to cut through him. "I have a mission for you, Major."

Von Schiffer quivered with anticipation and pleasure. Perhaps the waiting was finally over. "I am ready, Sire. Whatever you wish!"

King Richard reached into his robe and pulled out several slips of paper, placing them into the Major's open hands. "All of them . . . tonight," he commanded.

"Majesty." Von Schiffer stood, bowing deeply.

He backed away from the King quickly, holding the slips of paper like a fragile bird soon to be released into flight.

King Richard watched him leave. He turned back to the polished crucifix rising over the altar, meditating. For the first time in a long time, lost in thought, he allowed himself an unfeigned smile, like one whose prayer had been answered.

T

4

Lady Ainsley bubbled like a just uncorked magnum of Brut. She rarely behaved with such effervescence, but her personal patronage of English designers had set Paris fashion back on its heels. It was her holy mission to make English fashion preeminent. She held the delicate, champagne colored silk up to her face in front of the mirror and admired its flattering compliment to her cheeks through eyes long ago rendered myopic by age.

Still, she had to admit, she was a beauty even now. Other than the microscopic pink streaks at her hair line, behind her ears, and over her eyes, there was hardly any evidence at all of the many trips she had made to various Swedish cosmetic surgeons. Her hair, though somewhat listless, maintained its expertly highlighted blonde by a means which Lady Ainsley shared with no one. She was, after all, an aristocrat with a chicly long lineage and some things were just meant to be kept in the family.

"Oh, Aidan, the material is exquisite," Lady Ainsley warbled as she fondled the silken fabric. "The color is perfect."

Aidan stood behind her, trying not to frown as Lady Ainsley stroked the material over the heavy makeup covering her cheeks. "I knew it would be perfect for you the moment I saw it," Aidan said. He reached for the fabric before it could be damaged further.

"It's perfect with the scarf I bought in Hong Kong last month." Lady Ainsley returned the bolt to Aidan reluctantly. "This dress should put both of us in the spotlight, my dear," she declared patronizingly.

Aidan merely smiled and tried to look humble.

"Are the others boxed and ready for me?" Lady Ainsley almost drooled with delight. "I can't wait to get them home."

"Yes, ma'am. They're over behind the counter. I'll get them."

"Don't bother, dear. Oh, Horace," Lady Ainsley commanded to her able-bodied chauffeur, waiting patiently by the door. "Be a good boy and get my packages, will you?"

She pulled a compact from her purse and seized the moment to touch up her facial artistry. Horace lumbered over to the counter and picked up the stack of boxes obediently.

"I'll have the others ready before you leave for the continent, ma'am," Aidan said. He watched the powder dust over his freshly polished floor. "I'll call you for a fitting, probably around Tuesday."

"That will be fine, dear. I'm certain I can squeeze that into my day somehow. There's so much to do before Geoffrey and I leave." Lady Ainsley snapped the compact closed and returned it to her purse. "Will I ever find enough time?"

"I'm sure everything will get done," Aidan said sweetly. "You've always seemed to organize well."

"That's true." Lady Ainsley's head perked at the compliment. "Geoffrey always says I have a talent for organization."

"Lord Ainsley is very lucky," assured Aidan. "It's no wonder he's able to give so much time to the country."

Horace struggled to open the door for Lady Ainsley and balance the tower of packages he carried.

Lady Ainsley ignored him. "I'm just so glad he's in the diplomatic service." She shook her head plaintively. "It's so much safer for people like us to be out of the country right now—so much violence about."

"Times are difficult," Aidan agreed sympathetically.

"Oh, well," Lady Ainsley said hurriedly. "We'd best be off." She brushed out the door past her juggling chauffeur, almost toppling his burden.

"Pardon, ma'am," said a short, squat man she almost ran down on her way out.

Lady Ainsley stopped sharply, catching her breath at the near collision. She brushed a hand over the expensive tweed suit she wore and studied the unshaven, unkempt man who stood in her way. She stepped aside and darted past him with a dignified sniff as if trying to avoid a plague of lice.

"Come along, Horace!" she admonished, tapping her foot impatiently before the door of her vintage Bentley.

The unshaven man sniffed back at her, chuckling to himself and slipped through the door into the boutique. He shrugged at the unfamiliar surroundings. Pursing his lips, he thrust his stained fingers into his wrinkled jacket and began to browse through the small shop, examining the colorful array of patterns and materials with benign curiosity.

Aidan spotted the eccentric looking figure weaving in and out of his display as he came out of the storeroom where he had gone to replace Lady Ainsley's bolt of material. He headed for the stranger quickly. The constables were usually able to keep the shopping district free of vagrants, but every now and then one would slip by unnoticed to beg or shoplift.

"May I help you," Aidan called out, bearing down on him.

"Hello, Aidan." The man turned to face him with a toothy grin. "It's been a while, to be sure."

Aidan slowed his approach as recognition took over. "O'Dell!" he whispered hoarsely.

Aidan grabbed the man by the coat and almost dragged him to the back of the shop toward the storeroom. Moving behind some fabric displays, Aidan spun O'Dell around to face him. "What are you doing here?" Fire played wildly in his eyes.

"Aidan, me boy," pleaded the man mockingly. "This ain't no way to treat an old . . . friend and compatriot."

"Answer me, you fool!" Aidan shook him by the shoulders forcefully. "Are you trying to ruin everything?"

"I don't know what ye mean, child." O'Dell wrinkled his face with child-like innocence. "Can't a body visit an old friend without having to pay a tax for it?"

"Goddamn it, O'Dell!" Aidan turned away from him, furious. "I'll have to report this immediately."

"Now hold on there, boy," said O'Dell with a chuckle. "Don't worry so about nothing."

"Nothing!" Aidan turned back to him fuming. "Do you consider blowing my cover nothing? Do you think for a moment that I'm not being watched?"

"Calm down, son," O'Dell said, lowering his voice consolingly. The lower class inflections dropped suddenly from his voice. "No such thing is going to happen. We'll chat for a minute and then you can have the local police lead me away for some reason or another. No one will think twice about it."

"So you say." The steel was showing in Aidan's voice. "You take an awful lot for granted, O'Dell."

"Life is a series of chances, son. We play them as best we can."

"Save your sophomoric aphorisms for speech making, and I am not your son," Aidan snapped derisively. "You know the rules and you've broken number one."

"Let me worry about that, lad. It's important business that brings me here out of hiding. We're going to chat whether you like it or not. After all, I do have certain rights where you're concerned." He smiled at Aidan meaningfully. "You made me a promise once."

"Get to the point and go."

"Certainly, my boy. It concerns the latest set of orders to have come our way."

"What's that got to do with me? Speak to your contact about it."

"Not so fast," O'Dell said. "Contacts are fine for delivering and receiving messages but very poor in the explanation department. What I need are some answers and, knowing how close you are to . . . our friend, you seem the logical choice to play the middle man."

"What are you rambling about?" Aidan's agitation was growing with each second.

"Simply this, boy. We have reached the perfect moment for a final strike—a move that could well be the signal for a full scale armed uprising. Yet, for some hidden and mysterious reason we are ordered to sit on the situation . . . to wait . . . do nothing. We are losing the one historical opportunity to achieve complete separation. We've come this far and now we are to wait?"

O'Dell's fiery oratory only made Aidan angrier. "Your job is to follow orders," he snapped.

"Oh, very good, my boy. Whose orders?"

"You know whose." Aidan looked at him coldly. "You are in no position to know the complexity of the plans we are carrying out. The final strike will come when it is time."

"You know this to be a fact?"

"I know that this same wisdom has brought us up to this point. I'm not about to abandon it all because you're too impatient to wait out your orders."

O'Dell grew defensive. "You seem to have forgotten what it's like underground, Aidan. It's difficult to trust anyone. We, too, have a right to know the reasoning that stands behind the plans we risk our lives for."

Aidan tried a different tactic. "Rudy, this meeting was a foolish idea. I know your people can be very impatient, but that's not like you." He softened. "What's wrong?"

"We're so close, Aidan. Can't you see it?" His eyes glistened with a fanatic's pain. "So close to finally seeing our dream come true. It's hard to stay down and quiet when everything could be over within one last move on the board."

"Rudy, carelessness like this can blow the whole game," Aidan countered. "Go back and wait. We'll forget this meeting ever took place."

"And then what do I tell my people?" O'Dell shook his head furiously. "We need to know something now.

For God's sake, Aidan, the Royal Navy is flaunting itself on our northern coastline."

"It's just a show, Rudy."

"A show that's succeeding in making us all look like fools and cowards. We need to react."

Aidan put a hand on the man's shoulder. "We don't need to react just for the sake of reacting. We must follow orders, Rudy, and maintain the rule. This is what has kept our movement secure for so long. What your cell doesn't know can't hurt the next cell."

"If it were just me, Aidan, I'd go along with you. But there's a dangerous restlessness in everyone these days."

"You're one of our most important cell leaders, Rudy. Discipline is a problem you've had to cope with for a long time now. Your people respect you and what you say. You must believe that everything depends on your keeping them in line until the time is right according to the plan."

"You're assuming, then, that there is some master plan?"

Aidan nodded. "There must be. Have faith in it. Look how far we've come."

O'Dell took a deep breath and strutted out into the middle of the showroom floor. "Nice little shop you have here, Aidan. You always did have talent."

Aidan watched him warily.

"Shame to have a poor, lost slum dweller like meself loitering about all these pretty things." Rudy gave the younger man a wink.

Without another word Aidan headed for the door, preparing to play his part. He stepped out onto the sidewalk and glanced about for a policeman. Conveniently, there were two just across the street, conversing with several punkers, who were littering the streets with their outlandish dress and rainbow hair.

"Constable, if you please!" Aidan called out to them.

The two policemen turned in his direction.

"Yes, sir," answered one. They were both clean-cut and proper. "What can we do for you?" He pulled at his partner's jacket and they started across the street to the shop. "What's the problem here?"

Aidan opened the door for them to come in. "This . . . gentleman," Aidan gestured to O'Dell, who grinned drunkenly at them, "refuses to leave. I've asked him repeatedly."

One of the officers walked over to O'Dell, tapping his billy club against the side of his leg. "Is this true, sir? You wouldn't want to cause this taxpayer any trouble now, would you?"

"No, never, constable." O'Dell was suddenly speaking in a thick brogue. "I'm just a poor soul seeking gainful employment." He staggered forward. "Thought this young man could use a pair of good strong arms around the place. Just for a little spending money, ya' understand."

O'Dell fell against the policeman. "A man needs a little money in his pocket, ya' know."

"Easy there, old man." The officer grabbed O'Dell under the arm to hold him up. His partner quickly joined him, holding onto the other arm. "Come along, pops."

They started for the door.

"Sorry for the inconvenience, sir," one of the officers said to Aidan. "Any damage done that we'll need to press charges for?"

"No, no, officer, thank you." Aidan smiled engagingly at the young officer. "I'll appreciate it if you'd just show him off."

"Leave it to us, sir. Now come along, old man."

They carried the sputtering vagrant out the door and down the walkway.

Aidan shut the door behind them and stood leaning against it, watching them go. This was inexcusable, he thought, no matter who O'Dell was. Aidan knew he wouldn't report O'Dell. He owed him that much. Still, if his former patron ever did something like this again he'd kill the man himself, former lover or not.

5

O'Dell stumbled convincingly along with the two young policemen, occasionally spouting off some obscenity or pleading with them for a break. He had played this role before and felt very comfortable with it. The two policemen seemed to accept his performance with the pitying humor that characterized the socially superior and merely carried him along down the street.

A block away from the shop the two officers made an unexpected turn into an alleyway between two large brownstones. O'Dell began to worry that the policemen might be intending to rough him up a little before releasing him. Still he kept up his show. He had taken worse consequences in the past in order to further his fanatical goals.

"Boys, boys, where are you taking me?" O'Dell drawled drunkenly.

Suddenly one of the officers fell back against the alley wall pulling O'Dell up against his chest. O'Dell felt himself straining against an arm lock and a hand clamped about his mouth. He tried to fight but it was too late.

The other policeman stood in front of him, smiling down at him pleasantly. "Mr. O'Dell," he said, unbuttoning O'Dell's shirt. "You should learn to follow orders."

O'Dell struggled in vain. The hold on him was merely tightened. His face was grey with fear.

The young officer in front of him pulled a tapering, steel stiletto out of his boot and held it admiringly up to O'Dell's face. "Lovely, isn't it," the policeman said. "Easily concealed, very efficient . . . that is, if properly placed." He laid a hand on O'Dell's naked chest just below the collar bone and began slowly counting down the ribs on the left side. "My personal preference, Mr. O'Dell, is between the fourth and fifth ribs, though some would use the third and fourth," the officer said matter-of-factly. "Then again, I suppose it depends a lot on what instrument you are using."

His finger paused over the intercostal space between the fourth and fifth ribs of O'Dell's chest. He prodded the site carefully. "Yes, this should do it."

O'Dell was growing frantic. He struggled hard against the man holding him, trying to create some sort of opening, some slim opportunity to break free. He knew these men were professionals, but who . . .who?

"Stop relishing it so much, Toby, and get it over with," said the man who was holding O'Dell from behind. "My arms are getting tired."

O'Dell heard him laugh. A name, thought O'Dell. He searched his memory for a clue . . . Toby . . . but there was no such reference. If only they would let him speak . . . negotiate the situation.

The young Bobbie placed the point of his blade against O'Dell's heaving, sweating chest. He fixed his eyes on O'Dell's and with a smile, thrust his weapon forward. The razor-like instrument popped through the tight skin covering the open space between the ribs. O'Dell grunted against the cutting pain as the blade pierced neatly into the heart muscle.

An instantaneous weakness and lightheadedness overcame O'Dell as the blood exploded out of the torn heart wall. The injured muscle quivered spasmodically in chaotic fibrillation. The policeman quickly jerked the knife around to the side between the ribs bisecting the heart with medical precision.

O'Dell could hear the scraping sound of his feet slipping out from under him as his oxygen starved brain fought to stay alive and aware. The name . . . what was that name again? With incalculable speed the various centers of the brain began to die in succession and, with the last starved cell, went all that was left of Rudy O'Dell, IRA patriot. The name he had heard, died with him.

The two young policemen stood for a moment, looking over the body as if to appreciate the professional aspects of the death process. Finally one pulled a small square of parchment out of his pocket and laid it carefully on the body's chest.

"You think the wind might blow it away?" one of the men questioned, feeling the stiff breeze cutting down the alleyway.

The other man nodded, annoyed at the slight hitch in his otherwise perfectly executed operation. After due consideration, he reached down and plucked the stiletto out of the cooling corpse. He cleaned the blade briefly against the body's tattered clothing and then, holding the piece of paper against the body's solar plexus he thrust the blade downward through the small green shamrock, effectively pinning the paper in place.

"That ought to hold it," said the man, rising with a satisfied smirk.

"An excellent decision in the field," the other policeman agreed, slapping him congenially on the back. "Very neat."

Together they strolled back down the alley to the street.

"Lunch?"

"God, yes! I'm starved."

6

Michael Shane turned off the television. With a satisfied grunt, he slumped back in the grimy, over-stuffed chair which was his alone. The news contained nothing but update after update on the bombing, the IRA, the Roman Church and Arab terrorists . . . and the ensuing investigation. He pulled a crumpled cigarette from his pocket and lit up, sucking hard at the pungent tobacco. Stretching his short but solid physique out in the chair, he noted the indelible dirt lining the calluses on his hands and the new hole trying to open in his best work boots.

He exhaled long, filling the cramped and cluttered room with smoke, and kicked his boots off with disdain. He heard the dishes rattle in the kitchen and remembered to look about for an ashtray lest he be caught flicking ashes on the floor.

"Hey, Maddie!" he hollered at the noise. "We could use a pint in here, how about."

The rattle stopped abruptly and he heard the cabinets open and close and the sound of house slippers shuffling across the floor. His wife was a slender, small boned woman until you got to her hips which ballooned out rather meatily. She brought him a bottle, feigning her most severe and disapproving look. He flashed a gap-toothed grin at her, which was one of his best attributes, and reached out to squeeze a handful of buttock and hip.

"Give us a kiss, how about," he said sitting forward in the chair and trying to pull her to him.

"Get off and kiss yourself, Michael Shane," she said, laughing and slapping his hand playfully. She rubbed the subtle bulge of her pregnant belly. "You've already done enough damage."

Shane took the bottle of bitters from her and flopped back in the chair, laughing and trying to grab at her for another pinch.

"And don't be getting ashes on my floor." She turned and shuffled back to the kitchen, swinging her hips exaggeratedly, much to his enjoyment.

He took a long drink, remembering back a few years before when he had been nothing—just another invisible, ugly factory worker that women wouldn't even look at except for a price. Let the others join the underground for a free Ireland because of ideals. He threw his lot in with the new IRA for one reason and one reason only. A woman's pants always got wet at the prospect of sleeping with a man others considered dangerous.

Shane had risen quickly in the organization. A bombing here, a murder there, all added to the success both of his reputation and his sex life. His job at the factory provided the meagerest standard of living, but the prestige of being the commander of his district's cell of the IRA was a first class ticket to being somebody. More importantly, he fully expected his economic position to improve with the political changes others in his organization planned. The one important reality of revolution, of which he was certain, was that those on the bottom always got to trade places with those at the top. He planned to exploit his position in the New Ireland to the fullest.

Since he had married, his new family had come to mean everything to him. Before, he had never even let himself dream that a wife and two, soon to be three, children could possibly be a part of his fate. He thought of the little girl, almost four and the boy, barely a year old, sleeping soundly in the other room. The empty bottle slid from his hand and rolled across the floor as he drifted off to a contented sleep in his chair.

Maddie put the last of the dishes away and wiped her hands on the towel hanging over the sink. With a practiced eye she scanned the top of her spotless counter and small table for any sign of disarray. Satisfied she pulled open the icebox and rummaged about for the little jar of strawberry jam she had hidden in the back. It wasn't a big craving but every now and then a spoonful of the thick, tart jam seemed to relax her and satisfy the urge to eat everything else she could get her hands on.

She stuck a spoon in the jar and carefully skimmed a generous mouthful off the top. She almost choked when a light tapping on the back door interrupted her.

"Dammit, Alice! What now?" she said under her breath, quickly screwing the lid back on and pushing the jar to the rear of the icebox.

The rapping came again, more insistent.

"I'm coming, I'm coming!" She shuffled across the floor to the door trying to wipe the sticky residue from her fingers and lick any telltale signs from his lips. Grabbing the door knob, and at the same time throwing back the bolt lock, she pulled the door open quickly, expecting to find her neighbor and friend with another black eye, fleeing her drunken husband, again.

"What the bloody hell did he do this—"

A double edged combat knife ripped into her swollen belly almost lifting her off the floor. The stretched skin popped audibly as the carbon steel blade sliced upward to her ribs. One of her hands grabbed for the door jamb while the other flailed instinctively in front of her. She caught her breath one last time. Her eyes bulged wide but sightless, and the color drained from her.

Like a puppet whose strings had just been cut, she collapsed to the floor. Her hands, guided by survival, tried to hold her eviscerated body intact. Through her fingers, a small fetus, carried by the wash of fluids from her abdomen, made its untimely entrance into the world onto the cold kitchen tile where its delicate heart fluttered momentarily, then stopped.

The man, dressed in black camouflage, stepped into the little kitchen out of the night. He inspected Maddie for any sign of life before stooping to leave a small note, decorated with a lacy green shamrock, resting on her cheek. He signaled to two others waiting in the dark. They moved toward the sound of snoring in the other room, silent, except for the inconspicuous squish of rubber soles on a wet floor.

A loose floorboard groaned loudly, waking Shane with a start. His eyes focused on the three assailants a second too late and he felt his head snap back by the hair as one of the men rounded him.

"Maddie!" he managed to scream before a black-gloved hand clamped down over his mouth. He was aware of the flash of sharpened steel out of the corner of his eyes.

"Daddy?" A small girl with dirty blonde hair appeared at the bedroom door. The front of her night-shirt was clenched in her hands to her mouth in fear.

Shane watched helplessly as one of the men spun around to the little girl pointing a long black silencer at her. The gun hissed angrily firing its hollowed bullet into the side of her head. Her delicate face seemed to expand and contract in the same instant before slamming hard into the side of the door. The cry of a baby waking from its sleep rang out like an alarm through the small apartment. The other man pulled a knife from his boot and jumped over the little girl into the bedroom.

Shane jerked at the sharp sting across his throat and felt the rush of warm liquid on his chest. A wave of dizziness overcame him and his legs gave way. Before he hit the floor he realized the baby had stopped crying.

7

"What do you mean murdered?" Inspector Harlowe sputtered. "Almost in front of your eyes?"

"But they were Bobbies, Chief Inspector," pleaded the younger detective. "There was nothing out of the ordinary. Just another vagrant loitering where he shouldn't have."

"A vagrant!" The Inspector collapsed into his car seat. "Indeed!"

The younger man stood silently at attention in front of the window, fidgeting nervously.

"Well, let's have a look," said the Inspector, pulling himself wearily up out of the car.

He followed the young detective down the sidewalk toward the alleyway. The passage was roped off with police warnings and two Bobbies stood guard to shuffle the curious on their way. The forensic people were already on the scene photographing and tinkering with the body on their knees.

"What have you got, Sergeant?" growled the Inspector to a heavy set man standing over the scene and writing furiously in a small notebook. "More than Brewer here I hope."

"Chief Inspector!" The Sergeant ruffled quickly through his notes. "Not much to go on, sir." He flashed a nervous look at his younger partner. "It was a professional kill."

Inspector Harlowe studied the body for a moment. "Can we pull the knife yet?" he inquired of one of the forensic technicians.

"No problem, Inspector," said the cheery technician, reaching for the stiletto with a gloved hand. He carefully slid the thin blade from its perch in the corpse's abdomen and held it up to the Inspector.

Harlowe grimaced despite himself but reached to pluck off the small square of parchment impaled on the blade. He nodded to himself, noting the slips perfect match to eleven other such notes he had collected from eleven other bodies since the night before. There was no message, per se. Only the familiar stamp of a green shamrock. He quickly stored the paper in a small plastic envelope he produced from inside his overcoat.

He turned to his two subordinates who stood silently to the side. "All right. Let's have a rundown. I want to know what happened."

"Well, sir, we were . . ." Brewer began before being silenced with a look from the Sergeant.

"We were tailing O'Dell as ordered, sir," said the Sergeant quickly. "Your contact was right. We picked him up without any trouble. He didn't seem to be in any hurry and he walked the rest of the way from Victoria Station to this area. We observed him going into a dress shop down the square where some minutes later he had to be escorted out by two officers."

"What dress shop?" queried the Inspector.

"One down in the square, sir," answered the Sergeant thumbing through his notes. "Number 224. The two policemen brought him out and walked him down the street and into this alley."

"Nothing unusual, Inspector," chimed in Brewer. "It's not uncommon for vagrants to have a little lesson in manners, before being sent on their way."

"And where were the two of you while our man was being taught a lesson," asked the Inspector levelly.

"Well, sir —"

"Shut up, Brewer," the Sergeant snapped. He turned to the Inspector apologetically. "We waited across the way out of sight, Inspector. They were policemen. There was no reason to suspect anything like this."

Inspector Harlowe looked down at the body again. "Yes, well . . ." He fingered the small plastic bag in his coat pocket. "We had thought O'Dell was behind this rash of IRA murders that's been causing my desk files to groan." He looked up at the overcast sky in disgust.

"Obviously, we'll have to look somewhere else," he said to no one in particular.

"Got what he deserved, if you ask me," said Brewer, nodding to the dead man.

"No one did," growled the Sergeant.

Inspector Harlowe buttoned his coat against the stiff breeze cutting through the alleyway. He left his two subordinates to their argument and the technicians to their work and strolled back to the alley's entrance into the square. Experienced eyes scanned every inch of the passage. Criminal investigation required a great deal of patience and Harlowe was a very patient man. Still, even his was growing thin.

He scanned the shops around the square settling his gaze on the little dress shop at the end of the street which the alley intersected. Eleven murders in almost as many hours. Inspector Harlowe stood tapping his foot impatiently on the concrete. Nothing made any sense. Eleven known IRA sympathizers, murderers, cell leaders, innocent family members, all murdered apparently by the IRA.

He headed down the sidewalk toward the dress shop. Why was the IRA suddenly engaging in a purge of its most ardent supporters? They certainly were not the type to betray their cause, especially O'Dell. His list of mayhem and terrorist acts was too long and too committed. Perhaps these murders were a result of some violent, internal power struggle in the IRA.

Harlowe stopped in front of the shop's display window and eyed the swaths of expensive silks draped over mannequins in varying poses. Why would O'Dell have gone in here, he wondered? Did he know he was being followed or did he have some sort of business to transact inside? Harlowe pushed open the door to enter, ringing the small bell fastened at the top.

"May I be of assistance?"

Inspector Harlowe turned to the smartly dressed young man approaching him. He smiled broadly with the dawning of recognition. "How do you do ... Aidan Ennis, isn't it?"

Aidan studied him for a moment, unsure. "I'm sorry but ..." Aidan shrugged and shook his head. "You'll have to help me out. I can't seem to place you."

"No reason you should, Aidan." Harlowe smiled reassuringly. "I'm Chief Inspector Macklin Harlowe, Scotland Yard Special Branch."

"Chief Inspector?" Aidan's smile never wavered.

"Yes, I was at a party a couple of months ago at Downing Street. You came with Dennis Perkins. I remember asking who that well-dressed and well-bred young man was, hooked up with the likes of Perkins."

"Inspector," said Aidan, taking his arm and guiding him toward the counter. "You should have introduced yourself."

"Ah, I only wish I could have, but my wife was there and she's always had her heart set on hooking Perkins up with ... a different sort, it you catch my drift?"

Aidan laughed and poured two cups of tea, offering one to the Inspector. "Everyone who comes in is allowed one cup of tea, Inspector. Tell me you aren't disappointed in Dennis' choice and you might earn yourself a refill."

"Now, you're not trying to get me in trouble are you?" the Inspector asked lightly, accepting his cup.

Aidan allowed his hand to brush against the Inspector's in the exchange. "Now tell me. What has pulled you away from crime today and into my dress shop?"

"Oh, just in the neighborhood."

"You'd be surprised the number of married, straight men who come in here and say that same thing . . . before finding something in their size."

Harlowe laughed heartily. "I can't imagine you carry anything to fit an old horse like me."

"I'm a dressmaker, Inspector." Aidan eyed the Inspector up and down, gauging his size. "I'm sure I can fit something."

"Then you are talented." Harlowe sipped his tea. "No, I really was nearby on business."

"Now really, Inspector." Aidan teased. "You do want your refill don't you?"

Inspector Harlowe chuckled softly, stepping over to the rack of woolens. He ran a hand over an expensive bolt of silk. "A little murder down the street," he confessed cheerily. "Nothing too earth-shattering."

"Murder!" Aidan set his cup down on the counter carefully. "Where did you say?"

"In the alleyway at the end of the street," Harlowe said. He turned to study his reaction. "Happened short of an hour ago."

"Who was killed?" Aidan felt a wave of dread in his gut.

"No one special," responded the Inspector casually. "Some vagrant who had wandered into the area."

Harlowe noted the lines forming at the edge of Aidan's eyes. "I understand he had been in your shop earlier."

"In here?" Aidan gripped the edge of the counter unconsciously.

"Yes. Shortly before he was killed as a matter of fact."

"There was a man in here today," Aidan replied. He quickly regained his composure. "A rather pitiful man . . . unwashed . . . drunk . . . asking for work. I . . . had the police escort him out."

"I see."

Aidan moved behind the counter to freshen his tea.

"Can you describe the two policemen who came for him?" the Inspector asked.

"Well . . . I . . ." Aidan thought a moment. "They were young, very polite. They showed the man out without trouble."

"Nothing unusual about them?"

"Well, I don't recall anything. No . . . I can't say that there was. Certainly you don't think they are responsible . . . do you?"

"No, no, of course not," assured the Inspector. "Just questions I'm required to ask."

"It's hard to believe that we have a murderer lurking about our district," Aidan said, managing a shudder.

"Don't even let it concern you, Mr. Ennis."

"Please, call me Aidan."

"Aidan, then," said the Inspector with a smile. "How's Perkins been faring since his new appointment?"

"We don't get to see as much of each other. He seems to be even busier now."

"What a pity," the Inspector sympathized. "And knowing Perkins, when the two of you do get together he probably does nothing but talk about the office and affairs of state."

Aidan looked up at him with the barest tease of a smile. "Dennis never brings the office home with him, Inspector. We have much more important things to do with each other in our spare time."

"Indeed." Harlowe sat his cup down with a laugh. "I have a new respect for Perkins."

As the Inspector turned to leave, Aidan relaxed the grip he had on the fixed barrel, Ruger Mark I pistol he kept under the register.

"Take care Mr. Ennis . . . Aidan, and don't let Perkins work too hard."

"Thank you, Inspector. I do hope you'll keep some policemen patrolling nearby. This has totally unnerved me."

"Not to worry," said the Inspector, pulling open the door. "The area will be watched closely." He turned back to flash Aidan another smile before heading out onto the sidewalk.

He paused for a moment, jingling the change in his pants pocket. A very unusual young man, he thought. He would have to find out more about Aidan Ennis. One thing he was certain of, the boy was lying through his teeth.

8

"Well, Perkins, don't feel too guilty about your suspicions. There's certainly room to wonder here."

Dennis drummed his fingers on the phone, waiting for Harlowe to continue. "How so, Inspector? I mean, besides the fact that Von Schiffer was not exactly quick to respond." Dennis turned his chair toward the desk looking for something to take notes on.

"We've managed to turn up a few interesting tidbits on our assassin," continued Harlowe.

"Probably some poor malcontent, psycho—"

"Not possible, Perkins," said Harlowe. "Not this time, anyway. No, this man was a professional. The weapon was custom made from everything to the length of his fingers and the curve of his shoulder."

"Anything more?" Dennis doodled nervously on his pad.

"A few details that parallel your own suspicions, Perkins, nothing concrete . . . as yet."

"Don't be vague, Inspector."

"I just finished watching a video composite of the television coverage in the Abbey. Quite frankly, Perkins, I think our Major is manipulating the King and events around him for reasons I can't even begin to fathom. In any event I believe the King is in grave danger."

"This King is no fool, Inspector. If such a thing were true, surely he would suspect."

"Of course he's not a fool, Perkins, but he does appear to trust the Major implicitly. Such trust has been known to blind even the most discerning."

"What happens now?"

"That depends on you, Perkins."

"What do you mean?"

"The Prime Minister."

"Really, Inspector, we've been over that already."

"We need evidence, Perkins. Irrefutable evidence."

Dennis' head was pounding. He took the phone away for a moment and rubbed his eyes. "I've got to go now, Inspector. I'll get back with you later."

"Please do, Perkins." The Inspector did not sound pleased. "The next attempt on the King's life might be planned with a different outcome."

Dennis hung up the phone. He leaned back in his chair trying desperately to sort out the facts from his suspicions. He walked over to the window and looked out over the Mall. The crowds, for the most part, had dispersed long ago. Occasional pockets of the curious still stuck it out along the Palace gates, watching the second floor windows, patiently waiting for some fleeting glimpse of the new King. It was growing colder outside with the sunset and a light drizzle had begun to fall.

Dennis looked at his watch. He should have been home an hour ago. He wondered if Aidan had gotten in yet. Just thinking about his partner was enough to divert his blood flow to more sensitive extremities. He smiled at the intensity of his desire for Aidan and closed his eyes, recalling the last time they had made love.

A door somewhere close by slammed shut and the heavy fall of feet echoed out in the hallway. Dennis jumped up from his chair and hurried to the door. Trying not to be heard, he slowly turned the knob and pulled the door ajar.

Major Von Schiffer was heading for his rooms in the other wing. He stopped abruptly in the middle of the hall, standing perfectly still with his head up, like an animal trying to catch the scent.

Dennis swallowed hard, suddenly aware of how loud his breathing was. To his relief, Von Schiffer did not turn around but, instead, continued on his way, his long strides swallowing the distance. Dennis slipped out the door quickly and followed him. This was a switch, he thought. The mouse stalking the cat.

The Major entered his apartment without ever turning around. Dennis slumped against the wall, relieved. In no way was he looking forward to any more confrontations. He looked up and down the hall, listening carefully, trying to figure out what he was doing there in the first place. Without thinking he headed for the back stairs and crept down them to the basement. He felt like two people in the same body—the one with the sense being dragged along by the fool.

The Palace basement was actually a series of concrete-reinforced bunkers from the days of World War II, which now served as security bunkers against the possibility of terrorist bombings, assault and even as a fallout shelter. It possessed a War Room, communications room, infirmary with a fully equipped operating room, sleeping quarters, and a well-stocked emergency food and water supply.

Dennis entered the maze of hallways through one of the heavy steel, bomb-proof doors which could all be closed automatically from the inside. Naked light bulbs lit the stark white passageway. Dennis crept along carefully listening for the possible approach of one of the guards who would be enforcing the King's orders of no admittance. Since the infirmary would be the only area of the basement under heavy guard, there was really no need for Dennis to check behind any of the unlocked doors that he came across.

It was his compulsive curiosity, though, that was his reason for having come down at all, and Dennis rationalized his actions by the fact that his exploring might come in handy on down the road should he need a place to hide from the guards. He zigzagged down the hall, quickly opening one door after another, inspecting the contents. In general the rooms were mostly filled with old furniture being stored out of the way. One room was full of army-issue cots for sleeping.

Dennis' interest in the inventory consumed him for a moment to the point where he almost walked out into the hallway intersection without first checking. The sound of a radio playing not too far off made him jerk back out of sight. He leaned back against the wall panting at the shock of almost being discovered. He pulled himself up forcing his breathing to slow down and whispered a few curses at himself.

He peeked around the corner in the direction of the music. Ahead were the glass, swinging doors into the infirmary. One of the Major's ubiquitous security men was sprawled out uncomfortably in a straight-backed wooden chair next to an equally Spartan wooden table. He was cleaning his fingernails with a pocket knife and wagging one foot to the beat of the latest noise blaring from a small radio on the table.

Opting for the direct assault, Dennis clipped his security pass to his pocket and stepped out into the hall with as much authority as he could muster. His leather soles slapped against the tile floor ominously, snapping the security agent out of his chair and to attention.

"You, there! Get this door open immediately!" Dennis prayed the man could not sense fear.

"One moment, sir." The man eyed Dennis security pass.

"I'm the King's Private Secretary. He is in a great deal of pain," Dennis declared. "I have to get some medication quickly. Please open up!" Dennis stared hard at the man and tried not to sweat.

"Sir, I have no authorization for you," the man insisted. "I have strict orders directly from the King—"

"I am directly from the King, you idiot!" Dennis said, leaning into the man's face. "I don't need any other authorization."

The man stared at Dennis security pass, thinking it over. "Sir, I will have to check this out with the Major." He reached to the other side of his chair for the phone hanging on the wall.

Dennis had not seen the phone. "Major Von Schiffer is tending to the King right now," Dennis snapped. "I told you. Open this door before you make matters worse."

"Sir, I have to check..."

"Are you listening to me, man?"

"Sir, I have to check this with the Major." The man was like a robot.

"Goddamn it!" Dennis grabbed the phone from him and began to dial. "I'll get the Major for you, all right, you imbecile! I'll have your ass kicked from here to the Falklands for this delay." He watched the man from the corner of his eye and could sense a slight break in the agent's resolve. A gravely male voice answered the phone.

"Yes, this is Perkins. Let me speak to the Major immediately . . . I know he is with the King . . . I know that. I can't get in. One of his bloody security men won't let me through."

The guard was getting very nervous now.

"I can't help that," Dennis hollered into the phone. "The bastard won't budge until he speaks to Schiffer personally."

The guard began to fumble with his keys. "All right, sir," he stuttered. "Tell them to forget about it. I'll let you in."

"Tell Schiffer not to bother," Dennis tried not to smile into the phone. "I'm getting through now."

Dennis hung up the phone quickly before the security man could hear the voice on the other end hollering. Dennis smirked, looking at the phone. He needed a new bookie anyway.

"Sir, you understand I have a job to do here," the guard said, swinging the door open.

"I can see how busy you are," snapped Dennis, eyeing the radio in disapproval. "Don't let me keep you." He left the man muttering about proper channels and security and spun through the door.

The layout of the infirmary was very much like a doctor's office. Beyond the office area were several small examination and treatment rooms. Dennis looked about puzzled. After the hallway there were no other lights on. There were no nurses or doctors bustling about. He could hear no machinery going, no voices. He looked back at the guard out in the hall, who had sat back down to his radio. Where was the security one would expect about a head of state? Where was the medical support team necessary to maintain the life of an injured Prime Minister? The whole area appeared strangely deserted.

Dennis moved methodically from one exam room to another looking for any sign of recent occupancy. He began to wonder if perhaps the Prime Minister had been secretly transferred to an outside hospital or military facility, but this off chance optimism was hard to hold onto.

With increasing dread, Dennis pushed open a door into a small operating theater and felt along the wall for the light switch. His hand brushed over the switch, tripping the overhead incandescent lighting into a blazing glare of reflections off the polished metal and porcelain surfaces.

The room was small and most of its plumbing and counter fixtures were pre-world war. There were, however, several of the latest heart and respiration monitors, and a portable X-ray machine. He searched the room for anything that might suggest someone had been recently treated, but the entire area was spotlessly sterile. He checked the trash can by the door and found it empty.

Dennis stood silently with his hands on his hips, shaking his head in disbelief. What the bloody hell was going on anyway? The King had made no mention whatsoever about any kind of transfer. He continued to enforce the ban on visits with the Prime Minister as well as ventures into the cellar, period. He began to wonder if perhaps there might be two infirmaries in the basement.

The sound of a small compressor kicking on drew his attention to a medium-sized chest freezer sitting out of the way along the wall in the corner to his right. Dennis squinted to read the small red tag pasted on the front, "Blood and Plasma Products." A small clipboard sat on top, containing a running inventory of the freezer's contents.

Dennis picked up the clipboard and scanned over its entries. It occurred to him that if anything had been used from the freezer then it would be entered, or the list of the freezer's contents would not match the inventory. He could find no dated entries at all but each item on the list was, at least, counted. Dennis lifted the freezer lid open to check the actual items against the inventory. The haze of carbon dioxide was thick and Dennis waved his hand over the surface to clear his view into the chest.

He dropped the lid suddenly, stepping back, a chill of another sort crawling up his spine. He had seen this type of zippered plastic bag before. He closed his eyes recalling the many bodies he had seen being carried out in such bags following the bombing of Parliament. Dennis' hand clenched against the memory. The Prime Minister had been alive when he found him. Alive, he kept telling himself.

Hesitating, he reached to lift up the freezer lid again. The moisture in the air began to collect in a myriad of ice crystals over the shiny black surface of the bag, misting it like a snowfall. Dennis touched the bag lightly. There was something in it, all right. Something hard. The plastic zipper slid easily along its tracks. Dennis grasped the two sides and pulled the folds apart slowly.

The body was pale and rigid, every wrinkle and hair frozen into place. Dennis stared numbly at the familiar, aged face of the Prime Minister. He watched, mesmerized, as ice crystals from his own breath began to coat the body's eye lashes and brows.

Dennis felt the knot in his stomach trying to strangle his breath. He quickly zipped up the bag and dropped the freezer lid. A wave of panic took control of him suddenly from the inside and his lungs and heart began to pump out of control. Feeling the dizziness of hyperventilation, he broke and ran from the room, swatting at the light switch with his hand, plunging the room back into darkness.

Dennis stumbled out the door and went to his knees against the wall, catching himself with his hands. He stayed on all fours struggling to bring his breathing under control by holding his breath and forcing his mind to count slowly to ten. Free of the room, the episode passed quickly and he was able to stand again. He looked down at his hands, rubbing his fingers together. A trace of moisture remained where he had touched the frozen corpse.

On impulse, he fumbled along the wall to the small bathroom in the office, rolled up his sleeves and thoroughly washed his hands and forearms in the brown, liquid soap. After splashing a little water on his face he dried himself off, not daring to look at the mirror in front of him.

"Everything all right, sir?"

Dennis jumped, startled, and spun around. The security guard from outside was standing at the door, his gun drawn.

"Are you all right, sir?" The alarmed guard repeated cautiously.

"Yes . . . yes," Dennis stammered. "Everything is fine." He pointed to the gun. "Put that thing away."

"I got worried, Mr. Perkins. You took so long and then I saw you running out of the back."

"I was just in a hurry. It took me longer than I'd expected to find the right medication."

The guard holstered his weapon, disappointed.

"I slipped on the floor in the back and just wanted to wash my hands," Dennis added quickly.

"Well, sir, you sure seemed in a bloody hurry to get in here."

"And I'm in as much of a hurry to get out. If you'll excuse me now." Dennis brushed past the man and headed back out into the hall.

He wanted to run for the stairs but the guard stood at the door watching him suspiciously. Bridling himself, Dennis walked briskly down the hall and around the corner. Once out of sight, he broke for the stairs and bounded up them two at a time.

9

Reaching the top of the stairs, Dennis paused and leaned against the banister to catch his breath. He opened the door into the hall just a crack to peek out. The passageway was dark and no one was in sight. The day's office hours had long ago come to an end and the normally bustling office area was deserted. He crossed the well-worn carpet to his office and slipped in quietly, shutting the door behind him. Flipping on the desk lamp, he slumped into his chair, exhausted, cradling his head in his hands.

"Bloody hell," he whispered to himself.

Dennis sat up straight and took a deep breath to clear his head. He looked at the phone, still unsure. Someone had to be told. The situation was getting too extreme to let it continue. For a moment he thought about confronting the King with all the facts. King Richard should be consulted first.

Dennis slammed his fist down on the desk blotter. It was almost impossible to find the King alone without Von Schiffer nearby. Now he wasn't even sure it was wise to put his cards before the King. More and more, King Richard was looking like an opportunist who had used a grave national tragedy for his own benefit.

Dennis cursed himself for that thought. The King had really gained nothing from events except a shortened life span from the extra work and stress that were now his burden. The King lived and breathed the good of the nation. No, Bates had died, and the King only wanted to spare the nation another immeasurable loss. But now Dennis knew the truth, and it would be illegal, unethical, immoral, and career destroying to cover that truth up. Dennis nodded to himself. The next step seemed perfectly clear. Call Harlowe. Without further hesitation he picked up the phone and dialed the Yard.

The voice on the other end crackled behind a loud hum that slowly receded.

"Yes, I can barely hear you," Dennis answered, annoyed. "I want to speak with Chief Inspector Macklin Harlowe, please. It's urgent. This is Dennis Perkins, His Majesty's Private Secretary." He waited while the phone crackled again.

"I'm sorry," said the sterile voice into Dennis' ear. "The Inspector is unavailable at the moment. May I take your message?"

Dennis wanted to scream. "But I just spoke to him barely an hour ago."

"Sorry, sir."

Dennis could feel his headache returning. "Have him return my call, at home or my office. I don't care what time. He has the numbers."

The Yard operator hung up without answering him and the annoying hum returned in the receiver. Dennis hung up, wondering where the Inspector could be at this hour. He closed his eyes for a moment and massaged them slowly, trying to decide what to do next. He considered the safest place to wait for the Inspector would be in his office at Scotland Yard, but realized that his own presence there might raise too many questions in the minds of too many people once the inevitable word got out. He looked up from his desk. Major Von Schiffer was standing silently, directly in front of him.

Dennis caught his breath and jumped up from the chair. "Major!" He clenched his fists for calm. "How long have you been standing there?"

"I'm sorry, Dennis. Did I startle you?" The Major's smile made the small hairs on the back of Dennis' neck prickle up. He sat back down, straightening some papers on his desk.

"You should really knock before coming into someone's office at this hour, Von Schiffer," Dennis said heatedly. "Of course you startled me."

"I noticed the light under the door. I thought certainly you had gone home by now, Dennis." The

Major picked up a small letter opener and toyed with it absentmindedly. "I was concerned someone was about who had no business being here."

"No harm done," said Dennis, looking for a way out of the situation. "I was just getting ready to leave."

"A few last minute details?"

"You might say that."

"I couldn't help overhearing that you were looking for Inspector Harlowe."

"Nothing important," said Dennis, hedging. "Just trying to get an update on the investigation for His Majesty."

"Really." The Major leaned over the desk familiarly. "It sounded more . . . urgent than that."

Dennis met the Major's eyes for a moment and did not like what he saw. "I have to be going, Major," he said, grabbing up his brief case from the floor. "If you'll excuse me."

Von Schiffer stepped around in front of him, blocking his exit. A smile was frozen on his face, his voice low and menacing. "What were you doing in the basement earlier, Dennis?"

Dennis' heart hit the floor. His solar plexus tingled with the sudden rush of adrenalin. "Major, I'm expected at an important meeting. I don't have time to chat." He tried to get by, but the Major continued to block his way.

"The basement, Dennis."

"You're in my way again, Major," Dennis said. His fear was overtaken by anger. "What I do or where I go is none of your bloody damn business. Now step aside."

"Let's not argue, Dennis . . . I hope it's okay if I call you Dennis? You were in the infirmary against the expressed orders of His Majesty. Now why were you there?"

Dennis thought quickly. "For your information, Major, the Prime Minister is no longer in the infirmary. He has apparently been transferred elsewhere. I doubt seriously that the King's ban on visits to the cellar is applicable any longer."

Schiffer moved so close their faces almost touched.

Dennis was beginning to feel more than uncomfortable. He tried to step back but found himself wedged between the desk and the Major. "And goddamn it, Major, it's none of your goddamn business anyway!"

Von Schiffer straightened, towering over the smaller man. He pressed his groin against Dennis' belly bending him back over the desk. The briefcase dropped from Dennis' hand.

The Major laughed low in his throat. "Do I make you nervous, Dennis?"

"Get off of me, goddamn you, Schiffer!" Dennis struggled under the Major's weight. "Get off!" He drove a fist into the Major's side with little effect.

Von Schiffer pinned Dennis' hands to the desk. The light from the desk lamp gleamed off his teeth. "I was wondering just this morning, Dennis," he said, ignoring

Dennis' struggle, "about a conversation we had earlier . . . if you really are circumcised."

Dennis could feel the heat of his breath. He was so close. Its acrid smell was nauseating. Try as he might, he couldn't move except to twist his head from side to side. He could feel the Major moving against him in a perverse parody of copulation and was overwhelmed with anger and some new kind of fear . . . the fear of rape.

"Stop it, goddamn it!" Dennis tried to bring his knee up, but the Major had skillfully planted his own knees between Dennis' legs.

"Not until you prove it to me, Dennis. I told you, you would have to prove it to me."

"What are you talking about?" cried Dennis, jerking his head to the side in an effort to dodge the Major's advances.

"Whether or not you're circumcised, Dennis," the Major said, laughing. "Remember?"

"Get off!" Dennis groaned, making one last effort to throw the Major off balance.

Von Schiffer merely shifted his weight, keeping Dennis pinned to the desk. "A barbaric practice, don't you think? I understand it lessens sexual sensation."

Without warning, the Major released his grip on Dennis' arms. He grabbed Dennis' head in his vise-like grip and before Dennis could react the Major pulled Dennis' mouth into his own. Dennis struggled wildly, clamping his teeth and lips against Von Schiffer's wet, probing tongue.

Dennis arched his back, violently thrusting his buttocks against the front edge of the desk with all his strength. Bucking against the carpet the desk jerked away about a foot, spilling its cover of office paraphernalia onto the floor. Dennis moved backwards with the desk. In the same motion he brought his knee up hard into the intervening space and felt the satisfying thud as his knee slammed into the Major's groin. The Major slumped back with a grunt of expelled air, releasing his steely grip on Dennis.

Dennis slid to the floor, spitting and wiping his mouth. "Fucking bastard!" Dennis screamed, panting with fury. "Bloody goddamn bastard!"

Von Schiffer leaned back against the window sill massaging his throbbing middle. He managed a smile through clenched teeth. "I've often wondered, Dennis. Does that red hair go all the way down?" His eyes traced a line to Dennis' crotch.

Dennis pulled himself up by the desk and dove for the door, throwing it open violently. Von Schiffer made no effort to stop him.

"When I get through with you . . ." Dennis was too angry to finish. He knew he didn't stand a chance physically against the giant, and his only thought was to get away. Dennis slammed his fist against the door and stormed out of the room. "Fuck you, bloody bastard!" he spat, making all haste down the hallway.

He could hear the Major's taunting laughter echoing off the plastered walls. "No, Dennis, boy. Fuck *you!*"

10

Londoners have a definite talent for hard-core revelry against all odds. Despite the ink-black sky, overcast and pouring icy rain, the hardier populace continued to clamor through traffic in the narrow streets on pilgrimages to their respective shrines of thanksgiving. On most nights that would have meant one of several hundred pubs bottle-necked at every street corner in the city.

But on this night, worry furrowed the brows of those bartenders whose pride rested in their high volume trade. Rumor had it that the lines passing through St. Peter's and the various parish churches for communion wine were making a sizeable dent in pub receipts. These were, however, fears without foundation. It was doubtful the pubs could have handled any more than they were. For every communicant at St. Peter's sipping the blood of

Christ in honor of their latest national miracle there was a glass of ale being hoisted to the King's good health at the Dickens Inn.

Dennis had a different reason for decanting a bottle. His hand was shaking so much it took all his concentration to get the gin into the glass without sloshing it over the counter, while balancing the phone against his ear with his shoulder. He tipped the glass up to his lips and emptied it into his mouth quickly, dribbling a little down his chin onto the carpet. He slammed the glass to the counter and braced himself for the rebuke his body would offer the liquid fire he was forcing into it.

Aidan watched him quietly from the sofa. He could not fathom whether Dennis was afraid, angry, or nervous. Unsure how best to respond, he waited, passively, for more clues as to his lover's present mood. Besides, confident in his own talents at diversion, he felt sure he could placate his partner no matter what the problem.

The line was still busy. Dennis banged the phone down. Before the spasms in his throat subsided he poured himself another shot. He could still feel the Major's grip on him and could not shake the thought of what might have happened had he not gotten away. Where in God's name was Inspector Harlowe?

"Is this a private party or am I allowed to join?" Aidan asked. He stretched back on the sofa, allowing full view of his nakedness. Dennis tried to concentrate on the phone and ignore the younger man, without success. "What do you want to drink?" he muttered, trying to express disinterest while also trying not to notice the shifting exposure of skin as Aidan rolled onto his side.

"I'm a sympathetic person," Aidan purred, smiling up at the ceiling. "How about what you're having?"

Dennis covered the bottom of a tumbler with gin and brought it over to him. Aidan caressed his hand with both of his as he slid the drink out of Dennis' grip. He grabbed the waist band of Dennis' slacks and pulled him down on the sofa. Dennis sat stiffly, pouting into his gin, refusing to look at Aidan. Aidan cuddled next to him, laying his head on Dennis' shoulder and sipping his drink. He pressed close to Dennis, positioning himself where even the slightest turn of his lover's head would direct his gaze down Aidan's neck towards parts irresistible.

"You're not playing tonight?" Aidan asked, kissing Dennis lightly under the chin.

Dennis stiffened more and tried to down the rest of his drink unsuccessfully. "Bloody Christ! Is that all you think about?" He coughed from the liquor's bite.

Aidan pulled away from him. He eyed Dennis analytically, groping for the right button to push. "Well, it used to be all you thought about. Perhaps you're spending a bit too much time with that pretty little king of yours."

"Goddamn your mouth!" Dennis' hand lashed out at Aidan, stopping short of his cheek.

Aidan's hands went automatically to his face in defense. He stared at Dennis wide-eyed with surprise.

Dennis' temper melted immediately at the realization of what he had almost done. "Jesus, Aidan! I'm sorry."

The glass slipped from his hand onto the carpet as he reached out to him pleadingly.

Aidan recovered quickly enough but backed away for effect anyway.

Dennis held his arms gently. "Come on. I'm sorry, Aidan. I guess I'm a little drunk. I can't even think straight." He pulled the boy to him. "I'm sorry, Aidan."

Aidan slid his hand down Dennis' chest into the man's lap directing his fingers in their expert massage. Aidan was rewarded with an almost instant erection as Dennis' breathing grew more irregular in his ear.

"Oh God, Aidan!"

"So you like to play rough, eh?" Aidan whispered. Before Dennis' could respond, Aidan grabbed his lover's hard-on through his trousers and squeezed mercilessly while at the same time burying his teeth into Dennis' shoulder. Dennis cried out with a gasp. Instinctively his hands dove for his groin. Just as quickly, Aidan released his hold and fell back into the sofa pillows.

Dennis sat defensively, staring at the younger man for a moment, rubbing his sore spot. Aidan smiled up at him seductively stretching his leg out over the back of the sofa. Dennis stared at the boy's unabashed nakedness. In an instant Inspector Harlowe and the Major were gone from his mind. He caressed the inside of Aidan's leg just above the knee with his lips. His hot breath sent a ripple of goose flesh up Aidan's thigh which he followed relentlessly with his tongue. Aidan threw his head back.

He laced his fingers into Dennis' red hair and slowly guided his lover's lips to his own engorged member.

Any trauma to Dennis' masculinity from the previous events of the evening dissipated with every stroke of his tongue. Aidan was fast approaching climax and Dennis had brought him there with the technique of an expert. For the moment, Dennis put his own pleasure on the back burner and put everything he had into putting Aidan over the brink. Aidan cried out, pumping his hips upward, releasing his essence into Dennis' ravenous mouth. Dennis was so hard it hurt. With one hand he quickly released his belt and zipper, clumsily tugging his pants down to his knees.

Aidan raised his head and tried to focus on him through glazed eyes. "Hurry, baby! Give it to me!" He moaned as he adjusted his position on the sofa.

Dennis quickly resumed his attention to Aidan's needs. He loved the boy's sweet smell and he especially loved how noisy he was during sex. Dennis worked his tongue through the beads of perspiration forming on Aidan's belly upwards. He grasped one of Aidan's nipples between his lips and pulled slightly while at the same time plunging his sex deep into the warm chamber beyond Aidan's raised buttocks.

"Fuck me, for Christ's sake!" Aidan almost screamed in his ear, digging his nails into Dennis' butt.

Dennis did so with gusto, thrusting long and hard, pushing against the arm of the sofa with his feet. He couldn't control himself, so great was his need. Dennis collapsed on top of Aidan letting the spasms of pleasure/pain take over. He hadn't come so quickly since he was fourteen, trying to get through before his mother got suspicious and appeared, pounding on the bathroom door. Of course, at the time, his hand could only bring minimal relief. After Aidan, he felt like he had finished an afternoon of rugby with the pros.

The two of them lay pinned together, breathing hard, enjoying the warmth. The annoying cry of the telephone wedged its way into their cocoon.

"Shit!" Dennis pulled his head from the warmth of Aidan's neck. "Inspector Harlowe!"

"Is that who you've been waiting to call?" purred Aidan. "And I was starting to feel jealous."

Dennis withdrew from him, eyeing the sofa below his waning erection. "Christ! A wet spot. We should have used a towel," he said, trying to get his pants up and get to the phone before the caller gave up.

"You weren't thinking *straight*, remember?" Aidan stretched out yawning.

Dennis cast him an unamused look and propped the phone up to his ear with his shoulder freeing his hands to pour himself another drink. "Yes," he almost shouted into the receiver.

"I've got you now, you Irish bastard," fumed the voice on the other end. "I'm going to expose the whole stinking lot of you. I'll crucify the whole goddamn—"

"Who the bloody hell is this!" Dennis shot back, gripping the phone in annoyance.

"Don't play coy with me, Perkins," the voice spat. "Now it's my turn. You and all that kiss-Irish-ass scum you work for are going to pay dearly!"

"Look," Dennis responded with growing impatience. "If you don't identify yourself, I'll hang up right now. Who is this?"

For a moment there was no sound but a labored breathing. An icy chill passed from the phone down Dennis' spine as he waited.

"Who else knows you for what you really are?" the voice said finally. "Goddamn filthy IRA lackey! You and all those—"

"Conroe!" Dennis exploded.

Aidan shot up off the sofa with sudden interest. He slid up onto a bar stool next to Dennis and poured himself a drink. Dennis was too upset to even notice his lover listening intently to every word.

"Did you seriously think you could continue to operate so brazenly without being eventually uncovered." Conroe laughed across the distance. "I've known what you were from the beginning."

"You don't know shit, Conroe," Dennis said with equal venom. "This conversation is over as of now."

"You hang up the phone and I'll make my statements to the press. But then, maybe you'd prefer to read about your downfall in the *Times*."

Dennis hesitated. "You haven't made one bit of sense yet, Conroe. Get to it and quit wasting my time."

"Let me put it to you this way, you Irish poof," said Conroe, obviously enjoying his hold on the moment. "After your weakling of a King makes me the new Prime Minister tomorrow, you and all your cohorts at Downing Street won't stand a chance in hell of ever setting foot there again. Either that, or I'll go to the press and you can all spend the better part of this century in a military prison."

"You're drunk," Dennis said with disgust.

"I admit I've been celebrating ever since my informants pieced it all together. But don't entertain for one moment the idea that I don't know exactly what I'm saying."

"What exactly are you saying, Conroe?"

Dennis began to sit back on the bar stool only to discover himself in Aidan's lap. He shifted quickly to the other stool, pulling the phone over close to him.

"I'm saying that if you know what's good for you, you'll negotiate an arrangement with me right now, tonight," Conroe said. "That is, if you want to save your bloody Irish coward's ass, you will."

"You've got a lot of fucking nerve talking to me about deals, Conroe. I'm not talking shit with you!"

"You'll either talk to me tonight or you can do it with the world press tomorrow. I mean it."

"Why should I talk with you, Conroe? You tell me why?"

"Well, gay boy, let's start off with the fact that Prime Minister Bates is dead. I don't know where you bastards have been hiding the body, but I know now for a fact that he is dead. You and that prissy little king had better be prepared to work a real miracle tomorrow and produce a live prime minister for the press or you'd damn sure better talk to me tonight."

"Shit," Dennis cursed softly to himself covering the receiver with his hand while he thought for a moment. How could that lunatic know? Dennis could only imagine the problems this could cause. "Only a piece of scum like you would even consider blackmailing the King."

"I'm not blackmailing anyone, Irishman. I'm quite ready to discuss an equitable solution to the problem."

"Equitable! You as Prime Minister? You're not just drunk, Conroe, you're insane."

Conroe laughed bitterly. "I would be insane if I allowed this lie you murderers have been perpetrating on the British people to continue for one moment longer. I will be the next Prime Minister, Perkins—one way or another. You must agree that doing it this way will save the King considerable embarrassment, not to mention abdication."

"What kind of a fool are you, Conroe? You don't have any facts and you know it. If there is a problem, Scotland Yard will take care of it. Your meddling can only make matters worse. You don't give a damn about the people. You're just another power hungry fanatic out for himself."

"Your insults are meaningless, Irishman, considering the fact that you're the source of the problem in the first place. I've got all I need on you and all your terrorist cronies to put you away forever."

Dennis hadn't realized how totally mad Conroe was until now. Still his insanity only magnified the danger Conroe posed to the government and Dennis decided the prudent course was to get a look at all his cards, demented though they may be. "Personally, I think you've gone over the edge, Conroe, and I don't think you've got one damn fact on you that any rational person would buy. I think the press is going to laugh you out of Parliament.

"The only one who'll be left laughing is me, Perkins. I'm up to my ass in facts and unless you're willing to risk irreparable damage to the monarchy with the exposure of your little scheme, you'll take a look at what I have."

"Oh, I can't wait to see these so-called facts. That you can be sure of. When and where, Conroe?"

"As I thought." Conroe grunted with satisfaction.

"Stop wasting my time," Dennis fumed. "When and where?"

"Now, Irishman, right now. At my estate in the country. And do hurry, Perkins." He began to laugh again. "I'm anxious to get settled into my new flat on Downing Street."

Dennis' ear smarted from the loud click as the other phone was slammed down. He dropped the receiver onto its cradle and sat for a moment studying his gin. What could he do if indeed Conroe had some sort of tangible evidence of the Prime Minister's death? Hell, he didn't even need that. All he had to do was dispute the King's assertions loudly enough and the press would take over from there.

As he finished dressing, Dennis made the decision to make the meeting. All he could do was see the evidence, agree to anything Conroe said, and then high-tail it back to Inspector Harlowe. The two of them together could confront the King with their suspicions and hope he would make the necessary sweeping changes before Conroe realized he had simply been stalled and went to the press. He felt Aidan's fingers at the base of his neck massaging gently.

"Would you like to share this little dream with me?" Aidan cooed soothingly.

"Nothing to worry about," said Dennis breaking away to find his coat. "I just have to go out for a while."

"At this hour?" Aidan followed him to the closet. "What's going on, Dennis?"

Dennis slipped on his coat and tried to flash the boy his official smile. "It's just another meeting, Aidan. Government is twenty-four hours a day. You know that."

"It's not just another meeting if that meeting is with Gerald Conroe. He hates you and the feeling is mutual. What could you possibly have to meet with him for?"

"Look, Aidan, I don't have time to get into this with you." Dennis tried to reach into the closet to his other jacket, shielding his action from Aidan with the closet door. He felt in the pocket and pulled out the small pistol that Von Schiffer had given him in the helicopter on the way to Balmoral.

"Don't wait up for me." He slipped the small weapon inside his coat and stepped out, grabbing his hat from the wall rack. "I'll be back when I get back."

"That's very nice. What am I supposed to do?"

"Sleep," replied Dennis with another smile, pecking Aidan on the lips before making his escape out the door.

Aidan stood staring after him, thinking, his fingers drumming on the door sill. When Dennis was out of sight, he shut the door, pausing a moment to engage the slide bolts. He opened the closet and pulled out Dennis' tweed jacket, quickly checking the pockets . . . empty.

"Stupid fool!" Aidan threw the jacket back on its hanger and headed for the phone.

11

Dennis flexed his gloved fingers about the wide steering wheel of Aidan's sapphire Jaguar. He wasn't sure if it was the tension of driving for so long, or the cold that was causing his joints to stiffen and ache. Aidan loved to spin about the countryside, ripping around the curving landscape at dangerous speeds. Dennis preferred the use of taxis or chauffeured government transportation. Of course, he wasn't very impressed by the countryside anyway.

He had his fill of the gentry life as a child and had spent his adolescent years working his butt off to escape the drab, uneventful, predictable existence of the farm. The city was his domain now. Constant change, pubs, theater, politics, and the never-ending night life were the luxuries of his existence. He squinted through the rain-

soaked windshield at the dark, cold and dreary land-
scapes about him. His upper lip drew into a sneer. God,
he hated the country. He could never understand the
penchant of London's upper class for escaping the city to
damp and cold country homes.

He yawned at the hypnotic swish of the windshield
wipers and tried to remember exactly how much sleep he
had gotten in the last three days. He wanted to formulate
a plan in his mind for dealing with Conroe, but the bog of
exhaustion that was quickly enveloping his brain was too
much, even for his considerable powers of concentration.
A road sign flashed by for a second in his headlights and
Dennis veered the car in a hard right just missing a ditch
off to the side. For a moment his mind cleared, but after
the initial reaction time had passed, he found himself
back fighting the relentless downward pull of his eyelids.

After an interminable period, Dennis finally slowed the
car before the massive iron gates that fronted the
Elizabethan manor house, now fortress, owned by the
Honorable Gerald Conroe, MP. The location was infamous
with London Society. Conroe, the ambitious second son of
a Westminster green-grocer, had occupied the house as a
gift-in-trust from a wealthy and grateful London merchant.
He was riding the peak of his political career at the time, and
the salon gossips had it that this so-called merchant was
actually an Arab oil sheik and the house was payback for
favors done while Conroe was Minister of Finance.

All the talk proved harmless, however, until Conroe's
second wife was blown up with the Royal Yacht. The

resulting verbal and political assaults against all things Irish, that began to characterize both Conroe's public and private personae, began to wear thin with the public, the press, and personal friends. His obsession became so abstract that his hit list included everyone not engaged full-time in bashing the Irish. His comments about the Queen and finally the Prime Minister resulted in his dismissal from cabinet and his exclusion from the fellowship of Parliament in general.

For a time he became reclusive, hiding out in his manor house in the country. He engaged himself in augmenting the already imposing stone walls of his estate with barbed wire, free roaming Alsatian attack dogs, video sentinels, and a massive, and illegal gun collection. Only in the last few months had he begun to make public appearances again, lured from his self-imposed exile by the increasingly vocal anti-monarchy faction, who saw a covert use for his alarmist abilities.

Dennis sat with the engine running, considering the portents of such a man sitting at the head of government. It would have been unthinkable had it not been for the fact that Conroe just possibly had in his possession facts which, out of context and slanted the right way to the press, could catapult him to just such a position of power. Either that, or he might successfully blackmail the King into naming him the next Prime Minister. Knowing the King as he did, however, Dennis considered the latter out of the question.

He honked his horn several times hoping that some-one would come and open the gates for him without his having to step out into the rain. A blaze of light enveloped the car as a pair of powerful floodlights, mounted about the gate post, came on. Through the glare Dennis watched with fascination as a video camera mounted between the lights scanned his presence, its lens telescoping outward for close-up.

Dennis glared up into the camera's eye and lay on his horn again for effect. A high pitched whine signaled the start up of an electric motor, and the creaking gates began to retract with an almost painful slowness. Dennis was fully awake now, fueled by impatience. He skidded the car on through before the gates had finished their journey.

Tinebury Hall, or Shamrock Hill as it was mockingly referred to by the Right Honorables in London, was a somewhat grotesque creation, lovingly improved upon by successive generations of architects, much to its detriment. The Elizabethan facade of stone, wood, and mortar, masked a lengthening concoction of round towers, battlements and gothic spires in the rear. The current addition of halogen security lights, cameras, and ground sensors was a logical conclusion to the sense of eclectic chaos the manor house had achieved.

Dennis steered around the circular drive and brought the car up under a vaulting, stone porte-cochere extending from the west wing of the house. He climbed out of the small car into the cold and stood tentatively before the leaded glass door, curiously conscious of the bulk in his right pocket. He could hear dogs barking somewhere off in the darkness and prayed they were still securely locked in their pens. Dennis was reminded of his grandmother's Pekingese, Chang, whom he hated and feared from his earliest recollections. Though few could match the little dragon in meanness and ferocity, larger animals were a particular taboo with Dennis just on principle alone.

A middle-aged woman with stocky, peasant features and tightly braided hair heaved open the rain swollen door. She eyed Dennis blankly. Wiping her hands on a soiled, green apron, she stepped to the side of the doorway. Taking this as a cue to come in, Dennis brushed past her into the entry hall and stood waiting for his lead. She waddled down the hall without looking at him or speaking. Dennis followed as a matter of course, somewhat annoyed by her lack of manners.

The rooms beyond were mostly uninteresting and somewhat void of furnishings. What little there was served in a purely functional capacity, lacking any age or charm. The walls were depressingly bare of art and color with the hint of a once brightly floral wall covering, bleeding through the white paint that covered it. Dennis took it all in with a warming sense of satisfaction, attributing the Spartan quality of the place to a probable lack of vital support and funds for Conroe's peculiar cause.

The housekeeper stopped him in front of a double doorway framed on each side with a magnificent pair of elephant tusks, the first sign of genteel affluence Dennis had come across. Wiping her hands again, she rapped respectfully on the door, turned abruptly, and left Dennis alone. He watched her retreat down the hallway and started to call after her when the doors swung inward.

Dennis turned to the doorway and found himself staring down the barrel of an enormous elephant gun into the glazed eyes of Gerald Conroe. The palpable tension and silence turned the seconds into hours. Dennis did not budge. He kept his eyes locked on Conroe's, waiting for his antagonist to make a move. Terror crept up his spine as the possibility he had been set up for the kill by this dangerous paranoid flashed in his mind. Amused laughter erupted from the back of the room. Conroe swung the weapon over his shoulder and threw his head back joining in the laughter drunkenly.

"Good God, Gerry! Is that the way you welcome guests here?"

Dennis recognized the voice instantly. Devon Harper stretched out on the divan under a cathedral-like, diamond leaded glass window. He sneered at Dennis from across the room with a weaselly look of classless superiority that only a true socialist bureaucrat could muster.

Dennis pulled at the reins of his anger. Refusing to acknowledge Harper's presence, he directed the brunt of his undisguised hatred at Conroe. "You're certifiable, Conroe!"

Conroe turned his back on Dennis and walked away still laughing.

"You're the biggest goddamn asshole I've ever met," said Dennis coldly, sorting the mix of fear and anger he had experienced.

"And I'm going to get even bigger, Irishman." Conroe laughed again, slapping the heavy gun down on the ornate, French desk that was the room's focal point.

"I'm beginning to think the government can survive any embarrassment you might be able to cause it," said Dennis, remaining in the doorway. "I really doubt that an insane alcoholic with a penchant for threatening visitors with heavy artillery has a bloody chance in hell of ever being appointed Prime Minister. I don't think we have anything to talk about." He spun on his heels to leave.

"I wouldn't count on that if I were you, Dennis, old boy." Devon Harper sat up on the divan and yawned noisily. "It would be no trouble at all for us to include a goodly number of the current Cabinet in the taint of this little scandal."

Dennis paused, subordinating his anger to the purpose of his mission.

"Most would do anything to protect their meager political careers," Harper said with a mocking leer. "That fact, in conjunction with my own coalition, would almost virtually insure my colleague's chances of being Prime Minister."

Still laughing, Conroe poured himself into the leather chair behind the desk.

Dennis watched the scene with disgust before turning on Harper. "Your coalition might not be so quick to get behind you on this one, Harper. Surely your people have a bit more political savvy than to back an obvious nut case like him." Dennis gestured toward Conroe whose laughter turned to a near growl.

"Quite the contrary, I think," said Harper calmly. "We have found Gerald to be a very useful ally in our long fight for social justice."

"Social justice!" spat Dennis. "You forget who you're speaking to, old boy," he said mockingly. "I'm not one of your union radicals. You could care less about the plight of the worker. Christ, the two of you together wouldn't know a moral principle if it were to blow up in your fucking faces."

Harper stretched back out, picking his teeth, weary of debate.

Conroe stood, leaning across the gilded desk. "Your opinions mean very little here, Irishman." His eyes emptied of emotion and his face took on a wary, more calculating personality. "You and your IRA are responsible for the deaths of hundreds of innocent people, so I don't want to hear you preaching morality to me."

"God, you're totally fucked, Conroe," Dennis said.

"Shut up!" screamed Conroe, grabbing up the rifle again.

Dennis jerked a hand into his coat pocket wrapping his fingers around his own small pistol.

"Gentlemen, gentlemen." Harper was off the sofa like a nervous squirrel, heading across the room towards them. "This arguing is accomplishing nothing." He stopped beside Conroe and gingerly pushed the shotgun barrel down to the desk. "We have serious matters to discuss here. I suggest we get down to it."

Conroe's demeanor changed instantly as if by the push of a button. He laid the gun aside and then sat at his desk like any business man preparing to cut a deal. He pulled an itinerary book from a drawer and placed it open on the desk, slipping on his glasses to consult its pages.

Dennis relaxed enough to let go his grip on the pistol concealed in his pocket.

Conroe looked up at him as if he were addressing one of his parliamentary aides. "You will instruct the King to announce my appointment at a press conference to be called no later than tomorrow afternoon. This will allow me time to—"

"That's enough," Dennis interrupted heatedly. "I don't instruct the King to do anything and neither do you. And what's more, I have no intention of even suggesting anything to him until I've seen this alleged evidence you claim to possess to blackmail him."

"I don't have to show you anything," replied Conroe matter-of-factly.

"Then this meeting is over." Dennis turned again to leave.

"You're taking an awful risk, now, Dennis," Harper called after him. "We do have proof that Bates is dead."

Dennis stopped and turned back to them. "Then there should be no objection to my seeing it."

"To be frank, Dennis, Conroe is quite right. We aren't in a position to have to show you anything. You and your employer are the ones at risk, not us."

"I think it's rather obvious that this whole farce has been nothing but an ill-conceived bluff," Dennis said, displaying his coldest smile. "You have nothing."

"We have all we need," Conroe said, slamming the book closed. "An eyewitness from the Palace medical staff who saw the body."

"Some evidence," Dennis said derisively.

"But you forget the most important fact of all, Dennis." Harper walked around the desk to face him. "All we have to do is demand publicly, and on the floor of Parliament, that the Prime Minister be seen alive by a parliamentary delegation or one from the press, even if it means in a hospital bed." He smiled confidently. "The reporters will love it and needless to say they will not give up on it. The King will be forced to publicly show his hand. One which I believe to be quite empty."

Dennis felt his heart sink. These were his worst fears realized though he knew he should have anticipated it.

"There! What did I tell you!" Conroe shouted triumphantly. "This more than proves it in my mind."

Harper smiled benevolently at Dennis. "Your face betrays you, Dennis. Of course, I knew we were right."

Dennis rallied his defenses as best he could. "I don't know what you're talking about. You have proved nothing." He turned on Harper again. "All you see in my face, sir, is concern for the health of one of this country's greatest statesmen. You can do nothing but endanger the Prime Minister's recovery with this witch hunt you seem to be obsessed with."

"Hah!" Conroe sat, hitting the desk in disgust.

"Really, Dennis," said Harper. "Somehow I pictured you a better liar than this, having been under Bates' tutelage so long." He cocked his head at Conroe in mock disappointment.

"It is apparent the two of you intend to carry on with this fantasy," Dennis said. "I suppose it's no more than I should expect."

"Oh, indeed we shall, Dennis, to the bitter end." Harper picked out a chocolate mint from a crystal dish on the edge of the desk. "So, my boy. What will you tell the King?"

"You can rest assured the King will know of this meeting. And I am sure he'll do what is best for the country even though such grandstanding might be at the expense of Prime Minister Bates."

"Bates is dead," said Conroe, relishing the final consonant.

"We'll see about that," said Dennis, moving between them and mustering his most convincing tone. "One thing you can count on, gentlemen. It's going to give me the greatest pleasure to personally recommend to King Richard that he finally and permanently denounce the two of you and your respective cliques to the people, and use his considerable influence to have you censured in Parliament, and any hopes of a political career you may have, legislated out of existence."

Conroe sat staring at him with blistering hatred. It was Harper's change in personality that took Dennis off guard. Suddenly gone was the politician's jovial reserve. Harper stood gripping the edge of the desk.

Harper's face reddened with a sudden leap of blood pressure and his eyes and mouth became grim slits in a rancor-constricted face. "After tomorrow, Dennis," he said, drawing out the last syllable to a viperous hiss, "the King will have no influence to speak of. If indeed he is still King at all."

"You're as fucked up as Conroe," said Dennis backing away from the two of them. "I've bloody well heard all I intend to hear."

His attempted departure was interrupted by a calliope of alarm bells going off at once. He stopped dead in his tracks and turned back to the two men questioning. "What the hell?"

"Goddamn it!" cursed Conroe reaching for his weapon.

"Not to worry," shouted Harper above the din. "The dogs are released automatically. They'll handle any intruder problems."

Dennis jerked his head around at the sound of breaking glass. Harper, who had begun walking toward the sofa during the confusion, was standing frozen in the middle of the room with his back to Conroe and Dennis.

His hands twitched at his sides for a moment before he crumpled to his stomach on the floor. Dennis watched the slowly spreading black spot on the body's forehead in horror.

Conroe, cursing madly, turned on Dennis with the gun. "This is your doing, goddamn you!"

Dennis dove to the floor just as the lights were extinguished. Blindly, Conroe discharged a folly of shots from the powerful rifle in Dennis' direction, but with the luck of a slick, highly polished floor, Dennis had already skated on his belly across to the protection of the massive desk. He fumbled in his pockets for the small pistol and clutched it to his chest like a security blanket.

A deafening crash chased Dennis under the desk as black-clad bodies came flying through the windows. Dennis thought the roof was coming down. He could hear Conroe screaming obscenities into the darkness. The spit of machine gun fire lit the room for a split second and Dennis heard another body hit the floor where Conroe's voice originated. He tried to hold his breath in silence but his own fear was sending shock waves through his diaphragm, causing him to gasp noisily.

Dennis' eyes darted about the room looking for a way out, but he was still having trouble seeing anything in the darkness. He heard a scream and another burst of gunfire from somewhere in the house and thought instantly of the housekeeper. Padded footsteps scurried across the floor about him like squirrels on a rooftop. He listened but there were no voices, only the occasional rattle of weapons or the snap of a gun clip to drown out his heartbeat.

He could just begin to make out the dim starlight reflecting off the broken pieces of the huge window that stretched from floor to ceiling, just to the left of his position, about ten feet away. His mind calculated frantically, estimating the distance to the ground outside as minimal. If only he could make it out the window. He would need the car keys ready.

Without thinking he slid his free hand down his side to his trouser pocket and felt for the keys. He pulled them out quickly, unable to stifle the slight tinkling sound they made before he could get his hand all the way around them. They might as well have been a giant wind chime. The footsteps stopped abruptly along with Dennis' heart. He could feel the intruders listening, trying to identify the sound. Dennis tried but couldn't erase from his mind the picture of Major Von Schiffer sniffing the air.

He was screaming inside as he sensed a pair of feet start in his direction. Desperately he looked about him for some means to divert their attention, if only for a second. But there was nothing at hand. He considered opening fire with his little pistol, but knowing he had only an off chance of hitting one of the professional assassins bearing down on his hiding place, he returned the pistol to his coat pocket. He was quickly running out of options.

Mentally kicking himself, Dennis remembered the extra set of keys hidden in the little magnetic box under the left front fender of Aidan's car. Aidan, who was forever either losing or locking his keys in the car, had put the set there on his suggestion. He thrust his arm from under the desk and swung the keys up in a high arc across the room away from the window. They jingled and clattered in the darkness across the distance, smashing onto the glass top of a curio table against the far wall. The table was ripped apart in the ensuing gunfire.

Dennis was out from under the desk and across the short distance in three leaping, giant steps. He bounded out the window just as the last echo of gunfire faded away. In his previous estimate he had overlooked the height of the building's built-up foundation and the drop to the ground was a good six feet. He landed hard, twisting the same weakened ankle as before, crying out softly, but loud enough for the men inside to hear.

Without stopping he ran unevenly, like a peg-legged seaman, down the side of the house towards the car. There was no need to look back to know he was being pursued. Dennis was already pushing his pain tolerance to the limit. Any harder and he knew his body would shut down into unconsciousness. Several shots burrowed into the wall above his head in a spray of splintered stone and dust. He ducked his head even lower, fighting to keep his balance and his frantic pace.

Dennis rounded the front portico dragging his injured leg and fell to his knees beside the Jaguar's side, groping for the little box under the fender. He ripped the small container from its nesting place and fumbled to get it open. Dennis cursed softly as the keys popped out of his shaking grasp and fell to the driveway. The door key bounced out of reach under the car. As he hadn't locked the door in the first place he let it go and reached down for the ignition key.

A heavy booted foot stomped down on the back of his hand, pinning it to the ground. Dennis cried out in pain. All hope drained from him as he looked up into the eyes of the figure in the black ski mask standing over him. Teeth flashed through the small hole in the mask and the man slowly and deliberately holstered his pistol and began to draw out an ugly, jagged-toothed combat knife.

Dennis acted on instinct, surprising even himself when he smashed a fist up into the man's crotch. The assassin grunted in pain and staggered back, though still keeping his grip on the knife. Dennis propelled himself from his kneeling position, butting his head deep into the man's midsection. The breath exploded from the killer's lungs and sent him spinning back across the rear of the car. Wrenched free by the force of the impact, the knife slid across the trunk of the car and onto the ground far out of reach.

Dennis shot up from the ground again locking his arm around the man's throat. Gripping his head by the mask, Dennis tried to pull him backwards onto the ground. Immediately he realized how foolish it was to attempt any kind of close quarters combat. The professional struck backwards with an elbow into Dennis' ribs and spun around, with both hands clenched, striking Dennis across the chest. Dennis held on for dear life, but the blow sent him flying back, landing hard on the pavement, the mask clenched tightly in his hands.

"You!" Dennis cried out breathlessly, staring up into the face of the young lieutenant he knew as Toby.

Toby straightened with an amused look. "Me," he answered, laughing down at his victim. "Ready for the final surprise, Mr. Perkins?" He reached across with his right hand for the gun holstered under his left arm.

But Dennis had already palmed the small pistol out of his pocket and thrust it forward, firing haphazardly at the Lieutenant. At a distance of three feet, even he couldn't miss. The rounds emptied into Toby, striking him in the chest and abdomen.

At least one of the small caliber missiles found their way to a vital organ. Toby went to his knees, his expression more of surprise than pain. His mouth gaped open and he seemed to stare for a second with morbid fascination at the various small, bleeding holes dotting his black wool pullover. He made a last effort to extract his gun from its holster, looking up at Dennis in disbelief.

Dennis sat on his knees, the gun still pointing at the Lieutenant. He watched numbly as a small trickle of blood and spittle slithered out the corner of the dying man's open mouth and down his chin. Slowly, almost defying gravity, Toby collapsed forward onto the rain soaked pavement.

Dennis tried to shake himself free of the guilt and shock of having killed a man. He sat with his arms out rigid, still pointing the smoking gun. His muscles ached to be relaxed. Then the shout of other voices echoed around the building and jerked his arms back to his body. He quickly pocketed the gun and raced over the pavement on his knees, looking for the ignition key. Finally he rolled the Lieutenant over and found the blood smeared key under the dead man's chest.

From his knees, Dennis swung the car door open. He pulled himself up into the driver's seat, very much aware of the throbbing pain in his ankle. He jammed the key into the ignition and almost cried with relief as the powerful engine revved instantly. He threw it into gear and shot forward, feeling the dull bump and thud as the rear wheel rolled over the dead lieutenant's legs.

"Shit!" Dennis screamed into the rain as he steered the speeding car down the drive and through the open gates.

12

Aidan was sitting at the bar by the phone, waiting for the inevitable call when the knock came at the door. He stared at the door for a moment before setting down the cup of strong, brewed coffee that had been helping to keep him awake. The knock came again a little louder. He slipped off the stool with unconscious ease and tip-toed barefoot across the carpet to the door and waited for the knock to come again.

"Who is it?" Aidan called softly through the door.

The door rattled with the answering knock. Aidan's eyebrows knitted together in a frown and he glanced back at the phone. Carefully he slid the door chain into place, released the deadbolt, and opened the door a crack trying to make out the features of the tall figure standing in the dimly lit hallway.

"Who's there?" Aidan called again, louder through the crack.

A small slip of parchment paper slid through the door crack. Aidan pulled it in the rest of the way before shutting the door quickly. He had seen this calling card before, a small green, embellished shamrock stamped in the center. He studied it closely. The visitor had always phoned him before. Why, all of a sudden, a face to face meeting? Didn't the man know how dangerous this was, how senseless to compromise him this way?

Aidan took a deep breath and slid the door chain out of its socket and opened the door a little farther. A cold shudder prickled down over the tops of his arms as he looked up at the visitor smiling down at him. The visitor's affect on him was unnerving—fear mingled with a little revulsion. Aidan couldn't explain it. It wasn't so much the size of the man as his eyes—so cold and purposeful. The visitor pushed the door open completely and Aidan stepped back quickly out of the man's way. The visitor closed the door and turned the deadbolt back into position.

Aidan walked quickly back to the bar, trying to hide his annoyance at this unexpected change in procedure. "I was waiting for you to call," he said flatly. He felt more comfortable with the added distance between them. "I wasn't expecting to see you."

The visitor turned toward Aidan, the corner of his mouth twisting up in some caricature of a smile. "Dennis

has an interesting flat here, Aidan," he said conver-
sationally. "I must say you dress it up admirably."

Aidan looked down at his nakedness. If any other
man had noticed, he would have accepted the compliment with self-assured satisfaction. Under this visitor's
gaze, however, all Aidan could feel was the dread and
faint nausea trying to bore a hole through his stomach.

Aidan quickly retrieved his boxer shorts from the
sofa and pulled them on. "What's brought you here?
What if you were seen?" Aidan asked, at once trying to
get down to business as well as express his misgivings
about the situation.

"Nothing special, dear one." The visitor moved
further into Aidan's space, sitting on a bar stool by him.
"I come and go as I please. Who would, after all, question
me?"

Aidan reached for a match and put the small piece of
stamped parchment in an ashtray to burn.

The visitor reached over his shoulder and retrieved
the paper. "I'll need this later," he said matter-of-factly.

"Suit yourself." Aidan shifted on his stool and turned
his attention back to his coffee so he wouldn't have to
look at the man. He found the visitor's unblinking stare
oddly unnerving. "You must have some reason for taking
a chance like this and I wish we could hurry up and get to
it."

The visitor didn't answer.

"I have an early day tomorrow and it's very late," Aidan said, trying to pull some sort of response from the man.

"I wanted to hear your report first hand," the visitor said and reached out to touch Aidan's arm.

Aidan flinched perceptibly at the man's touch and tried to buffer his reaction by smiling at the ceiling. "Nothing has changed since I gave my contact the report earlier," he said. "What are you planning?"

"I was considering killing two birds with one stone," the visitor answered.

Aidan tried to muffle his feelings. "I think it would be a waste to kill him at this point," he said, hoping it didn't sound like a plea. "He's too valuable a source of information alive."

"Perhaps," answered the man. "But it would be so convenient now, what with all of them together in one place. Almost like before."

The visitor surveyed the room casually, slowly filling his lungs with air. Aidan took the opportunity to watch him out of the corner of his eye, relieved to have the man's eyes off of him. The visitor turned back to Aidan abruptly but the younger man was unable to turn his eyes away fast enough to escape the visitor's notice.

"Did you and Dennis make love tonight?" The visitor asked leaning closer to Aidan.

The question was like a slap in the face and Aidan met his eyes defiantly. He turned back to his coffee just as quickly. If it weren't for the freedom of his people, he would never have anything to do with this man. Why was it the men he had met in The Struggle all seemed to enjoy killing and other perversions more than simple lovemaking. He shuddered despite himself.

"I really don't know what that has to do with anything," Aidan said, trying, at least, to put the distance of aloofness between them. "Do you wish to discuss my report or not?" He wondered if he would regret his hardened tone.

The visitor laughed easily, though it might as well have been a snarl. "Certainly, Aidan, certainly." He stood from the stool and walked behind Aidan. "It just seems that Dennis cares a great deal about you and, for my purposes at least, that is very important to know."

Aidan kept his eyes forward for a moment, thinking about this. He could feel the man standing close behind him. "For your purposes, I think it's safe to say that Dennis and I are very close," Aidan answered finally. "He is somewhat naive to the political atrocities of the government he presently serves, but I have every hope of that changing when the truth finally comes out." Aidan's scalp prickled as he felt the visitor reach out and stroke the back of his hair. He willed himself to not pull away.

"I had someone I felt that way about too," the visitor said into Aidan's ear. "An intimate . . . a companion . . . someone to share the good times with . . . someone who cared for me."

"I let Dennis do all the talking," Aidan assured him.

"Still," the visitor added, smoothing the hair behind Aidan's ear. "You can't help but form an emotional attachment . . . a need."

"I assumed that is what you wanted," Aidan said with effort.

"Oh, indeed, my dear boy. Do I take it then that you have some feeling for our Mr. Perkins?"

"Dennis is a good man," Aidan answered quickly. "Politically he is somewhat idealistic and sheltered, but he tries to do the right thing. And he has treated me very well," he answered quickly, burying any further thought on the question deep away from his consciousness.

"And you no doubt have done the same for him." The visitor began to massage Aidan's shoulders.

Aidan stiffened at his touch.

"Relax, my beauty. Such situations are not uncommon. You have nothing to be ashamed of."

"I'm not ashamed." Aidan shook the man's hands from his angrily. "Why are you asking these questions? Have you suddenly lost confidence in me?"

The visitor massaged the nape of Aidan's neck. "Absolutely not. You are very valuable to me, especially now."

"I do what is necessary for our cause."

"And so do I," the visitor replied.

The man's arm blurred across Aidan's face for an instant, too fast for the boy to react. Aidan was aware of a faint zipping sound and a sudden burning airiness about his throat. The visitor lifted Aidan off the stool by his hair and stood holding him suspended in the air. Aidan tried to cry out but no sound would come to his lips. He strained his eyes downward, staring uncomprehending at the jets of dark red splashing about the bar.

For a moment Aidan was caught up in a consuming euphoria before the room began to spin away from him, leaving him behind, finally to be carried off into oblivion.

13

"Jesus," Dennis cried aloud, biting his upper lip. "That's hot!"

"Don't bellyache, now," Inspector Harlowe said as he poured a little more scalding water from his teapot into the large porcelain basin in which Dennis was soaking his swollen ankle. "You'll be as good as new in just a little while."

Dennis dug his fingers into his right thigh and massaged downward, trying to divert the throbbing nerve signals. "You don't think it'll need an X-ray?"

"No, no," answered the Inspector, returning the teapot to the hotplate by the window. "The doc said it's just a minor sprain."

"Minor, he says," grumbled Dennis, twisting slightly in his chair. He flinched at the extra shot of pain that cut up his leg as he tried to move the foot a little.

The phone rang and Inspector Harlowe answered it quickly, lowering himself into his well-worn chair behind the cluttered desk. Dennis watched him closely, looking for any sign of the information Harlowe was receiving, but the Inspector's poker face was unreadable. Dennis' gaze diverted out the tinted window behind Harlowe where the early morning sun was creating a spectacular corona of orange through the polluted cloud cover. He looked back at the Inspector, surprised to find that Harlowe had already hung up the phone and was sitting quietly looking at him.

"Well, Inspector?" Dennis asked.

"Well, Perkins." Harlowe pursed his lips and sat tapping the thumbs of his clasped hands. "It seems there has indeed been some unfortunate business at Shamrock Hill."

"Oh, for Christ's sake, Inspector! That we know already."

"Yes, well. It seems our people have only been able to identify three bodies; Gerald Conroe, Devon Harper, and the housekeeper . . . a Mrs. Jorgen—all shot to death. No other bodies have been found."

"Only three?" Dennis asked. He tried unsuccessfully to stand. "But I know that lieutenant was dead. He had to be." He fell back into the chair, wincing at the pain.

"I believe you, Perkins," assured Harlowe. "There were traces of blood on the drive under the portico where the rain couldn't reach."

The Inspector picked up a pencil and drummed it on his note pad. "I doubt seriously that they would leave something as incriminating as the body of the Major's right hand man behind," he said.

Dennis massaged his temples. "That makes sense." He lifted his aching foot out of the water and sat it down carefully on a towel to dry. "What do we do now? It's certain the Major can no longer afford to let me remain alive, knowing what I know."

"Right now your foot's the problem." Inspector Harlowe hoisted himself from his chair and walked around to sit on the edge of his desk facing Dennis. "I would suggest you keep it in the hot water a little longer."

"I'm already up to my bloody neck in hot water right now, Inspector," Dennis said without humor. "We have got to force the King into action, and now."

"And how would you suggest we do that? The only proof we have is your word linking the Major to all of this."

Dennis rubbed his eyes in exasperation. "If necessary we could use the leverage of Prime Minister Bates' death," he argued. "It may stink of blackmail but at least our end is a little bit more justifiable than Conroe's and Harper's."

"I'm afraid such a move would no longer be viable, Perkins." The Inspector pulled a sheet of paper from his desk and thrust it at Dennis. "The King certainly manages to get a lot of work done without his Private Secretary. Do you think he typed it himself?"

Dennis took the piece of paper, instantly recognizing the royal seal that decorated all news releases from the Palace. He read the release with mounting anger and frustration. "What in blazes is going on?"

"Oh, I think it's pretty clear, Perkins." The Inspector chuckled to himself with satisfaction. "The King has obviously made a brilliant move to beat his political opponents to the punch." Harlowe clapped his hands. "We regret to inform you of the untimely death of Prime Minister Bates this morning," he quoted aloud. "Imagine Conroe's face if he had lived to read this."

"But the Prime Minister has been dead for some time. Surely the King cannot expect that fact to go unnoticed."

"Ah, but that's the beauty of it, Perkins, my boy. One of the oldest tricks in the book. Bates' body has been on ice, so to speak. There is no way to prove the time of death. His Majesty has, of course, thought of everything."

"For someone who considers all of this to be illegal, you're certainly enjoying it."

The Inspector laughed again. "I have great respect and admiration for the King," he said. "He, more than anyone, has stabilized the nation and brought an iron hand and single-minded will to bear on the nation's problems. It's his casual disregard for certain written and unwritten tenets of Magna Carta that I take issue with."

Dennis sat quietly for a moment. "So, there we are," he said flatly. "We've got absolutely nothing to go with."

The Inspector picked a cassette tape up from his desk and toyed with it. "Oh, I wouldn't say . . . nothing, Perkins."

Dennis eyed the tape curiously. "What have you got?"

"A phone conversation that might interest you."

"Whose conversation?" Dennis sat up excitedly. "What? Tell me!"

"It's the result of a little wire-tap we've had," Harlowe said with a sly smile, "on your telephone."

"What!" Dennis couldn't believe his ears. "My phone? What the bloody . . ." His voice rose an octave. "You'd better have more than a good explanation for this, Harlowe. You have no right to—"

"Whoa, Perkins. Calm down." The Inspector walked over to his book case and the modular tape deck it held. "You're not under suspicion for anything."

"Then why the hell put a tap on my phone?" Dennis watched him slip the tape into the deck. "Does the word privacy have any meaning at Scotland Yard?"

Inspector Harlowe clicked his tongue admonishingly. "Such righteous anger, Perkins." He pressed the play button. "The phone tap was for a bird of a different color."

"A bit weak, Inspector," said Dennis. "I'm the only one who uses my phone." He tried to turn in his chair as the Inspector walked over behind him but the pain in his ankle caught him short. "It's my phone, dammit, Inspector. Except for Aidan, I . . ."

The stereo speakers hissed for a moment and then Aidan's soft, velvety voice filled the room. Dennis stared at the floor dumfounded. He listened intently with his eyes closed. It certainly sounded like Aidan but the caller didn't say his name. At first the conversation was essentially nonsense. But, as Dennis was preparing to dress down the Inspector even more, the conversation took a different turn.

"I think I have a letter that was sent by mistake," the voice of Aidan said, strangely lacking in its usual inflection and accent.

"By mistake?" answered the unidentified male.

"Definitely."

"Sent where?"

"Shamrock Hill."

"Strange place for your letter to go."

"I'm afraid of its not being returned." Aidan's voice had begun to tremble.

"Not being returned?"

"That's correct."

"We'll put a trace on your letter."

"Thank you." Aidan paused. "It will be returned safely?"

"We'll get back to you on that."

"I'll be expecting a call."

The male voice did not answer. Instead the call was ended with an abrupt click. There was another pause before Aidan hung up his end. The Inspector turned off the tape.

"When was that tape made?" Dennis asked, his voice tightly ill-at-ease.

"Close to midnight ... last night," Inspector Harlowe answered.

Try as he might, Dennis could not avoid the obvious. Despite the shallow, coded language, it was clear that Aidan had just informed someone of his meeting with Gerald Conroe. Above the hurt and confusion he felt, Dennis still could not bring himself to admit the truth.

"There's nothing in that call that proves anything," Dennis said adamantly.

"Except that your boyfriend informed someone of your meeting at Shamrock Hill."

"It was more like him telling someone he was worried about me."

"Indeed," the Inspector huffed.

"He could have been talking to someone in security."

"Security!" The Inspector was growing annoyed at Dennis' stubbornness. "I suppose that's why, shortly after your arrival, the Hill was hit by a death squad."

"Goddamn it, Inspector, I know Aidan."

"Do you?" Inspector Harlowe returned to his desk and flipped open a manila file folder. "How well?"

"What the hell does that mean?"

"I'm not talking about being intimate," the Inspector smiled. "I mean background."

"What's there to know?" Dennis said angrily, ignoring the folder in Harlowe's hand. He kicked the pan of water away and sat glaring at the growing puddle sloshing out onto the floor.

"For instance, anything about his family."

"His father's a wealthy Irish industrialist," Dennis said, trying to recall. "Hardly the IRA sort. He doesn't talk about his family much. I know they've had problems between them. His won't accept the gay thing and Aidan told him to go jump. Something like that."

"Perhaps," prodded the Inspector. "Any other family?"

Dennis shrugged his shoulders. "My interest is in Aidan, Harlowe. You *can* know another person without studying their pedigree." He began to put on his socks and shoes, pretending to ignore the Inspector.

"Perhaps, perhaps," the Inspector said. "However, I must say your boyfriend does have a rather interesting family tree."

Dennis eyed him with annoyance. "People aren't hung for their family trees, Inspector."

Harlowe merely smiled. "He had an older brother," he said, reading the file. "I note he was killed back during the Belfast uprisings in an attempted armored car robbery. An IRA attempt at fund raising, I believe. He had the dubious honor of being on our most wanted list at the time. IRA cell leader, you know."

"Christ, Inspector." Dennis held his head in his hands. "There's hardly a family around in Northern

Ireland that hasn't seen at least one member taken in by the extremists."

"True, true," the Inspector commented.

"All right, Inspector," Dennis said angrily. "Aidan has skeletons. We all do. He is a beautiful, apolitical young man who designs dresses for the titled and upwardly mobile classes. He runs a busy, well-established boutique and runs it mostly alone. He hardly has time for intrigue."

"Yes, that maybe true," the Inspector said. "However, his situation as your live-in lover gives him a—you must admit—wonderful perspective from which to gather information."

"Exactly what do you mean by that?" Dennis narrowed his eyes sharply at the Inspector.

"I'm not trying to slight your ability to keep secrets, Dennis, but much can be gleaned from casual conversation, overheard phone calls and the like. He has also accompanied you to almost every political affair you've attended in the last year."

"Good God, Inspector. You're trying to make him out as some sort of Mata Hari. This is ridiculous!"

"Consider one more fact, Dennis." The Inspector flipped a few more pages in the file he was holding. "One more coincidence to add to the stack." He sat back down on the edge of his desk, looking solemnly at Dennis over the rims of his glasses.

Dennis knew the Inspector was playing him, manipulating his mood and attitudes, but his own curiosity made it impossible for him to fight the pull of so much damning circumstantial evidence. He could see in Harlowe's eyes that the Inspector was preparing to set the hook even harder.

"Yes, one more little thing, Dennis."

"Only one?" Dennis turned his back on the Inspector.

"I was shocked the other day," said the Inspector, "to discover that your Mr. Ennis has an unfortunate . . . arrest record history as well."

"What the hell are you aiming at now, Harlowe?" Dennis shifted in his chair.

"Mr. Ennis . . . Aidan ran away from home several times. At sixteen he spent a couple of months in a juvenile detention center."

"So what! Kids do stupid things."

"Well, yes." The Inspector looked at the floor. "Turns out he'd been running off to join his . . . lover at the time . . . one Rudy O'Dell." Inspector Harlowe assumed his most sympathetic expression.

"Inspector, you are sounding goddamn provincial," Dennis said, almost laughing. "Do you think for one minute I don't know that someone as fucking beautiful as my boyfriend has had past relationships? What . . . do you think I was just a choir boy before meeting Aidan?"

"Rudy O'Dell is . . . was a top IRA command figure. Our intelligence places him as the planner and executor of the Royal Yacht bombing five years ago. Aidan was his lover at the time."

Dennis looked up at him, shocked. For a moment he couldn't speak. He wondered if Harlowe could be cruel enough simply to be playing with him.

"You bloody son-of-a-bitch," Dennis finally managed. "You bloody lying son-of-a-bitch!"

The Inspector merely shook his head regretfully, accentuating his pity for Dennis.

"What proof do you have?" Dennis started to stand, but the pain in his ankle and the Inspector's restraining hand prevented him.

"Easy, Dennis," soothed Harlowe. "I'm sorry to have to tell you like this, but it's true. MI5 has a very thick folder on your boyfriend. He has been under surveillance for some time. Your boss knew about him too."

Dennis shook his head. "I don't believe you," he stammered weakly. "Anyway, just because Aidan may have had a relationship with this . . . this O'Dell character doesn't mean anything now. The Aidan I know—"

"O'Dell was in Aidan's shop just the other day."

"I don't believe you!"

"Sorry, my boy, but here it is. Surveillance noted a vagrant enter Mr. Ennis' shop, for about fifteen minutes, and then be escorted away by constables. Not much was made of it at the time until the man's body was found in an alley nearby."

The Inspector shuffled some papers in the file. "Rudy O'Dell . . . one of three IRA cell leaders now coordinating terrorist activities here in London." Inspector Harlowe paused for a moment to let Dennis absorb these facts, before continuing. "The Yard really had no reason to investigate Aidan's past until now." He returned the file to his desk. "When we found O'Dell's connection to him, we immediately began piecing together his family background, and, as you can see, it became pretty colorful."

Dennis sagged in the chair unable to move. The weight of the evidence was overwhelming.

"Surely, Dennis, you'll understand now," the Inspector said, his tone growing even more gentle, "that my suspicions are not without foundation. These facts in conjunction with this taped phone conversation make things pretty clear, even to a person as closely tied to Aidan as you."

Dennis shook his head. "You'll have to excuse me, Inspector, but I simply can't accept this." His voice lacked conviction.

Tired as he was, his own memory was working overtime against him. Aidan's badgering for information on his meetings the last few days began to look more and more like something other than just feminine curiosity. Dennis tried to shrug off his increasing doubts, but even the guilt he felt for thinking these things weakened his ability to block it all out. A twinge of betrayal began to gnaw at his resolve like a maggot.

Many years experience at reading people's reactions told the Inspector that Dennis was at least straddling the fence now. He reached out and gave Dennis' shoulder a squeeze. "I think one thing is obvious, Dennis, and that is that Aidan does care something for you," he said in his best vicar voice. "That's clear from his concern on the tape. He may not be fully aware of the dire nature of what he's been doing."

"What he's been doing has yet to be proved, Inspector," Dennis said. He suddenly felt very much the fool. "At least not to my satisfaction."

"Others won't agree, Dennis. If we pick him up for questioning it won't be very pleasant."

"I warn you, Harlowe—"

"I said if, Dennis," the Inspector interrupted. "I'll give you a chance to talk to him first. Perhaps his feelings for you will give you the edge in getting to the bottom of all this."

"I'm not going to interrogate him like some criminal, based on mere circumstantial evidence like this," Dennis said, standing with effort.

Inspector Harlowe stood to face him. "You *will* talk to him, Dennis." His tone had a hard edge to it. "I want to know who he phoned, who his contacts are. You have one hour with him, at which point, if I haven't heard from you, my men will pick him up and we will find out the answers to these questions one way or the other."

Dennis tried to stare him down, but it was obvious the Inspector meant what he said. "Goddamn you, Harlowe."

"We'll all be damned if this mess is not straightened out soon, Dennis," the Inspector said quietly. "The King has named Hughen Fitzroy to head a caretaker government until elections can be held."

"Fitzroy." Dennis brightened. "At last a little good news."

The Inspector smiled at him. "I have a meeting with Fitzroy and the cabinet in a little over an hour," he said. "The Leprechaun will be the subject of that meeting." Harlowe looked hard at Dennis. "I need some answers, Dennis. You have to get me answers."

"All right, Inspector," Dennis said. He hobbled to the door. "I'll talk to Aidan. But I honestly don't know what it will accomplish."

"Don't worry, mate," the Inspector said. He picked up the phone. "I think the boy will surprise you."

14

Dennis slid his key into the deadbolt slowly, feeling in no particular hurry to rush the confrontation he knew was coming with Aidan. During the long drive from Scotland Yard to his apartment, he had divided his attention between practicing his approach with Aidan, and not losing the two bodyguards in the small beige sedan on his tail, which the Inspector had insisted on assigning to him.

As for Aidan, he had settled on nothing. Deep down he still wanted very much to believe that Aidan was in no way involved and, if that were true, he could think of no way to question his lover without making it seem as if he no longer trusted him. Knowing how exhausted he felt, he was sure that subtlety was beyond his abilities at the present time. He decided the best approach was simple, blunt honesty. If Aidan truly cared for him, he would get over the hurt of Dennis' momentary lapse in trust. That, assuming his boyfriend was innocent. If he was in some way tainted by the situation, perhaps his feelings for Dennis would allow him to be honest about his involvement, especially with Rudy O'Dell.

Bolstered by this resolve, Dennis turned the key in the lock and pushed to open the door. The door would not budge. He stood for a moment looking at it in consternation trying to see the problem. He turned the knob again and pushed but the door remained tightly shut.

"Damn!" he said under his breath, jiggling the door knob in vain.

He stepped back, cursing his own stupidity. The door was obviously unlocked when he got there and he had just locked it. He inserted his key again and turned it slowly feeling for the sensation of the deadbolt being pulled back. He made a mental note to chastise Aidan about leaving the door open, especially when he was home. He remembered his first week in the city of London, and the anger and disappointment he had lived with for many weeks after his most prized possession, a new flat-panel television set, was stolen.

This time the door obeyed and whisked open without resistance. He shut it quickly behind him and reengaged the lock. Shedding his hat and coat he made a beeline for the bar and poured himself a shot of gin. Not bothering with the tonic he tossed the welcome liquid warmth down in a swallow.

He looked around the room for any sign of Aidan but decided he was probably still in bed. He sat the glass down on the mirror polished bar and noted with satisfaction that the entire room had been straightened and cleaned. He smiled to himself at how out of character that was for Aidan. Dennis guessed that the boy had been up all night worrying with nothing better to do than clean.

He kicked off his shoes at the bar and padded over to the balcony window to check on his official protectors. He pulled the sheer curtains back with one finger and peeked out, relieved to see their small car parked directly across the street. The driver still sat at the wheel but the other man was nowhere to be seen. Dennis decided he was probably skulking about in the halls looking for IRA gangsters in the trash bins.

Dennis loosened his tie and unbuttoned his collar as he headed for the bedroom in search of Aidan. There was no sense putting off the inevitable, especially since the Inspector had only given him an hour to get his answers. He wondered what kind of mood Aidan would be in. The boy could out-bitch a dowager empress when riled.

The bedroom door was slightly ajar and Dennis, almost tiptoeing, pushed it open a little more to stick his head in. The shades had been pulled over the bedroom windows and the morning light caused them to glow with a warm, golden hue. The bed, however, was still in the shadows up against the opposite wall, but there was enough light from the windows for Dennis to make out Aidan's sleeping form tucked under the sheets.

He crept quietly into the room, relieved to have the insulated softness of the plush pile carpeting under his stocking feet. The bedroom was the only room Dennis insisted have carpeting, preferring the natural wood finish everywhere else. He hated waking up on a chilly morning and crawling out from under warm blankets onto an icy floor.

Dennis leaned over the bed, letting his weight settle slowly on his hands into the mattress. He bent down to lightly kiss Aiden hoping to ease him awake. Something made him pause, an instant before their lips met. It was as if some instinct of repulsion—an almost magnetic force of opposition existed layer-thin between them. He tried to will himself to complete his tender intentions, but a stronger drive from deep within prevented him.

His perception of the surroundings and even of Aidan took on an unreal, distorted dimension. As close as he was to the boy, the person into whose half-opened eyes he was staring, held only the vaguest resemblance to Aidan. His lover's parted lips were paler and thinner than he remembered. The skin and muscles of his cheeks and jaws seemed to sag toward the back of his head with gravity like an aged beauty queen. Something else was different. There was no warmth coming from the boy, and Dennis suddenly realized, no breath. He reached a hand up to touch Aidan's face. The skin was cold and stiffly unresponsive. His hand retracted from Aidan as if hit by an electric shock. Dennis backed away slowly, blinking his eyes as if to erase the unthinkable.

He grabbed the sheet and ripped it down off Aidan before his brain could rob him of the ability to act. He recoiled in horror, knocking over a menagerie of photo frames and music boxes on the dresser behind him. A guttural scream exploded from his lips before his larynx locked into paralysis.

"Jesus . . . Aidan . . . Jesus!" Dennis' voice caught in his throat as he stood frozen, staring at the cruel mutilation before him.

The bed was soaked with crusting, brown blood, surrounding the naked, spread-eagled body from torso to head. The neck gaped open from ear to ear. The left nipple and surrounding skin had been neatly excised and lay wrinkled on the bed between the left arm and rib cage. In its place lay a small, blood-soaked slip of parchment paper stamped with a filigreed, green shamrock that held Dennis' eyes transfixed.

A violent pounding shook the walls. It took a moment for Dennis' chaotic mental processes to pinpoint the fact that someone was trying to break down the front door. He staggered, dazed and in shock, over to the bedroom door.

At the same moment the body guard from the hallway came bursting in through the front door in a spray of splintering wood. "Mr. Perkins! I heard you cry out!" The young detective flashed his wallet identification.

Dennis clung to the bedroom doorway, momentarily blinded by too much adrenalin. "Aiden . . . Aidan!" he sobbed in broken syllables, trying to coordinate his hand to point the security guard into the bedroom. "Please . . . help!"

The man sprinted across the room toward Dennis, his gun drawn. He peered around Dennis cautiously, reaching in with his free hand to flip on the bedroom light. He glanced at the macabre scene only briefly before pulling out his radio. "Sarge!"

"Yeah, Brewer. What now?" crackled the voice from the radio.

"Better get up here! Our man's OK but there's some bad news you better have a look at."

"The boyfriend?"

"'Fraid so. It's a mess."

Dennis went weak in the knees and felt himself slipping down to the floor.

The voice on the radio began, "Whatever you do, Brewer, don't—"

The agent in the car was silenced abruptly as Brewer switched off the radio to catch Dennis and help him back to his feet. "Easy there, sir. Let's get you over to the couch." He gripped Dennis under the arm and guided him across the room.

"I . . . thought he was . . . asleep," Dennis said, stumbling beside him. He held onto the bodyguard with one hand and tried to hide his face with the other. In addition to shock and grief, he was also feeling some shame and anger at his seeming inability to get control of himself in front of the younger man. He had to think. Who could have been responsible for this? His mind seemed incapable of connecting the facts.

When they got to the bar, Dennis grabbed hold of the corner and pulled himself away from the security man, easing himself onto a stool. "Just leave me here for a moment. I'll be all right," he said and tried to pick up a bottle to pour himself another shot of gin. His hands were trembling too much to hold onto the decanter, and it slipped from his grip onto the bar.

"Here, Mr. Perkins, let me," Brewer said, catching the bottle before it spilt. He poured a generous portion into a tumbler which Dennis managed, with some difficulty, to balance in both hands. He left Dennis at the bar and returned to the bedroom for another look.

The gin proved a counter shock to his system, and Dennis calmed down enough to where he could once again attempt rational thought. The fear and anger seemed to wash out of him with each sip, but the ache of his loss could not be so easily erased. Despite himself, he kept trying to picture what his last moments must have been like, but the horror of what he had just seen kept invading his thoughts. For the first time he admitted to himself that, indeed, Aidan must have been connected very closely to the events of the last few weeks. Aidan must have been killed because he was a direct link, a threat, to the one person responsible for it all, the

Leprechaun, and Dennis was now more than certain this monster was the Major, himself.

Dennis was unable to stop the burst of laughter that erupted from him, laughter and tears. He refused to relinquish the hope that, despite his political betrayal, Aidan did care something for him, perhaps too much. It almost consoled him to think that perhaps Aidan was killed because of his love for him; a love which caused his comrades to doubt his reliability anymore.

"Looks like some handwriting on our perpetrator's calling card," Brewer shouted from the bedroom.

Dennis sat silent. He took a deep breath and looked up in the direction of the voice.

"An eye for an eye!" Brewer read.

Dennis jaw tightened to the point of pain. He understood very well what the message meant and who it was for as the recollection of his confrontation with Toby flashed to the fore of his memory. "Von Schiffer!" he said with more anger than he could contain. He lowered his glass to the bar with agonizing slowness. Dennis reached down for his shoes and slipped them on hurriedly.

"I'm gonna roll him over a little," Brewer called out again. "Looks like there's something else under him."

Dennis jerked around to the door as the agent who had been driving the car, a much older man than Brewer, came bounding through the broken front door out of breath. He bent over in the doorway gripping his knees with his hands trying to catch his breath. "Brewer!" the man yelled weakly.

"In here, Sarge!" Brewer answered with a grunt as he attempted to roll the stiff, sprawling body over.

The Sargeant started to yell, "Don't touch the—" A flash of light and the bedroom was ripped apart in a thunderous explosion. The blast wave knocked Dennis off the stool and onto the floor behind the bar. Plaster, debris, and dust were blown clear of the bedroom, shattering glasses on the bar above Dennis' head.

The Sergeant was also knocked off his feet but he was quickly up again and running for the bedroom. "Goddamn it!" he cursed, waving his way through the dust and smoke.

Dennis gradually got to his feet brushing the debris from his clothes. "What happened?" He coughed through the haze.

"Stupid kid!" the Sergeant raged at himself as he was driven back out of the bedroom by spreading flames. He turned to Dennis. "Get on the bloody phone and get some help up here!"

"What the hell happened?" Dennis shouted at him, grabbing the phone up from the floor and dialing the emergency number.

"Booby trap! These motherfuckers always leave a little surprise behind." He turned back to the burning room. "Don't touch the bodies! I've told him a thousand times!" He kicked some debris through the bedroom door. "Shit!"

Dennis slammed the phone down on the bar. "Fire brigades been alerted. They're on their way."

"A lot of fucking good!" shouted the Sergeant at no one in particular. He suddenly dashed out into the hall and returned with a fire extinguisher. "Stay put, Mr. Perkins," he said forcefully before taking a deep breath and reentering the bedroom.

With both hands, Dennis pushed a few wayward strands of red hair out of his eyes and back into place. The Major! The goddamn Major! His whole body tensed at the thought of Von Schiffer laughing triumphantly back at the Palace. He wanted the Major to suffer, suffer like Aidan must have, suffer even more.

Dennis could hear the pressurized hiss of the extinguisher from the bedroom. He pushed away from the bar and grabbed his overcoat out of the closet. He could still feel the weight of the pistol cradled in the pocket of his coat and pulled it out gently, checking the chamber for available ammunition. It was empty. He tried to count the number of times he had fired at Toby, but the incident had become such a blur in his mind that the effort was futile. He thought quickly but couldn't even come up with the location of a gunsmith where he might purchase some bullets. He wasn't even sure what kind of bullets he needed.

In desperation he turned back to the bedroom. "You! Sergeant!" he called out, taking aim at the bedroom door with his empty pistol.

The older man staggered out of the smoke coughing violently, shielding his eyes from the acrid fumes with one hand and lugging the heavy extinguisher with the other.

"Not going to have much luck in there with this little thing, Mr. Perkins. We better . . ." He looked up into the gun aimed at his chest. "What the fuck!"

"No arguments now, Sergeant," Dennis said calmly. "Your gun please."

"My what?" He stood staring Dennis in the eye.

"Your gun, Sergeant. Give it to me. Now!" Dennis held his aim and the man's eyes unwaveringly.

"You're making one hell of a mistake, Mister." The Sergeant reached slowly into his coat for his shoulder holster.

"You let me worry about that," Dennis said with a smile. "Very slow now. Set it down on the floor and step back. Please don't do anything stupid. All I want is your gun."

The man pulled his gun out carefully, wondering why the man he was supposed to be protecting was doing such a turn around. He held the gun by the muzzle and bent over, setting it onto the floor, never taking his eyes off Dennis.

Dennis waved him back and squatted down to pick up the gun. It was considerably heavier than Dennis' own and he tested its weight in his free hand for a moment before slipping it into his coat pocket. "I appreciate your cooperation, Sergeant," he said backing up toward the door. "I'll trust you not to follow me as I'm sure you'll have your hands full here."

"No sweat off my back," the Sergeant said, frowning at Dennis with contempt. "It's your own neck you're playing with."

Dennis tossed the small empty pistol into the room behind him and raced down the hallway for the stairwell. As far as he was now concerned the entire matter was out of the King's hands. The Major was a dead man one way or the other.

Dennis gave one last backward glance toward his apartment, his grief turning to hatred. Von Schiffer had to be stopped.

15

Buckingham Palace resembles a huge, sprawling, Edwardian hotel more than the seat of royal dignity which it serves. Other than its size, the princeliest aspect of the overall effect lies in the black and gold, decoratively Florentine iron gates and fencing that surrounds the facade in front of the Victoria Monument in the Mall. Beyond that, the Palace itself essentially consists of a series of rectangular boxes glued together at various ends and punched out with an array of windows and balconies of varying sizes.

Above this metaphor of the solid, marblesque foundation of state, there rises a single, spear-like pole topped with a golden coronet. It is from this vantage point that the monarch's royal standard is flown—or not flown as the case may be—a signal to the people whether or not the Monarch is currently in residence there.

Experienced Palace watchers also know that there are other signs and omens to take note of that can give further insight into what is going on behind the impressive architectural fronts of the Palace. For instance, a spurt of activity around any one of the garage gates is a definite sign that the King is preparing to depart in motorcade to preside at some official function. Windows being opened at various points around the Palace are indications of where the King is actually working at that moment, as he always insists on fresh, circulating air regardless of the outside temperature.

In the evening or even under the shade of cloud cover, taking note of the various office windows in which lights are burning can give the interested observer an idea of who is working. The Palace, after all, is something of a national fishbowl, with the King at its center. The other working members of his staff must, of necessity, share some of that public exposure as part of the job.

This was the first time that Dennis had ever considered a positive side to the nakedness of the Palace. For once, he found himself taking advantage of the same subtle aura about the Palace that journalists and paparazzi had long been exploiting. The window to the King's bedroom was opened about a quarter and Dennis guessed he was still lying in bed as was his custom, already wading through the sheaves of state papers that were in never-ending supply.

Dennis walked along the outer perimeter of the Palace grounds staring up into the windows, working out the interior floor plan in his mind, divining who was at work and where. If the reporters only knew half of what he knew, the Fleet Street tabloids would never lack for material. They couldn't, of course, care less about the state of the nation or the political maneuverings at Number Ten Downing Street. It was the little quirks and feuds surrounding the Royal household that made the front pages.

But Dennis had little interest in whether or not the cook was feuding with housekeeping or if the plumbing was again backed up in the private floors. He studied the run of windows along the first floor above the state reception rooms in the west wing just off the Royal Family's private compound. He thrust his hand into the pockets of his overcoat and slipped in through the private gate, nodding casually at the scarlet uniformed guard. He considered asking the guard for help but dismissed the idea, remembering that all the guards were probably Von Schiffer's men anyway. He walked briskly along the inside wall tightening the grip he had been keeping on the gun in his pocket.

A closer look assured Dennis that an overhead light was on in the Major's quarters. Von Schiffer's frugal nature would never have allowed this unless he were in the room at the time. Dennis tried to relax a little and a different, more rational plan began to develop in his mind. If he could get to the King with all he knew, proof or no proof, still it would be impossible for the King to totally disregard the matter. At least he would be with the King, armed and ready should the Major pick that time to complete what must be the finale to his sequence of murders.

Another thought stopped Dennis cold. The plan was viable only if the King were still alive. With things collapsing around the Major, as he certainly knew they were by now, he might feel the King's life was no longer a valuable front to hide behind. Von Schiffer may have already killed the King, thinking it was better to burn all his bridges quickly while he had the opportunity and go into hiding.

Dennis broke into a run back around to the staff entrance of that wing's ground floor. He brushed through the door into the servants' dormitory area and walked briskly down the narrow hallway fronting the many small cubicles the downstairs staff called home. He made his way around to the west pantry and hit the call button on the small service elevator nearby.

It seemed nothing in the Palace operated quickly. It was, therefore, no wonder that a hot meal never seemed to arrive hot. Dennis pounded the call button several more times as if his own impatience would bring it down quicker. He felt more anger at himself than at anyone else for not having comprehended the danger to the King before now. He considered trying to get a call through to Inspector Harlowe but knew that would be almost impossible once the Cabinet had convened. His only hope was that the Sergeant would report in and word would get through. The elevator continued to procrastinate and Dennis cursed audibly, giving the call button one more slam with his fist before springing around the corner to the stairwell.

The expansive hallway along the King's private quarters was empty of activity. Dennis moved quickly to the double doors that led into the King's study and bedroom. He knocked softly on the door, hoping the sound would not carry around to the Major's ears. There was no answer. He reached down tentatively to try the door.

A sharp cracking sound which Dennis immediately recognized as a gunshot reverberated from within one of the rooms down the oak paneled hallway. The echo was such that he could not identify the direction from which the shot came. The doorway in front of him opened without resistance and Dennis burst into the room with his pistol drawn.

The study was empty and unlit and Dennis, his heart racing, quickly crossed the plush red carpeting into the King's bedroom. The tell-tale window was still slightly opened and a stiff breeze blew across the room, ruffling the heavy drapes and rustling a few stray papers on the night stand. There was no sign of the King except for the fact that the bed sheets were pulled down and unmade. Dennis made a quick check of the bath and dressing room before returning to the study.

Dennis wrestled with the idea of trying the phone again but was afraid to waste the time. Instead he ran back out into the hall straining his ears for any other sounds. He headed back down the hallway toward the nursery, praying he would find everything in order. The door was standing open and he entered cautiously, his gun still drawn. The nursery, too, was empty save for an occasional large stuffed animal scattered in orderly disorder about the floor. Dennis' adrenalin-amplified hearing picked up a faint high pitched sound, like someone screaming, or yelling. He ran over to a window that overlooked one of the spacious inner courtyards and peered out.

Dennis caught his breath and leaned against the window sill, momentarily overcome with relief. The little prince, Bertie, was wielding a small plastic sword and shield, busying himself with the slaying of imaginary dragons as he ran round and round the baroque marble fountain that stood as a focal point in the center of the courtyard, yelling at the top of his lungs. His older brother, Prince Nicholas, sat at a small garden table to the side of the circular walk doing his lessons, occasionally looking up at his little brother's antics and laughing.

Dennis straightened to leave the room. For a second his gaze wandered across the courtyard to the apartments on the other side. A lone figure sat in the window on the first floor above the courtyard motionless, watching the children below. Dennis dropped quickly to his knees at the corner of the window squinting through the glass trying to identify the shadowy figure across the way. A dizzying chill wrenched through him. It was Major Von Schiffer's apartment.

Dennis stood slowly at the side of the window looking out with one eye, trying not to make any sudden movement that would catch the attention of his target. He pulled the heavy gun from his pocket and attempted to aim it through the window, but the distance was too great. He tried to shake off the advancing feeling of helplessness. The King . . . Dennis was almost sure of the worst.

He ran from the nursery and down the hall toward the Major's apartment. Rounding the corner with his gun ready, Dennis prayed that the safety was off and that the gun would fire. He could see down the hall that the door to Von Schiffer's quarters was standing open and he slowed quickly, keeping close to the wall. Approaching the door carefully, he held the gun high, pointing straight up in front of him. He worried about the door being open. Perhaps the Major had spotted him after all and was waiting for him, fully prepared to cut him down. Dennis leaned his ear against the door jamb, listening. There was no sound coming from the bedroom proper, though he could hear the faint noise of Bertie's play wafting in from outside.

He wondered how the Major might expect him to attack. Should he charge the room, firing, or should he drop to the floor as he had seen it done in the movies? Sweat began to roll down the side of his face and he swallowed hard. His mind drifted absurdly, considering possible headlines for the morning papers: King's secretary killed in shootout with professional assassin. He felt like a fool until the still vivid and painful memory of Aidan's mutilated body returned to haunt him. Leaving common sense behind, he spun into the doorway, dropping to one knee and bringing the gun up to bear on the window directly across from him.

The overhead light in the room had been turned off leaving the window as the only source of illumination. Dennis remained in firing position finding himself sighting down the muzzle of his pistol at the King, who sat undisturbed on a straight back chair, gazing out the window at his brothers. For a moment Dennis was unable to speak or move. The King slowly turned his head toward him, his face calm and impassive, his eyes betraying neither fear nor concern.

"Dennis. I've been expecting you," said the King softly. "Chief Inspector Harlowe was good enough to call." The King's eyes turned back out the window. He gave no hint of even having noticed the gun pointing at him.

"Your Majesty." Dennis slowly let the gun fall to his side. "I . . . you're all right."

King Richard did not move except to raise an eyebrow and clasp his hands together in his lap, continuing his watch over his brothers. "Should I not be?"

"Sir . . . Major Von Schiffer! I heard a shot. I thought he . . ." Dennis stuttered to a stop, flabber-gasted.

Richard turned to face Dennis. Dennis could feel the King's eyes cutting through him, absorbing his thoughts. Without speaking, the King turned his head slowly to the other side of the room and Dennis' eyes followed obediently. Pushed into the corner, up against the side wall, was a single, long narrow bed, neatly covered with a woolen army blanket, simply arranged without headboard. Stretched out over the full length of the bed lay Major Peter Von Schiffer. His hands were folded over his chest holding his own powerful Beretta pistol, protruding by its barrel out of the Major's mouth. The white linen pillow under his head was soaked black with blood and tissue and his face was grotesquely swollen and bruised.

Dennis' legs almost gave way under him as the tension and fear released him from their hold. He sat down onto the floor, cross legged, holding the gun in his lap, unable to take his eyes off the body. He was overwhelmed, and his face flooded with tears from the assault of conflicting emotions that possessed him.

King Richard sat watching him quietly for a moment before reaching for his cane to stand. With great difficulty he pulled himself up from the window seat to his feet. Dennis looked up at him from the floor. Even in the dim lighting, he was shocked at the physical deterioration that had taken place in the King during the short span of a few weeks. The King's cheeks and eyes were sunk in and the weight seemed to have melted off his body. A slight furrow in his brow was the only concession the King made to what must have been excruciating pain and he frowned down at his legs, seeming to will them to motion.

After a moment's rebellion, like loyal subjects, they finally obeyed and, leaning heavily on his cane, the King came up beside Dennis and placed a hand on Dennis' head. Dennis looked up into the King's face trying to gradually gain control over his spent emotions.

"I'm sorry, sir," Dennis said softly. He wiped his eyes with the back of his hand. "I expected to find you—"

"Dead?" The King smiled down at him. "Not yet. No, I've been quite safe."

"But the Major . . . suicide?" Dennis shook his head. "I don't understand."

King Richard looked over to the bed. For the first time his face, mostly his eyes, reflected a sense of personal loss and pity. "Peter has always striven to obey me to the best of his ability, in all things," he said in a hoarse whisper.

Dennis got to his feet quickly, returning his gun, which the King still seemed to take no notice of, to his coat pocket. "I'm afraid Your Majesty has been unaware of a great many things regarding this . . . this man," Dennis said, gesturing disdainfully toward Von Schiffer.

The King faced Dennis, his eyes carrying a gentle rebuke. "I'm afraid there are a great many things of which you are unaware, Dennis."

"Sir, this man was the worst of monsters, committing treason under our noses." Dennis voice hardened with each word. "He was responsible for the bombing of Parliament and God knows how many other acts of terrorism before that. Untold numbers of innocent people have been murdered at his behest."

The King took his tirade calmly. "And was it your intention to kill him?" he questioned.

Dennis looked down at his coat pocket. "He deserved to die. That and more." He could not seem to move the King. "Not less than an hour ago I found my partner . . . my lover brutally murdered in my apartment." Dennis' voice broke. "His body had been booby trapped with explosive charges meant for me. This animal was responsible for it. Surely the Inspector told—"

"Yes," the King interposed, slowly making his way to the corpse's bedside. "I regret that, terribly. He had no instructions to execute your friend. Though Mr. Ennis had been a valuable informant and liaison to a point, I'm afraid Peter was surely guilty of murder in this case. His motives were purely personal and without regard to the security or the good of the Crown. I believe you killed a close friend of his?"

Dennis reeled at the King's words. "Pardon me . . . Sir . . ." Protocol took its leave. "What are you talking about? What do you mean he had no instructions? You're not making—"

King Richard interrupted with a raised hand, motioning Dennis over to him. Obediently Dennis limped over beside him.

"Let's leave the Major in peace for now, Dennis." The King took his arm for support. "There are items of particular interest to you in Our study which will make events much clearer for you."

Dennis led the King out of the room, pausing a moment in the hallway to shut the door behind them at the King's silent command. Taking Richard's arm again he led the frail monarch toward the study in the other wing. Dennis felt a slight tremor in the King's hand and could hear his increased respiration from the strain of the short walk.

"Before Our succession to the throne, Dennis," the King said, rasping slightly, "how would you have characterized the state of the monarchy?"

Dennis looked at the King, puzzled. Richard inched along slowly with his head down, a practice which gave the public illusion of humility and prayerfulness, but which, Dennis was sure, merely reflected the King's intense concentration on getting his feet to move one in front of the other. Still he felt somehow that the illusion was not out of character for the man.

"Your Majesty knows, of course, that things were not at all very good. Though the late Queen was very much loved and respected, her heir was almost equally held in contempt. The feeling on Downing Street and Parliament for the most part, was that she would be the end of an era. There were plans already in the making among several political factions, constitutionally to do away with the monarchy upon her death. It was an institution that had outlived its purpose."

"Was it?" The King smiled down at his feet. "How would you characterize the state of the monarchy now?"

Dennis thought a moment before opening the door to the King's study. "Considering the mood of the people at present, I doubt seriously there's a politician in the country who could be elected without, in some way, expressing full support and loyalty to Your Majesty." He guided the King through the doorway. "But," he continued, "had the Prince of Wales lived, the monarchy would have died."

Richard nodded as if agreeing. "Help me over to my desk, please."

"Sir, there are still some puzzling statements you made back in the Major's rooms that I . . . I found disturbing." Dennis strained for the right words in which to frame his request. "Perhaps I might be allowed to ask some questions?" He eased the King down into the quilted chair behind the uncluttered desk.

Richard sank back into the folds of the chair, exhaling his relief at being off his feet. He raised an eyebrow at Dennis. "One doesn't question the King, Dennis. The King questions . . . and advises as it suits him."

Dennis stepped back from the desk nodding his head in a terse bow, his jaws clamped shut at the reprimand.

Unruffled, the King watched this display of ceremony, letting his eyebrow drop in satisfaction. He opened the desk drawer. "Let Us begin your enlightenment, Dennis," the King said. He pulled a small slip of parchment from the drawer and placed it on the desk. "I do this to ease my own conscience in the death of your friend. Let me caution you, however, on making rash judgments until you have considered all the facts."

He drew a stamp pad and a small wood block with a knob handle from the drawer. He rolled the block over the inked pad for a moment and then pressed it gently onto the center of the parchment. Dennis watched with growing apprehension. After a minute's drying, the King slid the paper over to the edge of the desk and motioned Dennis over for a closer inspection.

Dennis' features fell as he stared down at the small square of parchment. Stamped in its center was the familiar Florentine filigree of a lacy, green shamrock. He looked up at the King, who sat watching him serenely.

"You?" Dennis could barely get the word out.

"The Leprechaun? Yes," the King said without expression. "And before me, Our late predecessor, the Queen."

Dennis fled backwards to the fireplace, leaning against the mantle for support. "But the Major! Why . . ."

"The Major was following orders—Our orders, including the command to end his own life."

"Effectively removing any connection between you and all of this." Dennis noted.

"This is true," said the King without emotion.

Dennis stared down into the burning oak log, no longer able to look at the man he had grown to respect above all others. He laughed in spite of himself.

Richard toyed with the small woodblock. "It was a plan, Dennis . . . *the* Plan. My predecessor, the Queen, had begun to implement the entire process over three years ago. She, more than anyone, knew how close the Crown was to total eradication. She, along with others, also realized how fundamental to our way of life the monarchy is, as well as the constitutional safeguards it serves."

Dennis turned toward him, disbelieving. "You're saying that all this has been to preserve the monarchy. All the killing and—"

"You forget yourself, Dennis!" The King's voice rose above its frailty with the weight of authority. "You also forget that the Queen, herself, also gave her life, willingly, to preserve the holy estate to which she was born. My own father! My mother! Many others have sacrificed themselves, willingly or not, to save the future of this nation from the shortsightedness of political extremists, self-serving demigods, as well as terrorists from within and without!"

King Richard relaxed back in his chair again, exhausted. His voice grew gentler. "I regret the loss you have suffered and the pain that you must feel, but the losses I and my family have suffered, to ensure the future of freedom here, far surpass that of anyone else."

Dennis shook his head. He was too numbed by the death of Aidan and these revelations from the King to make any sane or meaningful judgments. "Sir, surely the monarchy will only be harmed by all of this. The people will not understand . . . I don't understand the reasoning behind this plan—that the Sovereign has been behind all this violence, controlling and manipulating the IRA . . ."

"But that, Dennis has also been a great triumph," the King said. "Because of the Major, the Queen's own security forces were able, over that period of years, to infiltrate the most vital cells of this so-called new IRA and bring them under a unified control. Violent acts were necessary to preserve the illusion that was the Leprechaun, and legitimize him in the minds of the IRA extremists—a leader they could all follow. Our people will never know the truth of these things."

King Richard studied the intricate etching of the small wood block as if admiring the workmanship. "The destruction of the Royal Yacht, though costly in lives, was the one event that cemented the IRA hierarchy behind the Leprechaun. The secretive nature and the limited knowledge of each individual IRA member concerning the whole, made it possible for the Queen to manipulate the circumstances and document the entire network.

"At this very moment, Prime Minister Fitzroy is making available to Scotland Yard and the internal security forces a complete outline of this network, and a census of each and every active member not already executed by the Major and his men—executed on my orders."

He motioned Dennis over to him. For reasons Dennis didn't understand, he obeyed. The King handed him the woodblock stamp and the piece of parchment. "Put these in the fire," he said softly.

Dennis looked at the objects in his hands, realizing that he held the only tangible pieces of evidence as to the Leprechaun's true identity. He carried them over to the fire, wondering if he were bewitched, and threw them into the flames. He stood watching the edges of the paper curl up in smoke and the intricate design of the woodblock blacken from the heat.

"The Plan has seen its culmination, Dennis," the King said, drawing him back to the present and motioning for Dennis' assistance. "The crown is secure and the one major threat to the people's safety has been effectively crippled." The King took Dennis' arm and stood slowly. "In due course, Scotland Yard, MI5 and the intelligence services of our allies will have the IRA and its Arab contingent fully dismantled and impotent."

"So it was the Queen's intention from the beginning that the succession go to you," Dennis said, supporting the King as they headed into the hall.

The King's mouth drew up at the corner in a half-smile. "Not really," he said, almost laughing. "Due to the nature of my illness, I should have been dead months ago, but I persisted in being stubborn."

They walked back into the nursery and Dennis helped the King into a chair by the window. Several minutes passed as the King sat quietly watching his brothers, still playing in the courtyard below. He nodded his head toward Prince Nicholas who, for the moment, had abandoned his studies to become Bertie's dragon adversary.

"The succession was meant for Nicky all along." King Richard smiled down at his brothers' play. "He is strong," the King continued. "Suited to carry the Crown with pride and provide the throne with many heirs."

Dennis sat at the foot of the window looking down at the princes. "Then why detour the succession to you?" he asked. "You could have easily been removed from the line just as your father was." He caught himself quickly, aware of how cold his statement may have sounded.

The King took no notice. "Nicky would have had to reign with a regent. He is not yet of age. He would never have been able to muster the support or authority to complete Our Plan and it is doubtful anyone else would have had sufficient motivation." He breathed deeply. "I had nothing to lose. Besides, it was felt that he would be better off not being tainted with the blood of so many should events not proceed as We wished them to."

"Does he know any of this?" Dennis asked.

"Nothing." The King smiled down at his brothers. "He will begin his reign innocent before God and man."

At that moment the young princes caught sight of their older brother in the window above them and waved excitedly up at him before returning to play. The King's face darkened with sadness. Dennis wondered if it was the sadness of one facing imminent death, or rather pity for the young prince, whose innocent life would soon be weighted with the heavy responsibilities of state and kingship.

"It is finished," the King whispered to persons unseen, his eyes closed, quoting from scripture.

Postlude

An early spring had put the farmers to work before they were ready, tilling up their fields and rushing to get the proper seeds into the ground. The rains had abated long enough for the ground to be able to be worked without being muddy and the sudden appearance of warmer weather shocked the wild flowers into premature bloom, swathing the surrounding countryside in a firmament of color.

Those who could be spared from the fields or assembly lines flocked to the capital, streaming down the Mall by the tens of thousands, gathering around Buckingham Palace or The Shrine, as those few remaining discontents on the fringes of government likened it to. The Pilgrims would take turns filing past the front gates to read the latest bulletins set out for public inspection, or listen to self-styled spokespersons read the bulletins to them the bulletins concerning the waning health of their king, from atop someone's. The tone of these bulletins never changed. From the beginning of the vigil on the evening before, they had stressed it was only a matter of time.

The King's bed chamber was also crowded to the point where official onlookers were forced to stand. Dennis walked away from the window in the King's study where he had been observing the crowd below. He looked over the various members of the Privy Council and Cabinet who had gathered to witness that immeasurable instant when the Crown of the Commonwealth was passed from one head to another.

Dennis made his way into the bedroom, trying not to disturb any of the small groups of power that stood discussing the affairs of state in whispers while the King lay gasping for breath. Dennis stared at the pathetic effigy of the dying King. He wondered what this assembly might say if they knew this man was also the feared and hated Leprechaun, responsible for the deaths of hundreds.

Of course, this fear was, to a large extent, in the past now. True to form, Scotland Yard had made expeditious use of the reams of evidence and names turned over to it by the King. Purportedly this information was the result of ongoing undercover work by Major Peter Von Schiffer and his security department. No mention was ever made as to the exact nature of that covert work.

It was bad enough that the Major was close to being hailed, posthumously, as a national hero. He was officially listed as killed in the line of duty. Dennis had remained silent, even with Chief Inspector Harlowe, who still harbored suspicions. What good would it have done to spout accusations without proof? After all, this was a King who had brought peace and stability, tradition and God, back to what had been a people torn by sectional violence, apathy, and little hope for the future. A politician who valued his political career, even his life, never spoke of the King except with the utmost reverence and respect. Anything else and the general populace tended to interpret it as certain treason.

Dennis spotted Hughen Fitzroy standing at the center of a small group of Cabinet officials near the bed discussing the various ceremonial details of a national funeral. He caught Fitzroy's eye, and the corpulent statesman, who seemed to have aged ten years, left his audience and signaled Dennis over to the back wall.

"Dennis, lad," Fitzroy whispered jovially, pounding Dennis on the back. "It's been a while."

"Mr. Prime Minister," Dennis said with undue gravity. "You look terrible."

Fitzroy laughed softly. "I'm due a little vacation. Thank God, with the elections almost over, I won't have to put up with these unruly politicians for very much longer."

"Unruly!" Dennis smiled at the older man. "I suppose this means that after you've successfully pandered this job off to some other poor fool, we'll be seeing more of you down at Abernathy's."

"Ah, not so lad," Fitzroy said with feigned sobriety. "I've been made a Lord, you know."

"Yes," Dennis said, bearing a woeful expression. "You're to serve as regent for Prince Nicholas."

Fitzroy pursed his lips in the direction of the King. "Sooner than I might wish, it seems." He slapped Dennis on the back again. "I hear you're making a bid for a seat in the Commons."

Dennis looked at the floor. "I had been thinking about it ever since the new laws were enacted. When the party caucus approached me about it, I decided, why not?"

"Good lad! The country can use an experienced hand like yours." He gave Dennis a wink. "Considering your highly visible association with the King, I'm sure your election will be a shoo-in."

Dennis felt a twinge of guilt. Fitzroy was apparently very aware of the extent to which that association was being touted in his campaign.

"I have been fortunate," was all Dennis could say.

"Oh, well, we'll have to get together soon and talk about it all, Dennis."

Dennis caught his eye. "Fitzroy." He leaned close, speaking in the old man's ear. "Did you know about . . . the Plan?"

Fitzroy stood very still, not looking at Dennis, his face blank of expression. "Whatever are you mumbling about, Dennis?" He suddenly broke out into his parliamentary smile. "You'll have to pardon me right now, lad—affairs of state and all that." He excused himself back to the impatient group he had abandoned earlier.

The King had begun to recite the Lord's Prayer, his voice weak and hauntingly disembodied. The two young princes, kneeling beside the bed, joined him, undisturbed by the crowd pressing in about the bedside.

Dennis walked over to the slightly opened window across the room. He looked out, amazed to see that the crowd had grown even larger. He became aware that on the last lines of the prayer, only one voice was speaking. He turned quickly back to the bed. Bertie was kneeling on the edge of the bed beside the King, head bowed and hands folded under his chin, dutifully finishing the prayer, unaware of the transition that caught everyone else's attention.

Nicholas bowed to kiss his older brother's hand before standing. No longer present were the gasping sounds of one trying to hang onto life. Fitzroy stood over the bed for a moment by the doctor. Having satisfied official formality, he turned to Nicholas, who stood beside the bed still holding the dead King's hand as well as his now sobbing little brother.

"The King is dead!" Fitzroy said, his voice thundering over the silent assembly. "Long live the King!"

Dennis turned back to the window to hide his face. "Long live the King," he whispered, echoing the others.

And let their heirs, God, if Thy will be so,

Enrich the time to come with smooth-faced peace,

With smiling plenty and fair prosperous days?

Abate the edge of traitors, gracious Lord,

That would reduce these bloody days again

And make poor England weep in streams of blood!

Let them not live to taste this land's increase

That would with treason wound this fair Land's

    peace!

Now civil wounds are stopped, peace lives again.

That she may long live here, God say amen!

W. Shakespeare, *Richard III*, Act V, Sc.V.

DOUGLAS KING
is also the author of
The Q Factor, The High Range, and
The Fabergé Conspiracy
He works as a medical investigator
and lives in Beaumont, Texas.